REDEMPTION

IN

BLOOD

A NOVEL OF THE PENITENT

TARA S. WOOD

TARA S. WOOD

ISBN-10: 061570395X
ISBN-13: 978-0615703954

BELLE OMBRE
PUBLISHING

CONTENTS

ACKNOWLEDGMENTS

Aron: My hero in real life. Your love and support have meant so much to me and without it, this book would never have been possible. I love you to the moon and back.

Lori: Three words. Friday. Night. Awesome.

CHAPTER ONE

Vesper Hyde delivered a well-placed kick beneath the doorknob and the apartment door burst open, sending the junkies inside scattering like roaches at the flick of a light switch.

She toed the door closed with the point of her black high-heeled boot and calmly ventured into the apartment, making no sound on the scuffed linoleum. Figures her tracking would bring her to a shit-hole project full of addicts and bangers. New Orleans was full of them. Her gaze pierced through the cloud of cloying smoke to focus on the young man lounging on the ragged yellow couch. *Stoned? Perfect. It's nice when they make it easy.* A loud, metallic clang came from the back of the apartment and she knew the junkies had found the fire escape. They were not her concern. However, the condemned vampire toking it up on the couch was very much her concern.

"Who the fuck are you?" he snarled.

"It's time to pay the piper, Wilson." Her voice lowered to a whisper. "You ready?" Vesper's hands slid behind her back, up underneath the soft leather of her jacket. Beads of sweat popped out on the vampire's forehead and his eyes darted wildly as he watched her calculated movements. Her stare never wavered as she pulled her hands down to her side, two large, curved knives now visible.

He pointed to the door behind her. "Look, bitch, get the f-"

The word cut off as his eyes focused on the silver pendant of crossed swords that hung at her neck.

That's right. Take a good fucking look. I'm here for you.

The symbol of the Penitent struck fear into the heart of even the coldest vampire. Coming face-to-face with a Penitent and the crossed swords they wore meant you were marked for death. The Archive knew your crime and sentenced you without your knowledge. Until the death-dealing Penitents came knocking, anyway. Then you were all too aware that you were busted. Permanently.

"What is this?" her target cried, popping up from the sofa. Sweat continued to drip down his forehead and his glassy black eyes were on the verge of protruding out of his skull. He was tall and skinny, and Vesper could see the creep of track marks on the inside of his upraised arms. Shaggy brown hair hung limply around his face, unwashed and greasy like his clothes.

Vesper kept her eyes on his face, glaring. She loved the stare down. She loved this moment, just before the execution litany, when she knew it was all falling into place for the target. The instant they understood that their actions had not gone unnoticed. The High Elder knew. The Archive knew. Their death was imminent. Her breath came faster, the blood beginning to rush in her veins.

"This is the end." Her low voice held no sympathy.

She held out her right arm, the tip of the blade pointed at Wilson's heart. The blade took on an eerie blue glow as Vesper spoke in the tongue of the Elders, her voice rumbling and echoing through the apartment. "You have been found guilty of the crime of murder, a transgression which carries the sentence of death. I am the instrument of the Archive and the agent of your demise. I am the absolution you seek. I am the Penitent."

The blue blade flashed brightly at the crescendo of her voice and the words reverberated through her body like a thunderclap. The declaration hung in the air for several long seconds then the glow disappeared from the blade and the echo of her voice dissipated.

Wilson began to stammer. "Ev..Evan Reardon. You want Reardon. I...I was only small-time, see? Some drugs and maybe a few chicks. He's what you want. He's got boys like me all over town. I'm nothing to you! Nothing!" His hands were wild in the air, a desperate pleading in his high-pitched voice.

"Nothing, indeed," she whispered. The weight of the knives felt good in her hands. Light glinted off the curved blades, their wicked symmetry making them fearsome. His panicked expression and the smell of sweat and fear in the air brought all of her heightened senses together and the blood lust grew deep in her belly. This was about to get dirty. She watched with satisfaction as the blood drained from his sweaty face as she ran the pink point of her tongue over the tip of an elongating fang. He understood how she was going to accomplish her task. Knives and teeth. He was practically pissing himself. She almost laughed. Very dirty, indeed.

Wilson rasped a fat tongue across his lips, hands still moving.

"It's not what you th-", he stammered, watching her gaze linger toward the bedroom.

Vesper's laugh was a low rumble. "Not what I think, Wilson? Maybe so. But I really don't care." She shifted her hands a fraction and caught his bulging eyes following the movement of the knives. His eyes widened until the irises were tiny black pinpricks in a sea of white, like a frightened animal on the way to slaughter. "I know you murdered one of our kind. I know you have another here. And I know she's a little young to be a 'chick'." Vesper's voice went even lower, "And I know you are dead."

The slight tic of his eyebrow caught her attention. *The idiot's going to run. The stupid ones always do.*

The glint of the knife coming up gave her away and Wilson darted to the side, managing to get around the couch and head for the back of the apartment. He turned the corner toward the open door of the bathroom. She was on him in two seconds, slamming one of the blades deep between his shoulder blades, riding him to the dirty tile floor. Wilson screamed in agony as she twisted the knife. His arms flailed behind him, but she danced out of his grasp. The scent of blood filled her nostrils and she inhaled deeply. She whipped her leg out and kicked the door shut, trapping them in the tiny room.

The blade made a wet, sucking sound as she pulled it free from his back and hopped to her feet. She muscled him over with the toe of her boot, taking great care to dig deep into his bony side. She whipped back the long strands of hair that fell forward into her face while Wilson moaned and wriggled on the floor. He thrashed around as if he were a snake trying to shed its skin, pushing away from her. But there was nowhere to go. He backed himself between the tub and the toilet, reaching, grabbing for something. Vesper leaned over him and found the prize. A Glock 9mm was taped behind the toilet.

"I don't care for guns, Wilson. They're so impersonal. And what we've got here, between you and I, that's personal. I'm sure it's personal for you when you snatch innocent young and sell them off as feed. Isn't it?" She ripped the nine from the porcelain tank, stuffing it behind her in the waistband of her pants. "No. No. No."

He worked his mouth to speak, sawing his jaw back and forth, but only managed a sick gurgle. Blood bubbled from between his lips, staining his fangs crimson. She crouched down in front of him with a cold smile that couldn't quite reach the depths of her eyes. More gurgling as he got a full on view of Vesper's fangs that had now reached their complete length.

"You know, Wilson, you might have managed to hang on a little longer before anyone found out about your little mess here. Your mistake was killing the girl. Or didn't you realize her death was a signal flare for the High Elder? Were you too high to remember? If the Archive had busted you for the trafficking, you might have had a shot at isolation, even rehab. No, the minute you took her life, you signed your own death warrant." Her chuckle was soft. "And I'm here to serve." Wilson's eyes flicked from her eyes to her fangs. "The teeth? Ah, yeah, I've decided to feed. But I've got something else in mind for starters. You like guns." She held up the bloody knife in her hand and ran her tongue along the flat of the blade, keeping her gaze on his. "I like knives."

6

Vesper ran her hands under the trickle of cold water and splashed it on her face. She grabbed the washcloth from the edge of the sink and wiped away the last traces of blood from her mouth. Wrinkling her nose at its musty smell, she dropped the dingy cloth into the porcelain bowl and raised her eyes to the reflection in the mirror. She stared at herself for a moment, then took a deep breath and focused her attention on the dead vampire on the bathroom floor.

She had waited for him to render to ash, but the corpse still remained. Too young. Too stupid to realize his mistake.

The law was kill, and be killed. Vampire lives were too precious to waste with murder. And even though he would not ash, his fangs would recede, leaving no evidence of the race he'd been. Lifeless eyes rolled heavenward and puddles of blood spread from him like a spider web, running in slow, thick rivulets on the dirty tile. The knife wounds glared back at her, pounding home a vicious reminder of the violent deed. Another corrupt soul sentenced to death, carried out by her hand. Vesper closed her eyes and blew out a deep breath. Another successful execution.

A small whimper sounded from the bedroom, snapping her to attention.

"It's all right," she called, opening the bathroom door. "I'll be right there."

Vesper rushed into the room, kicking beer bottles, dirty clothes, porn magazines, and other trash out of her way. The whole apartment was foul with layers of dirt and grime, but the bedroom was the worst. The greasy smell of unwashed bodies and clouds of marijuana smoke lingered in the air and in her nostrils. The whimper was louder as she reached the tiny closet door on the other side of the room and she felt the pallid taste of fear coat her tongue. The last trickles of sunlight managed to stream through a filthy window onto the closet door, filtering in through the wooden slats. She pulled the door open with a hard yank, and the light spilled on to a mass of dirty, tangled blond hair.

Vesper slowly crouched down. "It's okay, now. You're safe."

A sniffle. The little girl raised her head and leveled fearful blue eyes on Vesper, then glanced past her into bathroom where Vesper had been moments before.

"I promise. You're safe now," she said, understanding what the little girl's look meant. He wasn't coming back.

The little girl nodded. Vesper eased to a stand, holding out her hand. Like a bird, the tiny girl unfolded herself from the closet floor and grasped onto Vesper's outstretched hand. In one smooth motion, Vesper pulled the girl up into her arms, pressing the tear-streaked face against her shoulder.

"Don't look. Just keep your eyes closed. We're leaving." The girl nodded, her face buried from the scene. Vesper glanced one more time at the squalid room and blood stained sheets. With dawning horror, her hand curled around the back of the little girl's thigh and she pressed her closer. The slight grit of something dry on the girl's leg came off on her fingers and she lifted her hand to inspect the residue. Blood. They had raped a child. Bile rose up in her throat and she closed her eyes.

Enjoy being gang raped in the seventh circle of hell, asshole!

Vesper turned to exit and felt the vibration of her BlackBerry. She hefted the girl a little higher and pulled out the cell from inside her jacket. She checked the screen. A text message from the High Elder was never good. Artemis always preferred conversation.

Meeting. Archive. Now.

She sighed hard, tucking the phone away. Vesper pressed her face into the girl's hair, breathing in the sharp, clean scent of innocence. She'd spent the last two days tracking Wilson and the junkies, running on adrenaline and fatigue from hunger. She needed rest and time. She had a nagging feeling she wasn't going to get either.

The black Aston-Martin Vantage roared through Belle Ombre's wrought iron gate, almost clipping the side mirrors. She kept her foot on the accelerator as she barreled down the last quarter mile of gravel drive, and then braked to a smooth halt in front of the mansion.

The BlackBerry in her jacket beeped again, and the message was received with relief. The little girl was now reunited with her family and Archive law enforcement would be looking into the trafficking ring. If Wilson's mutilated body was found by human police, given Rampart Street's reputation, his death would be chalked up to a drug deal gone bad. She'd have to keep her ears open about Evan Reardon and let the Archive know, if they didn't already. It was entirely possible that once they had their proof he was behind the trafficking and the facilitating of vampire deaths, she would be his assigned Penitent. His death would be hers. The sweet scent of sunshine and innocence lingered in her nostrils and she thought that was a pleasing possibility, indeed.

The Louisiana night surrounded her like a wet blanket as she got out of the vehicle and placed the phone back in her jacket. Taking the front steps two at a time, she pushed open the massive oak doors and walked inside.

The imposing Antebellum styled home was actually built in the early twenties and retrofitted with state of the art technology and convenience, but it was a replica of a plantation home that had stood on the River Road in the early eighteenth century. The mansion and its buildings lay on several hundred acres of land along the famed byway.

The fortress-like gates, armed guards, and heavily monitored perimeter kept the tourists and other wandering eyes at bay. Although her early childhood was spent in Europe with her parents and brother, the River Road and south Louisiana were home.

The staccato of her boots on the marble floor echoed in the immense foyer, announcing her arrival better than any of the acolytes ever could. It had been a couple of crap days all around and the High Elder's terse summons could only mean there was trouble. She found him in the downstairs study, exactly where she knew he would be.

The wooden door eased shut behind her and she leveled her eyes on the tall, silver-haired man behind the ornate mahogany desk. He didn't look up.

"I hope this is good news, Artemis," she said, depositing herself in the leather club chair across from him.

"Your task is finished, I presume?" Artemis Harrow's voice was low and even. Was it her imagination, or did it waver a bit, too?

She shifted slightly. "You know it is." As High Elder, Artemis *knew* when each Penitent carried out their respective sentence.

"Yes, well done." He looked up from the desk, his expression hard and firm. "What do you know of Evan Reardon?" he asked slowly.

"Reardon? Then you already know. My target tried to bargain with his name. Drugs and trafficking. The Condemned was all too eager to point him out. They're always itching to lay blame elsewhere. Nothing I haven't heard before." She drummed her fingers on the arm of the chair, watching the High Elder's face. The lines around his eyes and mouth were tight and his shoulders were taut, tense. Unusual posture for the ever-confident Artemis.

"That doesn't surprise me," he replied.

"What's the story, then?" She leaned forward, trying to discern more from his face.

He sat back in his chair and placed his hands on top of the desk. "That's just it, Vesper. I don't know. I only know he's dead."

Vesper's brow wrinkled. "What do you mean, you don't know? How can you not? I mean-"

"I don't know why I couldn't see it," he barked. "It's disturbing. It was only brought to my attention a few hours ago. Marcus said he heard it on the police band, letting me know a Condemned corpse was found so we could keep tabs. But, Reardon wasn't a Penitent target. Not a Condemned. He wasn't even on the Archive watch list." He rubbed a hand across his face. Despite the outburst of emotion, his hand was steady.

She tread carefully; she had never seen the High Elder this upset. "You didn't *see* anything?" she asked.

"No." He let out a deep breath. "I didn't get a vision. I didn't feel his death. And what's worse, I can't recall any visions of him at all. It's like he didn't exist among us." She noticed his eyes softened a little when they met hers, and the gesture warmed her heart. "I don't know what the hell has happened, Vesper, but if the humans are on it, we've got to do damage control."

With his close-cropped silver hair and ex-Marine physique, he normally carried the ease of a fit man in his fifties. Tonight, Vesper could see the weight of his years making him look so much older. Her heart ached for him.

"Who else knows within the Archive?" She kept her voice soft.

He gave his head a little shake. "Just you and your brother." His brown eyes hardened and he stiffened. "This is dangerous. I need to know what the humans know and if Reardon's killer is one of us. There's got to be a reason I didn't see any of this, and I need to know what that is." The intensity of his gaze and the urgency of his words made her skin prickle.

"Do you want me to take Marcus, since he's already involved?"

"No, that won't be necessary." He stood, coming around the desk. "Vesper…if the Council finds out about this-"

"They won't," she countered, rising to her feet. "I'll take care of it. We'll get to the bottom of this."

He nodded. He raised a hand to her chin, tilting it up. "I know, child. I trust your judgment. And your discretion."

"Always, Artemis." She wrapped her arms around his shoulders and embraced him in a tight hug. She rested her head against his chest and closed her eyes, the sound of his heartbeat still able to soothe her after all these years.

The High Elder was not her father. After her parents' death as a little girl, Artemis had brought her here and acted in their stead, taking an interest in both her and her brother, Marcus. He shaped her, guided her, scolded her, and taught her, preparing her for their world and her place in it. It was Artemis who had called for her to become a Penitent like her brother, to become one of the few members of the vigilant order created to uphold Archive law and deliver its sentences. And when the Archive's Council would not support her, it was Artemis who pulled rank as High Elder to ensure her place.

In six hundred years, he had never overridden the Council. But he did for her. So far, she'd only let him down once. She'd be damned if she let him down again.

The drive back to New Orleans was a quiet one, giving Vesper time to think. It was unnerving to see Artemis so uneasy. As High Elder, he was privy to the innermost workings of their society. A quirk of the DNA that was the office. His visions allowed him to see the most heinous crime among their society. Murder. Vampire reproduction was spotty at best, females and young highly regarded and protected. Any senseless death of their kind did not go unnoticed. Between Artemis and the Council of Elders, they kept law and order within society. When murder, or any other crime that could jeopardize the balance of their existence, the Penitent came into play.

By all accounts, Reardon was dead and Artemis didn't know who or how or why...well, it was easy to see how that could become a problem. If the High Elder showed any weakness, any sign that he was unable to keep society safe as a whole, either from themselves or from humans, the Council would to remove him and call for his execution. Vesper shuddered at the thought and went cold. Her hands gripped the steering wheel tighter as the headlights of the Aston-Martin cut a narrow path through the Louisiana night, the old River Road twisting out in front of her, seeming endless in the darkness.

The corpse of Evan Reardon slumped over the expensive glass-topped desk, the head barely attached to the rest of the body. Tugging on a pair of latex gloves, Detective Decker Price put his hand to the victim's head and turned it gently to the side, examining the damage.

A low whistle came from the doorway. "Pretty nasty, huh Deck?"

Decker looked up from the body to his partner and then let out a whistle of his own. "Christ, C.C. You poured into that thing?"

Smoothing her hand down the front of her little black dress, Detective C.C. Anderson gave him a slow smile. "Yes, I know. I'm hot. My date certainly thought so. In fact, I had to rush to put this back on to get here." She winked. "He was not happy."

"I'm sure he wasn't. What do you make of this?" he asked, gesturing to the body.

"C.S.U.'s still processing the rest of the front office, but so far it looks pretty clean. Lots of prints, but you expect that. They'll compare it to the employee list and see if anyone's out of place." She looked at the massive blood pool around Reardon's head and body that had spilled onto the carpet. "Looks like he bled out, but the M.E. can give us an exact cause of death."

Decker came around the desk, carefully avoiding the blood soaked carpet at his feet to look at Reardon's body head on, pulling off the gloves. He raked a large hand through sandy hair and scanned the large room. The office sported a high end Scandinavian vibe with lots of simplicity and sleek lines. Ultra contemporary. The entire back wall was floor to ceiling windows, the twinkling lights of the city below like fireflies. Not much on the walls except for a few black and white prints of cityscapes. Minimalist. He looked left from the desk to the metal and glass modular shelving units to the four large black steel filing cabinets on the right. "Computer's missing. None of the bookshelves or file cabinets looks like they've been disturbed."

"This place is locked down pretty tight, Deck. Security system and cameras all state of the art. They had to know how to get in here, or were let in by Reardon himself. The camera footage is on its way back to the precinct for examination. What do you think they were looking for?" she asked.

Decker glanced at the body. "It's hard to say. The lack of disturbance to the office seems to suggest that, but what if what they wanted could only come from Reardon himself?" Decker paced through the room, avoiding the desk, looking again at the photos on the walls. The place was too clean, too quiet. Nothing to support the evidence of break-in. No, Reardon knew his killer.

"Reardon Pharmaceuticals has been in the news lately with that new Alzheimer's drug they're testing, and then the Fortune piece. Business could've been getting rough. Trade secrets, corporate espionage and the like. Could've escalated to murder. You want to start there?" C.C. scribbled on a notepad.

"Yeah, let's do that. It's going to take some time to weed through, but I want to know every move Reardon made in the last six months." Decker turned back to his partner and added, "But you know C, I got a feeling this was personal. Very personal."

Her gaze moved to Reardon's corpse and on the ragged and torn flesh of what used to be his throat and neck. "Yeah, Deck, I'm feeling that, too." She flipped her notepad shut and headed out into the front office. "Does this mean I can go

back to my date now? We were...getting to know each other."
She flashed him a quick smile.

"Yeah. I'll probably go ahead and recon with the unit at
his residence. I'll meet you at the station later." He walked her
out to the elevator bank in the hallway and pressed the down
button. The gray steel doors opened with a slight whoosh and
C.C. stepped inside. "And C," he grinned, "I didn't see any
pockets on that dress. You want to tell me where you been
keeping that notepad?"

She wheeled around on her stilettos to face him with a
dirty look. "Same place I keep my gun, ass-" The doors closed
on the expletive and Decker chuckled. Whoever C.C.'s date
was, he was in over his head.

Back at the station, Decker leaned back in his desk chair,
folded his hands behind his neck and let out a long sigh. The
clock on the opposite wall hit two a.m. and the ticking of the
second hand echoed throughout the quiet of the floor.

The canvass at Reardon's house on St. Charles had
provided little in the way of evidence, but he left a uniformed
officer at the premises just in case.

Blinking, his gaze caught the photo of the beautiful
blond-haired woman on his desk. Her soft doe eyes and wide,
bright smile made him sigh once again. Even two years after
her death, Miranda's smile still got to him. He touched the
corner of the frame with a long finger, the gesture gentle as if

the frame were a piece of her. This was the last memento he had, guilt having driven him to put away all her other things, the little things too hard to bear. Guilt warred with memory in his gut. The damn job got in the way, but he couldn't leave it. Couldn't leave Miranda, either. But she put up with it like a trooper and it had cost her life. She was gone, nothing left but the photo. A small reminder that no matter how he felt, she would have wanted him to keep going. And so he did.

The desk phone rang, startling him.

"Price." His voice was thick, foggy.

"I knew you'd be at your desk," the medical examiner started. "Get your ass down here, son. You're going to want to see this."

He cleared his throat. "What is it, Cal?"

"Just get down here. Pronto."

The line went dead and Decker shot out the door, making it down the three floors to the morgue in record time.

He pushed open the double doors to the autopsy suite with a swish and walked in to see Dr. Calvin Wheeler, a large African-American man, standing over a sheet-covered corpse on one of the autopsy tables.

"All right, Cal. Give."

Wheeler's face was grim, a mean feat for the normally jovial man. Decker frowned at his expression. The M.E. blinked and leaned his six foot four, two hundred seventy pound frame over the body. He blew out a breath as he pulled the sheet back from the head of the corpse to its waist. "I don't know what to say, son. I called you as soon as I finished." He lowered his eyes and waited for Decker to notice.

Decker's brow furrowed and his blue eyes swept from Wheeler's pinched face down to the corpse. Evan Reardon lay on the table, eyes closed in eternal sleep. He took in the ragged scraps of flesh at the throat and then looked lower to the chest.

He stopped breathing. His eyes fluttered, trying desperately to make sure what he was seeing was real. Because it couldn't be real.

Just above Reardon's right nipple, staring back at him, a jagged heart had been carved into the chest, deep into the muscle. Wheeler's Y-incision slashed through it with purpose, but there was no mistaking that mark. All at once, a thousand anguished memories came flooding back. His vision went red and fuzzy and he lurched forward, nearly falling onto the side of the table. The slow roll of bile burned in his throat and he suppressed the urge to turn and vomit.

Blurry vision finally gave way to flashes of clarity in his mind's eye. It played along in black and white, the gritty images flapping about like 8mm footage from a bad indie flick.

Miranda. Clear, bright laughter. Summer at the beach, the wind in that long, beautiful hair. God, it was like silk in his fingers. Miranda smiling. Eyes shining, so full of love, so full of life. Color slashed through the film, red streaking the happy scenes, time slowing down to reveal the ultimate horror.

Miranda, limp and lifeless, a rag doll covered in blood, the same angry red heart carved into her still form.

Decker closed his eyes against the onslaught of emotions he thought he'd put away for good. It wasn't possible. It just wasn't possible. Howard Grainger had been rotting in solitary up at Angola for the past two years and would be for the rest of his life. Miranda's killer could not have done this. It was not possible.

He must have a made a sound because Wheeler replaced the sheet and came around the table. The ex-Tulane fullback was gentle as the big man gave Decker's shoulder a tight squeeze.

"Come on. I've got some bourbon in my office," he said. "Might take the edge off."

Decker sniffed, pushing himself from the table and patting Wheeler's arm. "No thanks, Cal. I'm going to need a clear head." He rubbed a hand over his eyes and composed himself.

"Fine. Autopsy's finished. I'll keep him in storage while you do your thing. I'll write up my report and leave it on your desk. I assume you'll want it to compare."

Decker caught the knowing edge to the M.E.'s tone. "Damn straight." His own voice was firm. Determined.

"Let me know if you need anything else. I'm done here, so call me at home if you need to." He looked Decker in the eye. "I mean it. Call me."

"Thanks, Cal. I will." Decker nodded, extending his hand. They shook and Decker turned and headed for the double doors. He called out over his shoulder, "I'm headed back to Reardon's residence. See if I missed anything, given the circumstances. I'll be back later. I'll get the report then."

Wheeler laughed, a throaty rumble coming from the older man. "You should get some sleep first, son. He'll still be there tomorrow. Pace yourself."

He heard Cal's voice fading behind him as he shoved the doors aside. Miranda's face loomed again in his brain. Her lovely, smiling visage filled his head and new purpose entered his heart. His footsteps echoed against the tile of the empty hallway, the heavy stride a hallmark of a man on a mission. God help anyone who got in his way.

Vesper parked the Aston-Martin a block from Reardon's and walked down St. Charles to the house. It wasn't hard to slip past the uniform out front; he was snoozing in his cruiser. She shook her head. Humans. They made it too easy.

According to what information she gathered on Reardon, it appeared he was a model private citizen, able to head a profitable business and still live on the fringe of human society. After that, nothing concrete. Nothing on Council radar, either. There had been no suspicion at all that he was running drugs or girls. If she was lucky, she would find more information here. If not, his office in the Central Business District was her next stop.

She picked the lock on the back door and quietly stepped inside. The back entrance led her into the kitchen, immaculate with shiny, new appliances and the air of infrequent use.

Vesper sniffed and wrinkled her nose. *Strange.* She couldn't detect a vampire scent. He must have been gone a long while for the scent to dissipate. She did, however, pick up the scent of a number of humans. They tended to blend together after a while, but she did detect a prevailing note of something a little different.

It was there on the edge of recognition. A dark scent of spice lingered in her nostrils. She breathed in deeper, the need to discern more knotting in her stomach as the air rolled over her tongue, coating it with the rich flavor. She shook her head, getting back to business.

From the kitchen, she made short work of the living room and the downstairs bedroom. Two French doors opened into the study and she inspected the bookshelves first.

Based on what she had seen so far, Reardon wasn't the type to leave things lying around, or in the habit of having a lot of clutter. There wasn't even a phone or a computer in this room. The desk was almost backed up against the far wall, leaving little room behind it. Cherry, obviously an antique, it was intricately carved with front wood panels of scroll work and leaves.

A slight dulling of the finish in one small spot caught her eye and she crouched down low, bending to inspect the woodwork. Engrossed in running her fingers along the myriad of scrolls and design, it took her a moment to realize the warm tickle of that intriguing scent had grown stronger and more potent. And a lot closer.

Just as her fingers found the hidden mechanism on the wood panel, a deliciously low and sexy voice that matched the scent in the air stopped her cold.

"N.O.P.D. Put your hands where I can see them, chère."

CHAPTER TWO

Vesper managed to palm the empty glass vial that presented from the secret opening in the desk. She deftly slipped it inside her jacket pocket and rose to her feet. Turning around slowly with her hands in the air, she was careful to keep her movements lithe. Mentally, she shook her head. The cop from out front must've come in for a walk-through. *How in the hell had he gotten the drop on her?* She expected to be confronted with a nervous uniformed officer. Not so much.

What she got was a full on blast of the exotic scent that had been at the edge of her consciousness wrapped around the darkest blue eyes of the sexiest man she had ever seen. The fragrance assaulted her senses with a vengeance, striking her hard in the chest, stealing the breath from her lungs. She gasped as their eyes met, trying to keep the shock off of her face. Those sapphire eyes were somewhat amused, but his expression was firm. The scent was so strong; she wouldn't have been surprised to see tendrils of it in the air, like smoke.

That had to be the reason she didn't notice his approach. The reason he was able to sneak up on her. The reason, she realized with a jolt, *she* was nervous. It had to be the scent. Sure as hell wasn't the SIG Sauer he had pointed at her.

She tamped down the butterflies. He did have a gun aimed at her, after all. Time to clear the cobwebs and focus. It would be a shame to get shot this evening.

He spoke, and damned if she didn't get all fluttery again.

"You want to tell me who you are and what the hell you're doing here? This is a crime scene." His voice was low and rich, the kind of hot, sexy man voice that could persuade a woman to do all sorts of things she wouldn't normally do. Like have sex in public or lend him money.

She swallowed and said, "Vesper Hyde. I'm a private investigator." The lie rolled off her tongue.

He looked her up and down and she knew what he was thinking. The tight, all black ensemble was her trademark style, even if it was a little severe. It certainly didn't say 'private investigator'. People were afraid to approach her, and she preferred it that way.

"Private investigator?" He held out a strong, tanned hand. "Show me some I.D. Slowly," he added.

"Okay." She reached into her jacket pocket and pulled out a small leather wallet and handed it to him.

He kept the gun level and flipped open her credentials.

"You work for the Séraphine Consortium?"

Vesper nodded. "I handle security for a few of the firms. My primary work is for Crescent City Investigations." The lies were so easy to tell, they were almost true. She knew if he bothered to run a background check, everything would come up clean.

He looked closely at the wallet, and then back to Vesper's face. Satisfied, he handed it back to her and she tucked it away.

"I noticed you didn't have a concealed gun permit on you." He arched a chiseled eyebrow at her. "You packing?" he asked lightly. The corners of his mouth turned up in a wry smile.

Was that flirting? He had a gun on her, and he was flirting? *Outstanding.* The realization should have bolstered her confidence to talk herself out of here without incident. But he was just too much. He smelled too good, sounded too good, and definitely looked too good. Those three small factors were short-circuiting her brain in all sorts of fun ways. If she didn't snap out of it soon, she'd be handing over her Amex and begging him to do her in the driveway.

The sexy rumble was back.

27

She gave her head a little shake. "I'm sorry...what?"

"Gun. You carrying?"

She let out a breath and focused on his eyes. "No. I'm not carrying a gun."

He nodded toward the desk. "Turn around and place your hands behind your head, please. I'm going to pat you down."

Turning to face the desk, she said, "I'll bet you say that to all the girls. Does it work for you?"

He chuckled. "You'd be surprised, chère."

She heard the slight swish of his coat as he pushed it aside to holster the SIG. Vesper felt the surge of something on her skin as he came up behind her. It wasn't heat that radiated from him, but it was definitely some type of electricity because the nerve endings in her body snapped to attention as if he flipped a switch.

She felt the wide span of his hands on her shoulders as they slowly worked their way down her back. She held her breath as he crouched, his strong hands traveling down over her rear and legs. Either her haywire brain was playing tricks on her, or his hands were lingering a little too long and with a little too much pressure for a pat down.

He stood up, pulled her arms down and put his hands on her hips. They stood that way for just a second and Vesper's nose picked up a surge of the scent in the air. *He felt it, too.*

He turned her around, slowly.

"Take off the jacket." His silky voice was just above a whisper.

She had to give him some credit. Even looking right at him, he managed to move faster than her, sliding the black leather jacket off her shoulders and onto the desk in a second.

Her eyes never left his and she stared into their dark blue depths.

He frowned at her, the angles of his face tight and hard. "You said you weren't carrying any weapons," he growled.

The breath she'd been holding came out in a rush. At least he wasn't going to shoot her. She batted her lashes at him.

"No, I said I wasn't carrying a *gun*." She smiled. "Those aren't guns."

His eyes focused on the slim leather holster strapped to her upper body. She had six small throwing knives at her abdomen, three on each side, just below her breasts. The two really scary knives were snapped in behind her back. That must have been an interesting find. Not to mention the three others securely tucked away around her legs and ankle. They were designed to avoid detection. And they did.

Her smile got wider. Finally, she'd gotten the drop on him. That's how it was supposed to work. She was the vampire, for chrissakes.

"You know all my secrets, and you haven't even bothered to introduce yourself," she said tartly.

He stepped back from her and held out his hand. "Detective Price. Homicide."

She placed her hand in the firm grasp. If he felt the same tingle she did, he didn't show it.

"You haven't mentioned what you're doing here," he said. "Besides breaking and entering, I might add." He pulled his hand back. The loss of contact was disappointing.

She picked up her jacket and folded it over one arm. "I'm looking for a missing girl."

"And you think the C.E.O. of a pharmaceutical company might know where she is?" he crossed his arms over his chest. "Interesting theory. I assume you got wind of Reardon's death through police channels?"

"Of course. Your people apparently blew up the police band. You would have to be deaf not to have heard it." There was truth in the lie somewhere.

He nodded. "How do you figure he's involved with your missing girl?"

Vesper took a step toward the door. The glass vial in her jacket was burning a hole in her pocket, and no matter what sort of sparks were flying off the detective, there was work to do. Might as well throw him a bone. "My intel suggests at least part of the pharm lab is in the manufacture of several nasty street drugs and he's heavily into sex trafficking. Mostly eastern Europe, we think." *Happy hunting, handsome man.* She almost waggled her fingers to shoo him away.

He pulled a quick body block and kept her from reaching the door. "Narcotics and Vice haven't mentioned anything. I would have gotten a call," he insisted.

She shrugged at him. "It's almost three a.m. Maybe they'll hit you tomorrow." Vesper put her jacket on. "If you'll excuse me..."

"If you've got an informant, you need to share. Especially if it's vital to a murder investigation," he urged. "You don't want an obstruction charge hanging over you."

Vesper snorted. "Do your own detective work, *Detective* Price. Make your call, someone on another squad can fill you in." She shook her head in disapproval and stepped around him. "And FYI, I don't scare easily, so pointing your piece and threatening me won't make me play nice." She moved again and his hand shot out and grabbed her arm. Instinct prevailed and she palmed the hilt of a dagger in a flash.

"Careful, Ms. Hyde." His arm tightened like a vice, jerking her against him and she felt the nose of the SIG against her belly. *Fine. Point taken.* She pulled out her empty hand, showing it to him.

She looked down at his hold on her arm and her eyes darkened with anger. "I won't be man-handled, Detective. By anyone," she warned.

He released her and holstered the weapon. "And I won't be brushed off." He raked a hand through his sandy blond hair, sniffing. "It's Decker, by the way."

Vesper eased back a bit. "I thought all detectives had names like John or Frank or Harry," she said wryly.

He grinned, all seriousness gone. "You've read too many crime novels. What about Vesper? You're not exactly standard P.I. fare, either."

She could feel the shadow cross her face and couldn't stop it. His eyes narrowed on her, watching. The clarity she saw kept her from a snarky comeback. Finally, a truth emerged.

"My mother was very devout. She always said she felt the most spiritual at evening prayers."

"Sounds like a mother."

Vesper shook off the memory and eased back on her heels. "Double check through Narcotics. I got it first hand from one of his dealers. It shouldn't be too hard for you to verify. Good luck with your investigation." She moved past him into the hall and started back toward the kitchen. A new jolt of confidence sparked through her. It was time to get home.

He fell into step behind her. "Give me a lift back to the precinct?" he asked. "I had a patrol drop me off."

No. No. No. Tempting as it was to get into close quarters with him, she could do without the distraction.

"M.E. should have the autopsy report ready. If you're interested, that is," he suggested.

She kept moving toward the back door. He might be onto something. Getting a look at the file might give her something to go on. He followed her out the back door and into the street without waiting for a response.

"Well?"

There it was again. The damn sexy man voice. No way. Not. Going. To. Happen. Whatever N.O.P.D. had discovered, someone within the Archive could get for her. She wouldn't have to deal with Detective Sexy Voice anymore. Time to get rid of him.

Vesper wheeled on him, a tart kiss-off on her lips, and slammed into the hard wall of his chest. A chest that did not move. Liquid pools of blue stared down at her, leaving her in danger of getting lost in their depths. His hands were steel bands around her upper arms gripping her tight, steadying her on legs that had mysteriously devolved into Jell-O.

The night air was heavy and damp, daring her body to breathe. The pressure of his chest so close against hers made her dizzy. She sucked in a deep breath and was rewarded with a mouthful of hot, humid spice. The taste of the air across her tongue sent a change rippling throughout her body. She felt the steady drum of his heartbeat, heard the blood pounding in his veins. It called to her.

Something low and deep in her growled, calling forth feelings she kept a careful lid on. She could see the flicker of the pulse at his neck as its rhythm pulled her closer. Her fangs itched with longing. She wanted to taste him. Wanted to see if he tasted as good as he smelled. Her mouth watered at the thought, because God, he smelled like heaven.

Heavy emotion surged, overwhelming her senses. The thin layer of his shirt couldn't disguise the wall of corded muscle she felt underneath. She had resisted his hands on her earlier, but now she wanted him to pull her even tighter against him, joining them together. Magnolias in bloom couldn't overshadow the scent that emanated from him. It rolled over her in waves, chipping away at her willpower. The mix of spice and desire were coming together in an onslaught of sensory input she needed to fight. Hard. It would be a mistake to leave with him now. Huge mistake.

Her mouth suddenly went dry. "The car's a block over."

There were two things, Decker realized, he knew with absolute certainty about the woman sitting next to him. First, no way in hell she was a private investigator. No P.I. would ever dress like that. Sleek, stylish, and lots of expensive black leather. A haute couture female Johnny Cash. Not to mention the car. The only Aston-Martin he'd seen was in a Bond flick.

Second, and not to be underestimated, he was attracted to her. The violet eyes and thick mane of silky brown hair put her in an exclusive class of beautiful. She was stunning. And to be honest, attracted was too meek a word for what was going on below the belt of his khakis at the moment. Their little body brush back there had him jonesing for more of the bump and grind, as crude as that was. The feeling unsettled him a little; he wasn't usually like this with women. Basic southern upbringing had pounded home the gentlemanly ideal. Miranda hadn't even elicited this kind of visceral response and he loved her deeply. He sickened. *Miranda.*

It always came back to Miranda. Her death nearly killed him. For the first two months, he drank his grief, the misery so all-consuming his chief nearly chained his ass to a desk for eternity. After that, gentleman be damned, it was solace in the faceless bodies and hollow hunger of mindless sex to drive away the demons, even for a moment. And when her killer was tucked away to be forgotten at Angola, he thought the torment would end. It did for a while, but over time, in a hundred different ways, she kept creeping back into the edges of his mind, fraying his fragile hold on sanity. A song on the radio, the sound of a woman's laughter, and the smell of the damn Chanel perfume she wore. It was all too much, so he simply packed away the memories, praying to a God he no longer believed in for peace.

He was almost there, he thought, if not for the alluring enigma in the driver's seat.

Decker gave her a sidelong glance and felt his body quicken. Her pale skin glowed in the moonlight, its luminosity drawing him in. Flawless. Danger lurked beneath her violet eyes and the easy grace of her movements as she shifted in her seat read to him the story of a woman who knew her body well. That knowledge alone was enough to stoke the fires of his arousal. For a second, he imagined her lithe body pressed against his, knotting together in an erotic tangle of limbs and mouths, submitting to the pleasures only flesh against flesh can bring.

He shook away the sultry image from his mind and quickly came to the conclusion that where Vesper Hyde was concerned, peace was not forthcoming.

She was quiet and relaxed, her eyes focused on the highway ahead. Vesper made no move to look at him, but he knew she was watching him.

Decker cleared his throat. She didn't startle.

"So, your work for the Consortium? Security, right?"

She nodded, eyes never leaving the road.

"That's got to be interesting, I imagine. What sort of protection do you provide?" he asked.

"I'm not a bodyguard. I deal mainly with corporate security and intelligence." Her voice was clipped.

Decker arched an eyebrow. "Corporate espionage? How John Grisham. Tell me, does 'private investigator' translate well into 'illegal enforcer'?"

Vesper's eyes flicked over to give him a pointed look. "What makes you think I'm doing anything illegal?" she snapped.

The annoyed glare she gave him made him smile. He rolled his eyes at her and continued, "I'm not sure. Maybe it's the nighttime B&E, the black leather cat burglar ensemble you're sporting, or possibly it's the small arsenal of nasty looking cutlery you have strapped to your lovely little body. Take your pick, chère. Either way, none of it smacks 'legit'."

Vesper sniffed and tossed her head to the side, revealing the soft curve of her neckline highlighted alternately between the moonlight and the lights on the freeway. Decker found himself staring into that small expanse of skin and noticed the ink there. He couldn't make out the image fully since her hair blocked part of his view. He wanted to take his fingers and brush the silky strands aside to see what she had hiding beneath the chocolate curtain. It looked like the hilt of a sword or some type of blade. Another flash of moonlight caught his eye and he redirected his gaze to her chest. The flash had glinted from the silver necklace she wore. The same emblem, he noted. Silver crossed swords on a delicate silver chain.

Now, he'd seen a lot of ink on a lot of women and it ran the gamut from serious connoisseurs who regarded it as body art to the ever popular tramp stamps. This was a badge, a military mark, the kind a Marine or Army Ranger would use to brand themselves with pride. Her air of mystery was growing by leaps and bounds and he found he was eager to learn more.

"See something you like?" she asked, exiting the freeway.

"I'll admit," he sighed, "you've definitely got my attention."

She gave him a wry smile but kept quiet. They remained that way for the last few blocks until she pulled into the precinct's parking lot and veered the Vantage into an empty space.

He unsnapped his seat belt and got out. Peering over the roof of the car at her he said, "You'd better de-bling, Ms. Hyde. Your knife collection is bound to short circuit the metal detectors."

Vesper frowned and held her chin high. "They stay. Deal with it."

Decker held his hands up at her. "Suit yourself. I hear the night shift does a mean frisk."

She smiled knowingly and passed through the open door he held. She watched as he unholstered the SIG and removed the clip and set it down on the conveyor. He grinned at the night guard.

"Hiya, Frank. Quiet tonight?"

The skinny uniform nodded. "Pretty much, Deck. You doing all right? Kinda late for you, huh?"

"Nah. Can't complain, can't complain." Decker winked at the younger man. "Hey, you tell Sarah and the girls hello for me, you hear?" He passed through the archway of the device and assembled and holstered the weapon.

Frank smiled at him. "I sure will. Ma'am." He glanced down at Vesper's credentials and nodded at her as she stepped through the opening without incident.

Decker's eyes came up to stare blankly at her as she nodded her acknowledgment to Frank and walked confidently past them to the elevator a few feet away. He charged up behind her and jammed the up button hard with his finger. The doors opened and he grabbed her arm and pushed her inside.

She twisted in his grasp, but he managed to grab both of her hands and pin them behind her. He elbowed the button for the third floor and maneuvered quickly to trap her against the back wall of the elevator.

"Get off of me," she hissed, glaring up at him.

He could feel the rapid rise and fall of her breasts beneath his chest with every breath she took. Her lips parted slightly at his roughness and their lush fullness was almost enough to distract him. They touched from chest to thigh and the contact started a slow burn in his body.

"What in the hell was that? Who are you?" he insisted.

"Get. Off. Of. Me."

"The blades?"

"I'm special," she sneered. "They're treated."

"Bullshit." Decker frowned and tightened his grip, causing her to gasp.

The soft, seductive sound did it. Blood rushed to his groin and desire knifed through him. Her upturned mouth was plump and inviting and her body was heaven against his. She was breathing in little shallow gasps that timed perfectly with the pound of the pulse in his ears. Decker felt her nipples tighten through the fabric of her T-shirt and he resisted the urge to groan. Her lashes fluttered for a moment and he was drawn inexorably lower to her lips. He wanted to kiss her. Kiss her good. Decker opened his mouth, readying for the feel, the taste of her.

The elevator jolted to a halt, jarring them both. Vesper took advantage of the moment and wrenched free. She whirled and ground out, "I warned you about the manhandling. Next time, you'll be using your teeth to pick your fingers up off the floor."

He ignored her, pushing past her onto the empty floor, stopping at one of the six desks in the open area. He flipped open the folder on the desktop and quickly scanned it. He closed it, snatched it up and crossed back to her. Decker shoved the file in her hands and headed back to the elevator. She followed in step behind him and they entered the opening doors.

He punched a button and turned to face her. Anger crossed his face.

"That's the autopsy report. I'm taking you down to see the body. Now, I expect some reciprocation." He shifted on his feet and reached out a finger to her necklace. She met his eyes with an icy glare. "Again, who are you? There's no way you can treat a blade to avoid metal detection." He lowered his face to hers. "Why are you on my murder?" The chill in her eyes couldn't disguise the glimmer of arousal he saw there. Frustration was building a swirling knot in his gut.

Vesper didn't flinch. "I don't know what-"

"Do not bullshit me, Vesper." Her given name rolled off his tongue too easily, he thought. "I want answers."

The elevator dinged and she followed him out. "I don't have any to give you. It's need to know. And you don't."

Decker swished aside the double doors to the autopsy suite with a heavy hand. He was thoroughly pissed. It was bad enough Howard Grainger was coming back in some way to bite him in the ass; it was even worse that it looked like he was going to be muscled out by some as-of-yet unknown organization. The image of those damn swords were burned into his brain. *Who was she working for?*

Vesper was no longer paying him any attention and was checking out the photos in the autopsy report. Decker stopped against the back wall of drawers, and tapped on one with a finger.

"Here you go. Pull him out and take a look for yourself," he said, shoving his hands in his pockets.

She laid the file on one of the metal tables and walked over and opened the drawer and slid the body out. Decker watched her face as she inspected the corpse, trying to discern any change. Her eyes lingered longest on the savagely torn flesh of his neck and hardened. She glanced at the heart-shaped cut on the chest and arched an eyebrow in question at Decker.

"What's that about?" She gestured to the mark.

"You are looking at the signature of one Howard Grainger, sexual sadist and serial killer," Decker replied.

She leaned over to look more closely. "You're telling me Reardon was murdered by a serial killer?" Her frown of disbelief lingered.

Decker shook his head at her. "I'm telling you that's his signature. There aren't any signs of sexual trauma to the body, which Grainger usually leaves in spades, but there's just one other thing." He pulled out his cell phone from the pocket of his khakis and flipped it open. He looked away from her long enough to push a button for speed dial and then returned his gaze to hers. She opened her mouth to speak, but he held up his hand. "It's Decker Price. Yeah, I know. Wake up the warden," he said into the phone. He paused and acknowledged her questioning look. "Did I mention Grainger's been in solitary at Angola for the past two years? Saddle up, chère. We're going to The Farm."

CHAPTER THREE

For all his pissiness and mancentric ego, she had to give it to him. He was adorable when he slept. His chest rose and fell under the heavy cloak of sleep and Vesper could only shake her head and wonder how she managed to wind up on a crack-of-dawn road trip to the Louisiana State Penitentiary at Angola. With a human, no less.

It did, however, give her a delicious feeling of guilty satisfaction to know he thought she was part of a secret government organization he wasn't privy to. She hoped it would make keeping her cover that much easier.

She resigned herself to the fact that the vial in her jacket would have to wait just a little longer. Once they returned, she'd rid herself of Decker and get back to work on the vial's origin.

Her dear friend and witch, Lorelei Masters, would be the one to help her. She could tell when she palmed it that it was probably spell-ridden, given that Reardon had taken great pains to conceal it. And frankly, when you were dealing with spells, you needed a witch. Hence, Lori. Artemis would hate having to enlist a witch's help, but he'd have to get over his little vampire versus witch issue and deal. Especially if he wanted answers. Given what was at stake, she guessed the High Elder would be able to suck it up long enough to get them. After all, he had only frowned and nodded when she informed him she'd had Lori use magic on her blades.

Decker woke about halfway through the trip, but didn't speak, instead keeping his gaze fixed on the rolling Louisiana landscape out of his tinted passenger window. Small talk wasn't her strong suit either, so she kept her mouth shut and kept driving. She had ample time to reflect on the current situation and decided that the growing attraction she was feeling was definitely a problem. Keeping their distance from the human race had served her kind well for a very long time. It was precisely this distance that had kept the two races from a possibly disastrous collision course. Vampires just did not meddle in the affairs of humans. The more separate their worlds could be, the better. And the sooner his usefulness was over, the better.

Once she got what she needed and sent him on his way, these unsettling feelings would be gone and she would be on to another assignment. *Keep telling yourself that, babe.*

Decker straightened in his seat and cleared his throat as she made the final turn, heading onto the prison's grounds. She slowed at the main gate and Decker leaned over her chest and flashed his badge and credentials at the security bunker.

"Detective Decker Price, NOPD Homicide. Warden's expecting me." They were waved in, passing through multiple gates and winding through the parking area to one of the buildings.

Even her spell-disguised blades didn't go unnoticed at the maximum security prison, and she was relieved of them via a detailed and almost harassing body search. After raising several eyebrows from the burly guards, they were led into a small holding area with a table and chairs and telephone. A few minutes passed and one of the guards, a heavy-set white man, came in.

"Prisoner's ready for you. Warden won't be in. He's on an early call with the Governor's office. Said to tell you hello, Detective. If you need anything else while you're here, just let us know. Now, if y'all want to follow me, we'll take you to him."

The walk down the corridor was quiet and the sound of her boots on the tile floor echoed down the long hallway. They were whisked through several electronic doors before being led into a small interrogation room.

Howard Grainger sat handcuffed to a metal table in the center of the room directly in front of a large, two-way mirror. The guard stepped out and closed the door, leaving Decker and Vesper alone in the room with the restrained killer.

"I see your tastes have changed for the dangerous, Detective." Amusement glittered in Grainger's eyes as his hard stare flicked over Vesper with keen interest. "Well, well. Aren't you just a dark vision of loveliness?" He cocked his head to one side and smiled directly at Decker. "Not quite the bright, sunshiny day that dear Miranda was, but I imagine it's all the same when you close your eyes, I'm sure. Am I right?" He chuckled softly, an eerie sound that had Vesper's hand twitching for one of her knives. Damn maximum security.

She saw Decker's body stiffen slightly at the mention of the woman's name. Sister? Mother? Wife? Definitely someone close. *Interesting.*

Parking herself in the corner, she stood back, ready to watch things unfold. Decker strolled in and casually sat down at the table. He folded his hands and looked across at Grainger.

"How's it going, Howie?" he asked happily, as if the two were old friends.

Grainger visibly bristled at the nickname. "Detective, surely you didn't have them rouse me so early this morning simply to exchange pleasantries?" The prisoner folded his hands together, the handcuffs clinking.

"I can't recall it ever being pleasant, Howie," Decker said.

"On the contrary, my dear detective, some of my happiest moments have been our little chats," Howard responded. "But, I don't think you're here for a trek down memory lane. If you're in the mood to reminisce, however...." He opened his tethered hands in an inviting gesture.

Vesper tilted her head to the side, careful not to draw attention, to get a focus on the killer. The orange jumpsuit was a little baggy, but the span of his shoulders gave away the toned physique underneath. He had a sharp, angular face with a slight point to his chin. Pale, but otherwise fairly attractive. Dark gray eyes, a full pout to his lips and a thick head of short, dark hair served to add to his slightly-cuter-than-the-boy-next-door look. It wouldn't have been too hard for Grainger to coerce his victims. Human women tended to blindly trust good-looking men. A fatal flaw in their design, she supposed. Vesper saw right through his facade and zeroed in on the glint of suppressed psychopathic rage in his stormy eyes.

Decker took the close-up photo of Reardon's shredded neck out of the file he'd brought and slapped it down in front of Grainger.

"Tell me about this." he said.

"Looks like someone was hungry. I prefer the other end for snacking." Howard said.

"So you've seen this kind of thing before, then?" Decker drummed his fingers over the photo.

Howard considered the question for a moment and leaned back, the flimsy metal chair squeaking under the adjustment. "I've indulged in some....blood play on occasion. Those chalky Goth girls really go for it. Low self esteem, I suppose." He smiled. "But that's a little much, even for me." Howard ran his tongue along the inside of his mouth as he spoke, the gesture adding volumes to his air of restrained instability. Vesper's fingers twitched again, longing for her confiscated cutlery.

Decker looked genuinely interested. "Really? Sounds like you need a willing participant for that. How'd you manage it?" he asked. "Pay for play?"

Howard wrinkled his nose at Decker's smirk and gave a small, wistful sigh. "Oh no, in the end, they were all willing. It's amazing what they'll bargain with for a little hope."

"I find that hard to believe," Decker said. "Damned arrogant, if you ask me."

Howard's eyes flickered in annoyance. "Arrogant is such an ugly word, Detective. I prefer the phrase 'supremely confident'".

"Right," Decker drawled. "But then again, you're not exactly a ladies man, now are you? I always thought your tastes ran to pole rather than hole. Did they all laugh at you? 'Cause you couldn't get it up?"

Grainger shrugged lightly, as if he didn't catch the veiled insult. "Well, I suppose it's all a matter of perception, isn't it?" He leaned forward slowly, the cuffs scraping loudly on the metal table. His gray eyes were cold as he locked on to Decker. The thin lines of his face contorted to a twisted mask of suppressed rage. His voice was hard as steel. "They all wanted it. Every bitch, every time."

Vesper caught the whiff of a new scent in the air. One she was all too familiar with. Tart and rich, like cranberries at Christmas, Howard Grainger was exuding vampire! *What in the hell was that about?*

Unfazed, Decker slid the autopsy photo across to Howard. His demeanor changed from predatory to cool and relaxed in an instant. Howard looked at it for a moment, considering the gray-blue tint to Reardon's skin, and the sutures from the M.E.'s Y-incision which dissected the ragged heart carved into the chest.

"This," he sniffed, sliding the photo back to Decker, "does not interest me. I'm sure there are others that would be more to my liking. Some that might stir up some feeling of, say...nostalgia?" Howard smiled smugly.

Decker made a slashing gesture with his hand. "No can do, Howie. This is all you get."

Grainger gave a loud mock sigh. "I suppose I should have expected that." His eyes narrowed on Decker. "I'm well aware you don't bargain. Isn't that right?" The undercurrent of

49

sarcasm got Vesper's attention. If it ruffled Decker, he didn't show it.

Right now she was more concerned with how Grainger smelled like vampire. She pressed back into the wall and focused. Her eyes cut over him slowly, taking in every detail of his body. She rested on his hands and looked closer at his fingers. They were slightly curled into his palms, but she was able to see the nail beds. Almost white, the light glinted off of them, making them look almost like glass. She craned her neck forward a little to make sure her eyes weren't deceiving her.

Grainger caught the movement and met her gaze. He gave a slight, almost imperceptible shift of his head. The collar of his jumpsuit had come away from his neck a tiny bit, revealing a small opening of skin.

What was it he said? Blood play?

Her eyes shot to the mirror behind him, and there it was, concealed by the collar of the jumpsuit. Two small holes about two inches below and behind his ear. Her mouth opened in surprise and she let out a small breath.

Fang marks.

The marks were easily dismissible to the untrained eye. He had been fed on, often, and for a while, judging from the condition of the scars. A bite mark from a single feed would fade on a human, but repeated trauma of the area would leave marks. Soft scars just like those.

Grainger cleared his throat and she met his eyes. The knowing smile chilled her. *He'd made her. Damn.*

And the nails? For that to happen, Grainger must have fed from the vampire as well. Transformations like that took time, not to mention they were strictly forbidden. Only the High Elder had the power to turn a human. What the hell had she stumbled on to?

"All this concern over someone who's taking an interest in my work?" Howard asked. "I'm flattered. Maybe I'll get a fan club and start signing up members." He glanced at Vesper. "You interested? I do get one visit a month, you know. We could make it conjugal. Bring the leather, because that outfit is hot." He licked his lips at her suggestively.

Decker chided, "That's enough, Howie. Has anyone contacted you recently? Anything unusual?"

"Other than the marriage proposals and offers to help me find the Lord? But there's always hope. I would really like to know that I've inspired others." He traced the heart in the photo with his finger and looked up at Decker. "I'm so glad you brought this to me, Detective." The storm is his eyes rumbled and darkened. Real emotion was coursing through Howard, she could smell it. "So glad." He let out a slow breath. "I don't suppose you'll let me keep this, will you?"

Decker snorted. "What do you think?"

Howard nodded. "I didn't think so. But no harm in asking, right? And in answer to the question buzzing around your brain, no." His demeanor changed again, this time all business. "They read all my mail. Screen all my visitors, of which I've had few. I've got nothing for you. Nothing. You're wasting my time. All this fuss and I could be playing mah-jongg."

"That's not true." Decker tapped the photo. "Your little trademark was never made public. Makes this a lot more interesting." He leaned forward and locked his gaze with the killer.

Howard paled, then quickly regained composure. "Yes, well....the heart wants what it wants, Detective. Maybe this gentleman didn't give them what they wanted." He sniffed, sat up straighter and said, "I think we're done here."

"Not by a long shot, Howie. Now-"

"He's right, Decker. We're done," Vesper said, pushing off from the wall. "Let's go." She moved to the door.

Decker looked at her with suspicion and growled, "Fine." He snatched the photos from the table and shoved them roughly in the folder, scraping the chair back as he got to his feet.

Decker had one foot out the door and Howard called, "Detective? I hope you find what you're looking for. Let me know when you do. I want to hear all about it." Grainger's face slid into a twisted smile. "It's been so very long."

"Fuck you, Grainger."

The sound of Howard's laughter was cut off by the slam of the door.

Decker stormed out into the hallway and went to the guard that had been standing outside. He yanked his wallet from his back pocket, whipped out a card and shoved it into the guard's chest, damn near pinning the man to the wall.

"That's my card. You give that to the warden and tell him I want Grainger's visitor log. I want to know every person that's been here to see him in the past two years. I want every piece of correspondence *to* him and *from* him. And I want it yesterday. Fax it, email it, fuck, send it by carrier pigeon. But I want it on my desk in New Orleans by the time my ass hits the chair," Decker snarled.

"Will do, boss. Harper," he called to a younger guard just down the corridor, "see the detectives out." He held up the card. "On my way now, Price."

Decker watched him leave and turned to Vesper, fire blazing in his eyes. He leaned down to her face and spoke, soft and deadly. "I am not in the habit of being pussy-whipped, and I'm damn sure not going to start now." Her jaw clenched in defiance and he continued, "I don't give a rat's ass who you are working for, the next time you interject yourself into my interrogation like that, be prepared to reap the consequences, because I will have your ass on a platter right next to your knives, chère. Do not presume to fuck with me on this."

He turned away then, bracing himself on the wall with one hand and a deep, heavy sigh escaped him.

"He wasn't going to give up anything else." She said, unapologetic. "I don't know what else you hoped to gain, but-"

"But nothing, Vesper." He stepped away from the wall and brushed a frustrated hand through his hair. He gestured to the door. "He could've....I was...Fuck," he stammered. His voice cracked roughly and he rasped, "He's got more answers. You don't understand. There's more he's not telling. You saw that." There was strained pleading in his voice.

A twinge of sadness touched her heart as he lowered his head and shook it in futility. She realized with a start this case had consumed him for whatever reason and he thought it had been over. Reardon's death was dredging up hard and painful memories, memories he buried instead of facing. The agony was written on the lines of his face, the sorrow mirrored in his eyes. This Miranda, she was the key. However Reardon and Grainger were connected, she knew she would find Miranda somewhere in the fray. She knew this pain. Guilt. Loss. She placed a hand on his shoulder and turned him to face her.

His soul was laid bare and her heart lodged in her throat at the anguish she saw. A silent cry howled deep in her belly, a call to arms steeling her for a bond as old as time. With a clear, yet comforting realization, she knew that whatever happened from this point on, they were linked inexorably on a course neither of them could imagine. Their worlds were about to collide and there was nothing to do but brace for the fallout.

He pulled away from her and followed Harper down the hall, his heavy footfalls drumming out his irritation. He didn't look back as he snapped, "Let's get back. I've got things to do. And just so you know, your shitty cover about the missing girl, yeah, that's pretty much blown to hell."

The glare from the morning sun was irritating, even through the blackout tint on the Aston-Martin's windows. The whole "sunlight kills vampires" thing was a myth, but it did manage to tire them out faster than normal and force them into feeding more often. It was common for young just coming into their change to have trouble adapting; old habits die hard. Learning to live nocturnally wasn't for everyone, and if one wasn't careful, it was easy to get caught up in a vicious cycle of fatigue and hunger, which usually ended badly. Vesper knew from experience it was no way to live.

So, when it was necessary to be out and about in daylight hours, she relied on a pair of Gargoyles Downforce sunglasses and the heavy tint on the car. It was not optimal, but functional.

"He's working with someone." They were the first words Decker had spoken since they left the prison over an hour ago.

"You're sure about that? How do you know he wasn't just screwing with you? He seems to enjoy it and you seem to fall for it."

He dug out his cell and snapped, "You don't know shit about it."

"Enlighten me."

He pushed another button on speed dial and waited. Vesper could hear a muffled voice on the other end and Decker said, "Hey C, it's Deck. Yeah, I know. I'm sorry. There's been a lead." He paused as the voice on the other end spoke. "You got the logs? Yeah, Grainger. I'll explain it when I get back. Start running backgrounds on those names. I'll see you in a few." Another pause. "Yeah, I'm okay. Thanks." He hung up the phone and tucked it away.

"Partner?" Vesper asked.

"Yeah."

"I take it they sent over the logs and letters?" She tried to sound casual.

"Yeah."

He was still angry. *Oh well.* The too-handsome detective was going to have to man up for now. She wasn't up for a pissing contest even though fangs beat dick every time.

They were silent for the rest of the drive.

Vesper sat quietly across the desk from Decker while he flipped through the printouts. His anger was still rolling out with each hard turn of the pages. He'd glared at her again as she passed through the precinct's metal detectors, but had kept quiet.

There was no way around it. She was going to have to tell him. And soon. Artemis was not going to be happy. This was getting more complicated by the minute. The fang marks on Reardon were obvious and coupled with the big feeding no-no that was Howard Grainger; the truth would make her options very limited, indeed. If she came clean and it all went south, there was a very real possibility that Decker would have to be neutralized. The Council would demand it. The Archive and its secrets would have to remain safe, no matter the cost. Her stomach turned at the thought. She would do her best to see that he remained useful and hope that he didn't fuck it up. Because if he did, she couldn't help him.

"Tell me what we're looking at, Deck."

Vesper looked up to see the voice belonged to the striking dark-haired woman who had appeared at his side, leaning casually against his desk. *The partner was a woman?* The knowledge left a bad taste in her mouth.

"Hey, C.C." Decker looked up and smiled at her with genuine affection. Vesper's irritation ratcheted up a notch.

He nudged his head at Vesper. "C, this is Vesper Hyde. She's a security consultant for the Séraphine Consortium." He didn't elaborate further.

The tall woman smiled at Vesper, revealing pageant-perfect white teeth. Irritation was becoming a hearty dislike.

"Vesper, this is my partner, Detective C.C. Anderson." C.C. extended her hand to Vesper.

"Nice to meet you, Ms. Hyde." C.C.'s voice had a gritty phone-sex kind of tone. Vesper's mind flashed to hot, erotic images of Decker and the woman detective. Images equally disturbing for their intensity and their players. The two women clasped hands. "Thanks for making the road trip to Angola. He would've been good to make it back in one piece if I had to spend that long in the car with him," C.C. laughed.

There was no strong arm in the handshake, no unspoken bitch-that's-my-man warning. They weren't lovers. Why was that a relief? "He snores."

C.C. laughed again and pulled a chair over and sat down. "Grainger's a real piece of work. Every time I see him, I feel an unholy need to shower afterward. He's creepily unnerving." She paused. "So what's with all the backgrounds? Most of them came up clean."

Decker shifted in the chair, agitated. "I think he's working with someone."

C.C.'s brown eyes darkened. "You're serious? That's how he's connected to Reardon?" Decker handed her the autopsy photo and she looked at it and let out a low curse. "Christ."

Vesper leaned forward. "Did anything in your prior investigation point to anyone besides Grainger? Someone who just wasn't as good for it?" she asked. Decker shook his head. "Could you have missed something?"

His head whipped up to face her. "No," he snapped, jamming a finger down hard on the desk. "This case was solid. One perpetrator, that's it. There was no evidence to prove otherwise." His blue eyes were stone cold. "I didn't miss anything."

Vesper met his steely gaze and turned to C.C. "Is he always this pissy or is it just me?"

The other woman gave a perfunctory nod. "When it comes to Howard Grainger, yeah."

Decker frowned, "What about the background checks again?" he huffed, shooting a furtive glance between them.

"Like I said, most of them came up clean. Except," C.C. rifled through the paperwork, picking up a couple of sheets and laying them out, "for this one. He only visited once, shortly after Grainger was transferred up. I couldn't past a really good paper trail that went nowhere fast."

Vesper reached over and took one sheet. "What's the name?"

C.C. scanned the documents. "Um...here it is. Vincent Destrehan. He-"

Vesper didn't hear the rest. The world shifted in focus and she placed a hand on the desk to keep from falling out of the chair as icy realization set in.

Vincent Destrehan. No, Victor Delacroix. *Victor Fucking Delacroix.* Her heart pounded in her ears and her stomach plummeted to her toes, daring her to vomit. Her only Penitent failure. The one the Council nearly had her head for. The one that almost killed her. The one that got away.

Everything shifted again, and to her relief, neither Decker nor C.C. seemed to notice her inattention.

"-and that's all I could find. I'll need a warrant for the financials, though," C.C. finished.

"Well, get on the phone to the A.D.A. and make it happen," Decker said.

She needed to go. Now. Vesper looked at the Patek Phillipe watch on her wrist and stood. "Here's my contact info. Hit me with a copy of that." She took her card from her jacket and handed it to C.C.

Decker looked surprised. "You're leaving?"

Vesper nodded. "Yeah. I need to get back." She looked at C.C. "It was a pleasure, Detective Anderson." The women shook hands again.

"Likewise." C.C. smiled. "I'll get it together for you and email it ASAP." She gathered the papers together as Decker got up to follow Vesper to the elevator.

Decker blew out a harsh breath. "Where are you going?" he demanded.

She stiffened. "I have to get back." That was an understatement. Victor Delacroix drastically changed the playing field. She raised her chin and looked him in the eye. "I have a job to do. I'm leaving to do it." It wasn't a lie, exactly. Executing murderous vampires was the crux of her job description. And now was not the time for plot exposition. That would come later. Much later, she hoped.

"You're hiding something, Vesper." He leaned in a little and his damn scent assaulted her one more time as he pressed the elevator button. "I will find out."

"You do that." She turned on her heel as the doors opened and stepped inside. "Goodbye, Detective." The doors closed and Vesper sagged against the wall, weak with the knowledge of remembered pain and new complications. She didn't know which was worse.

Decker narrowed his eyes at the elevator bank and walked back to his desk. Without hesitation, he picked up the phone and dialed.

"Yeah, Brick, it's Price. There's a black Aston-Martin leaving the lot. Can't miss it. Tail it and let me know where it ends up. And keep it off the band, would you? Thanks."

He hung up the phone and met C.C.'s questioning, almost disapproving look. He shrugged. "What can I say? I don't trust her."

CHAPTER FOUR

Vesper woke with a start and looked at her bedside clock. Seven p.m. She'd come home in a rush, the need for sleep outweighing the need to see the High Elder. She needed a little time to rest and focus before she dropped the bomb.

She flipped back the silk coverlet and walked naked to the bathroom. She reached in and started the shower and went to the sink to brush her teeth. Staring at her reflection as she brushed, her gaze focused on the dark circles under her eyes.

A storm was coming, far out on the horizon of her consciousness, the rumbles of things to come weighing heavy on her heart. She spit, wiped her mouth and straightened and looked at her naked form in the mirror. There were no visible scars on her body, prompt medical attention and rapid regeneration were to thank for that. The scars that remained were deep beneath the skin, etched forever on her psyche.

She ran a trembling hand down her chest, over the fullness of her breasts and began to remember. Each cut, each slice, each scream. It took a hell of a lot to kill a vampire and Victor Delacroix had done his damnedest. But his mistake was in not finishing the job, his arrogance getting the better of him. He'd inflicted pain she could never imagine and her body quaked at the memory. Not out of fear, but sheer agony. It was a miracle her brother Marcus had found her, broken and bleeding, her life seeping away in pools of blood on a slab of concrete.

If Marcus was a minute later, if he hadn't stopped the bleeding, if he couldn't have given her his vein, she would be dead. But she had recovered and Victor had disappeared. More importantly, she had failed.

She swallowed the hard lump in her throat and stepped under the hot spray, desperately trying to scrub away the memories.

Feeling somewhat cleaner and ready to face the past, she dressed and headed for Artemis.

"I've made an....unsettling discovery."

Artemis drummed his fingers on his desk, waiting for more. Vesper could see the tension that lay beneath the calm exterior of his face. She took a deep breath and stepped off the cliff.

"Victor Delacroix killed Evan Reardon." The fingers stopped their drumming but there was no change in his expression. She took the vial from her jacket and placed it on the desktop. She continued, "I think he was looking for this." Artemis broke eye contact for a moment to consider the vial and then looked back to her, still silent. "I'm going to take it to Lori." She noted the eyebrow arch at the witch's name, but finished, "I think she may be able to shed some light on it."

The calm visage faded, making her feel very much like a child about to be scolded.

"You're sure it's Victor?"

Vesper nodded, and recounted the events leading from her encounter at Reardon's to the discovery of the alias in the visitor logs. She steeled herself against the tirade she knew was coming.

"Humans. Witches. You've been very busy." The drumming resumed and Vesper lowered her gaze. "This detective, does he know what we are?"

She shook her head. "No, he thinks I'm with a secret government organization." Another eyebrow arch. "*Human* government organization," she stressed.

"You will not be able to keep this secret."

"I know."

Artemis frowned. "Will he be a problem?"

She thought about Decker, the scent memory lingering in her brain, causing her skin to flush. He was already a problem.

"I don't think so," she answered. "But I can tell you, he's not going to let this go. This Grainger case is very important to him. He's going to follow this down the rabbit hole, regardless of where it leads."

The frown deepened. "And you're leading him straight to us, Vesper. The Council will have to know."

"I know," she whispered.

Artemis laid his hands flat, palms down on the desk and pinned her with his gaze. "Fine. Keep him close. He stays until it's over, whatever the outcome, for his own sake. If he can't be trusted, well....you know how it will end." She nodded at the ugly truth. "See the witch, as much as it pains me to say, and find out about this Grainger and how he's involved with Reardon and Delacroix." He sighed heavily. "I don't like this. This cannot end well. For all parties involved."

A frantic knock at the study door got both their attention.

"Excellency!" a voice called. "I must speak with you! Please!"

Artemis threw open the door onto an agitated acolyte.

"It's the front gate! Security says there's a man – a policeman demanding entry! He says if we don't allow him in he's bringing a SWAT team and – *gasp*- the ATF!" The young man was white with fright.

Artemis put a hand to his forehead and closed his eyes. "Let him through." He turned to Vesper with a grim face. "It appears Daniel has entered the lions' den. Make sure he doesn't get eaten." He checked his watch and began to make his way to the double staircase in the grand foyer. Two steps up, he turned back to Vesper. "The Council will not be with us on this. Both our fates are in your hands. Ensure this ends to our satisfaction." He walked upstairs, leaving her in the empty space.

Vesper turned to the waiting young man. "Leave."

The shell shocked acolyte suddenly found somewhere else to be as the doorbell chimed.

She pulled back one of the large oak doors and there he was, smelling like sin with a look to match. The door was large, but so was Decker and he nearly filled it with his size. She took a step back to let him in and her nostrils were rewarded with the familiar scent determined to wreak havoc on her senses.

"Welcome to Belle Ombre, Detective. One hell of a tail you've got," she said dryly.

"I thought I was gonna have to call down the law to get in here, chère. Didn't know the Delta Force was running your checkpoint," Decker said, waltzing past her into the foyer.

She shut the door. "I thought you were the law."

He ignored the comment and looked around with an impressed eye. "Nice digs out here on the River Road. Not too far from the big city. Guess it's nice and quiet. Don't have to worry much about the neighbors, right?" He smiled at her frown.

The foyer was immense and circular, with the double staircase leading to the next level of the mansion. He made the circle, tipping his head into open doors along the way, taking a quick peek inside each one.

She followed a few steps behind, watching the lines of his body. The man had an ass she could swear was carved from Italian marble. He was poured into those damn jeans. The rest of him was just as cut underneath the long-sleeved black t-shirt. Neither garment did anything to try to hide the physique he rocked. She recognized the SIG he'd flashed in her face strapped to his belt. He probably slept with the damn thing.

"Is this a social call, Detective?" She crossed her arms over her chest and cocked a hip to the side, feeling slightly perky. The look on his face when she fessed up was going to be, pardon the pun, priceless.

Her lighthearted mood quickly deflated as he stepped forward with purpose, bringing himself into her personal space. For a split second, her mind went blank. Her brain kick started in a flash and her consciousness filled with nothing but him. Chocolate and dark spice swirled in the air, lulling her into a hazy fog. She was frozen as he pulled her arms to her side and bent his head ever so slowly. Frozen, indeed, since her eyes could not tear away from his. He knew the spell he was weaving, she could see it. It was written in the glimmer of his gaze and in the upturned corners of his mouth as his lips beckoned her forward. She cursed him for being able to read the signs her treacherous body was sending out like signal flares.

"You owe me answers, chère." The richness of his honeyed voice primed her like someone had smacked her with a tuning fork, the reverberations barreling through her nervous system. "I've come to collect."

Yes, it was past time for answers. He asked for it, and she was going to give it to him. Damn him for dredging up feelings she had no right to feel for a human. Served him right. Vesper blinked and pulled back, licking her lips. She smiled at him, very cat who caught the canary. "Fair enough, Decker. Let's talk."

She motioned him into a comfortably appointed parlor underneath the left wing of the staircase. Vesper followed him inside and shut the door behind her.

"I could use a drink. How about you?" she asked.

"Just coffee."

She pressed a button on the intercom and waited for the voice. "Coffee for the downstairs parlor," she said into the speaker. "Service for two, please." She watched him out of the corner of her eye as he sat down on the red velvet chaise.

"Now," she said, leaving the doorway and settling into one of the chairs across from him, "what is it you wanted to discuss?" She clasped her hands together and placed them on her crossed knee, waiting.

"I want to know what the hell this," he said, gesturing to the surroundings, "is all about. And why you're interested in my murder case. What does the Séraphine Consortium, if that's really what you are, want with my serial killer and my victim?" His face was quiet, but serious.

A knock sounded at the door a few moments later, and at Vesper's "Enter", a young man dressed in black fatigues entered with the silver tray of coffee. He set it down, bowed to Vesper and left as quietly as he'd come. Decker stared after him and then turned his questioning look back to her. Time to put it out there.

"It's very simple," she said, pouring the coffee from the pot. "We're interested in Reardon because he's one of us. We take it very seriously when one of us is murdered." She smiled softly and handed him a cup and saucer. "Cream and sugar?"

"No, thanks. Um, what do you mean 'one of us'? Is he an agent with your organization? Who the hell are you people?" He frowned again, deeply agitated.

She sat back with her cup and took a sip from the streaming brew. She looked him straight in the eye, widened the scope of her smile and let her fangs drop. "Nothing that nefarious. We're vampires, Decker."

He set the cup down with a rattle and gave her a furious glare. "I have reached my bullshit quota with you, Vesper. I-"

The rest of his tirade stopped abruptly as his eyes hit her teeth. Decker's brows furrowed as he leaned forward, staring at the gleaming pointed tips of her fangs. He swallowed hard and sat back. "Those are real?"

She arched an eyebrow at him. "Does anything about me look fake?"

He stood up and raked a hand through his hair. Anger blazed in his eyes as he paced the room. "You lied to me. You made me think-"

"You thought what you wanted to. I just didn't correct your assumptions," she interrupted, getting up to face him.

"Correct my assumptions? That doesn't even fucking begin to cover it! Vampires?" He blew out a long breath. "Shit." He stormed over and placed his finger underneath the tip of her pendant, raising it to eye level. "Then what the fuck is this? This is military grade. Yeah, I saw the tat. Explain."

She lifted her chin and took the necklace from his grasp, her eyes boring holes into his face. "I do belong to a militant order. I deal in execution. We are the Penitent." She felt the pride in her voice.

He shook his head at her. "You're an assassin?" His eyes were wide. "A fucking assassin?"

Her eyes narrowed coldly. "Tread lightly, Decker. I carry out the death sentence against those of our race who commit crimes that warrant it. I don't slink around and sell my trade to the highest bidder."

He snorted loudly. "So you're government sanctioned. You only kill *bad* vampires. I'm supposed to be okay with that?"

She stiffened. "I sure as hell don't recall asking for your permission. Or your absolution. Our world is different from yours."

"I'll say."

"We do our best to stay out of your way and keep ourselves hidden among you. We have survived like this for thousands of years. Despite what you think, death is serious business to us." She walked back to her chair and sat down. "If you've finished with your petulance, I will give you some more answers."

Decker snorted again and walked to the door. "Lady, you and your 'race' can go fuck yourselves. I have a murder to solve." He reached for the handle.

She couldn't let him leave. Not now, and certainly not like this. She took a shot.

"And what about Miranda?" she asked quietly, her back to him. "If this is all connected the way I think it is, don't you want to know how your *wife* figures in?" She paused, waiting to see if she touched the nerve.

"Don't you ever mention her name to me, do you hear?" he growled. *Bingo.*

Vesper picked up her coffee again and sipped. "I would think you would be willing to compromise in order to find closure."

He whipped around the chair and got down in her face. "You don't know shit about my closure."

Victor's mocking laughter echoed in her ears and she recalled flashes of memory, remembering the pain, the blood, and the defeat. "I know more than you think I do, Decker." She set the cup down. "This Vincent Destrehan, he's not who you think. He's one of us, a vampire, and he is deadly. And I can promise you, he will not think twice about cutting you down if you get in his way."

Decker was quiet as he sat back down, a myriad of emotions running wild on his face. There was a lot to tell, a lot he needed to understand. She didn't have that kind of time.

"How did you know about my wife?" he asked softly.

"I took a guess. What Howard said and your hard-on for this case...yeah, wasn't too hard to figure out. Plus," she nodded when he looked up at her, "you've still got a line from your wedding ring on your left hand."

He looked down at the thin white line. "Am I that transparent or is that just part of your vampire powers?" he scoffed. "Super great eyesight and hearing and all that?"

"We're not dogs, Decker." She crossed her legs. "You ready to talk about this now?" He needed to be brought up to speed. Her heart went out to him for the confusion and the anger she knew he was feeling, but it had to be put aside.

"Do I have a choice?" Defeat was heavy in his voice.

She drained the last of the coffee from the cup, set it down and folded her hands together on her knee. "Like I said, our race has existed for thousands of years among you. Despite your urban legends and B-movies, we do not feed on humans to survive. We're self-sufficient in that aspect."

He held up his hand. "What? You feed on each other?"

She nodded. "Yes. The blood of other races has a high potential for danger. Think of it like a street drug. Some tolerate it fine, some become severely addicted, or some even die the first time. It can be an issue."

"So what happens when one of you goes insane and starts killing people?"

"Depends. We have local law enforcement of our own to deal with that, but if it's something deemed worthy by our Council, or if a vampire is murdered, then I do my job." It was an unusual feeling to be sitting here, calmly discussing the inner workings of her society to an outsider, but the more she talked, the more she wanted him to know, to understand, and even more strange, to accept. "I carry out the death sentence. I am an executioner." Her voice was grim and the words, for the first time, tasted bitter in her mouth.

He let out a deep breath. "You execute all murders?"

"Our birth rates are extremely low," she explained. "Our females are only fertile twice a year, and we suffer from a very low conception and a very high mother and young mortality rate. Women and children are vital to our existence. We ensure procreation through population. Any senseless death threatens that balance."

"And this Vincent guy? What about him?"

The sudden lump stuck in her throat. She did not want to relive this. "Vincent Destrehan is really Victor Delacroix, a vampire who committed a multitude of crimes. He killed several human women. Prostitutes. That was bad enough, but then he killed a female. A female vampire."

Decker's eyes widened. "I see."

"He was my assigned target." She looked at him intently and steeled herself. "And I failed. He's still alive because I failed to kill him." Her voice quavered. Coffee wasn't going to cut it. She needed something stronger to walk this road. There was a definite shift of the mood in the room as she walked to the corner cabinet and poured herself a scotch.

"And that's your interest in this? This guy, Reardon, not Grainger?"

She took a long sip of the liquor. The burn felt good. "It was. Until I saw Grainger."

"What do you mean?"

"Someone's fed from him, and they've done it often enough to leave marks. My guess is Delacroix, which is strange, but I don't have proof of that. I saw the fang marks on his neck and more importantly, he knew what I was. That was why I pushed to leave. They're all connected somehow, Reardon, Delacroix and Grainger. I have to figure out how and why." she said.

"So you weren't just trying to be a high-handed bitch?" he quipped. Before she could respond, he added, "Look, this is a lot to have to comprehend and I don't even know where to begin to start processing it." He got up and went to her. "I have a feeling there's much more that you're not telling me. Is that right?"

Her heart was pounding so fast she thought it might explode. She nodded. "There is." She shook her head and set down the drink, bracing one hand on the cabinet. "However it has happened, our paths have intertwined. I'm prepared to help you get the answers you need, but you have to do this my way. Period." Shadows darkened his eyes but she continued, "That means you have to follow my lead. You have to disappear from your world. Are you capable of that?" Vesper could see him visibly tighten.

"I've never been good at taking orders." He moved closer, bringing them face to face. The proximity of his body was starting to set off alarm bells in her brain. "Then you need to understand one thing very clearly. If you do anything the Council deems threatening, or if you cause any sort of unnecessary trouble, make no mistake, they will kill you without so much as an afterthought to protect themselves." Another slash of shadows stormed across his eyes as they narrowed to dark points at her threat. "If that happens, I won't be able to help you. Got that?"

She could see the frustration and the anger in his face, tempered with another, darker emotion. "Yeah." The finality in his voice said it all. "I will have my answers, Vesper. One way or another."

She flashed her fangs at him. "Don't push me, Decker. I've laid a lot on the line to bring you in on this. Your ass isn't the only one at stake here," she hissed, poking him hard in the chest.

He grabbed her wrist and pulled her to him. "I've agreed to your terms, but I won't be shut out while you use me as bait. This works both ways, and let me tell you I have no qualms about manhandling you to keep you in line," he said.

She pushed against him. "Are you threatening me? I thought we agreed that would just end badly for you."

Decker's eyes glittered with amusement and she smelled the hot surge of his scent in the air. "No, Vesper. I am telling you that if I have to, I *will* seduce you to get my way. And I think you know I can." He murmured and she felt a rush of heat clamor through her body. Heat she wanted to feel.

She ran her tongue across her lips and was pleased to see his eyes widen a bit. "Don't think I won't do the same," she replied, bringing her mouth inches from his.

He nodded. "So, we're in agreement, then?" Vesper curled her hand at the nape of his neck, letting her fingers play in the short, sandy locks.

"Complete." She tightened her grip and felt him harden, grinding his pelvis against her.

"I'm going to kiss you now."

"Oh, yes."

His mouth came down on hers, rubbing and plundering; stoking ancient fires back to life. His mouth was hot and wet as she opened for more, taking the thrust of his tongue with fervor.

She gave him a small, teasing stroke of her fangs and her name became a throaty moan on his lips, the erotic rasp of his voice like a choir of angels in her ears. Decker maneuvered her over and down onto the chaise with the easy grace of a key and a lock, driving her to distraction with his hands and mouth, seeking, touching, tasting. Want, a greedy and reckless thing, pulsed through her and urged her arms and legs to tangle tightly with his.

He returned the embrace, clutching her hard against him, mastering her with the kiss. She surrendered to it blindly, following him where he led, savoring the feelings his touch was springing to life.

Time would have stood still and they would have ended up in her apartments upstairs, if it weren't for the weight of his gun digging into her hip and for the sobering thoughts that doused the flame that was burning. This was a complicated and dangerous game they were playing, with a very real chance someone wasn't going to make it out alive. He was getting under her skin in ways she discouraged, sneaking in through the cracks in her armor. How would she feel if she lost him? She realized she didn't want to find out.

His mouth moved over hers once more and then he broke the kiss, staring down at her with eyes blurred by passion.

"You okay?" he rasped. She gave a little push and he hauled them up to sitting with no hesitation.

She nodded, her head still reeling from the atomic bomb of a kiss. This attraction between them was leading her down a lust-laden path of destruction. And she was skipping all the way. Decker was dangerous in more ways than one and he was getting ready to rush headlong into a fight he could not imagine. Vesper looked at the mixed emotions of desire and concern in his face and knew she could not do this without him.

She sniffed and stood. "We're going to see a friend of mine. She's a little unusual, but you're going to learn a lot of new and interesting things. Do us both a favor and try not to get us killed."

Decker eased up off the chaise and pulled her back into his embrace without a struggle. He planted a quick kiss on the top of her head and tucked it beneath his chin. She relaxed and he wound his arms around her. She sensed the comforting gesture was more for him than it was for her. He sighed.

"It's going to be hard to accept this world of yours, Vesper. I just need some answers for mine." He gave her one more quick hug and pushed her toward the door. "Let's go."

The woman in the chair moaned and shifted, causing the handcuffs to scrape loudly on the metal of the chair. *Good, she was coming to.* For a moment, he thought he'd struck her too hard when he'd cornered her in the alley a half hour ago. *Not dead, just unconscious.*

Victor Delacroix got up from the cot and stretched lazily as he headed to the table on the other side of the room. He loved these old warehouses on the riverfront. They were a perfect place to play, even before the hurricane. Condemned now by the city, they were virtually deserted. The whores and the dealers populated the alleys with their respective trades and without decent citizenry to complain, the police concerned themselves with other areas of town. A studio for the artist at work.

He opened the worn leather doctor's satchel sitting atop the table, his fingers brushing across the engraved metal clasp. They lingered for a moment and traced the initials.

H.G.

A fine sheen of sweat broke out over his bare chest. It just wasn't the same. He heard more clinking behind him. He turned to the woman, now fully awake, her terrified eyes wide and luminous with unshed tears. The cloth gag in her mouth muffled her gasps of fright as her breathing began to quicken. More scraping as she moved her hands against the restraints frantically, discovering with terrible realization that they were bound behind her body. Likewise, her ankles tinkled with metal on metal, shackled to the front legs of the chair.

Victor turned his attention back to the satchel.

"Be still," he said in a comforting tone. "It won't be as bad if you're still." He smiled, knowing she couldn't see his face. It was a lie. He liked it when they fought, and he liked enticing them to do so. It heightened the experience, feeling their fear, relishing their terror. He could smell the rank emotion oozing from her skin and he grew hard with the knowledge. The mastery. The control. It was thrilling.

He took a suede bundle out of the bag and set it down gingerly. An artist's tools were his trade. He pulled the tie and opened it, unfolding the contents. A dozen or so gleaming metal instruments winked in the fluorescent light, each tool more gruesome than the next.

He laid his palms down on either side of the cloth and bowed his head in reverence. She wasn't worthy, but he was needy and alone, so the whore would have to do for now. The luxuries of time and choice were not on his side. Hunger gnawed in his belly and her muffled noises were spurring the need, making him grow harder in anticipation. He sniffed and stood up straight, his moment of reflection gone. He pulled a small blade from its pocket and held it up to the light as he inspected it for her benefit. He was rewarded as the woman gasped through her bonds and bucked wildly in the chair. He turned to face her, eyes glowing with evil triumph.

She stopped moving and whimpered as he came forward. He slid the blade in the waistband of his jeans and savored the stinging feel of the cold surgical steel teeth against his flesh. *Oh, yes.*

She shook her head erratically as he reached to untie the gag. Her mouth finally freed, she let out a raspy scream. He waited. She screamed again, louder this time. The sound echoed off the concrete brick walls and went nowhere. He smiled a slick, snakelike smile and chuckled at her efforts. He watched as she took a deep lungful of air and gave it one more shot, this one loud enough to hurt his ears and throw a crack in the veneer of his fantasy.

Like a whip, his hand whistled up, backhanding her with enough force to snap her head back and rock the chair on its legs, effectively shutting her up. He smelled the tang of blood in the air and as her head lolled forward, a bright river of crimson pooled from her mouth. He inhaled sharply at the sight and his erection surged forward, threatening to break through the fly of his jeans.

He whipped out the blade and made a quick slash in her skin from her sternum to her abdomen. This time, the cry of pain was a balm to his dark soul and the shallow cut between her breasts bloomed and dripped. The first cut was always the sweetest.

Victor raised the blade to his mouth and wound his tongue gently around it. She tasted gritty and earthy and the beast within hungered for more. His hand came down to his side and he stared at her with cold, dead resolve. The blade came up and she started screaming again.

Hours later, it seemed, but he really didn't know, he stood before her, naked and bloody and panting. The rest of the tools lay discarded around the chair, covered with the evidence of the carnage.

He took a final, ragged step toward her limp form. She was still breathing and even better, still conscious. His cock strained forward, beckoning for a release that, until now, had been denied. He stepped behind her and fisted a bloody hand in the wet, matted mass of her hair and pulled it back and to the side, exposing the flesh of her neck. Ah, the part he'd been waiting for. His right hand gripped her hair tighter and his left wrapped around the base of his cock.

A sharp intake of breath brought his head down and he plunged his fangs into her vein. He closed his eyes and drank deeply, swallowing her last weak cry of protest. His bloody fist pumped the rigid length of his shaft with an evil vengeance. The taste, the sensation. It had been too long and he wanted it too much. He blinked hard as his balls tightened and his mouth popped free of her still form, his climax thundering over him.

As his body jerked with each spasm, the name rolled off his tongue in a soft whisper.

Howard.

It just wasn't the same.

CHAPTER FIVE

The Poisoned Apple lay nestled among various other Victorian homes on Magazine Street. On the outside, it looked much like the small businesses of the area with only a little painted sign and some wind chimes on the porch to direct visitors to the interior. Vesper opened the door and they walked inside.

"Cain, you bring one more emo chick in here for some Spanish fly, and I swear by all that is unholy, I'm giving you a set of elephant balls and setting them on fire!"

Lorelei Masters stood behind the granite counter frowning severely at the spiky-haired young man on the other side.

"Aw, come on, Lori! I know this chick down in Storyville who is into some *freak*-y shit. I just need-"

"Am I interrupting?" Vesper cut in.

Lori brightened as she noticed her friend. "Not at all, love. Cain here is just being a royal pain in my ass, as usual."

"V!" Cain shouted, rushing over to hug Vesper. He wrapped his arms around her tightly in a big bear hug and set her back, casting a suspicious glance at Decker, who stood with his arms folded and an unhappy look shadowing his face. "Who's the gumshoe?"

Vesper opened her mouth as Decker said, "You made me, kid?"

Cain sniffed loudly. "Please. Your permanent ass clench reeks of cop. Hey Marcus," he called over his shoulder. "Your sister is consorting with law enforcement."

"I'm sure she has her reasons," said a low voice from the other side of the store. "And they had better be good." Marcus sat in an overstuffed velvet chair, thumbing through a large book. "Do tell, Vesper."

Decker turned to Vesper. "You have a brother?"

She glared at Marcus, who returned the sharp look. "For now."

"So, what's up?" Lori asked, breaking the tension. "I'm not usually graced with so many of you. Artemis likes to steer you clear of my corrupting influence."

Decker followed Vesper to the counter. "I need your help, Lori," she said. "We all alone here?"

Lori's face lost her smile. "Cain, get the door." He obediently went and locked the front door, flipping the sign to closed. She met Vesper's gaze. "We are now."

Marcus ceased his thumbing and watched them carefully, but didn't go over.

"I'll admit when Marcus and Cain showed up, I was a little surprised, but you've got my attention, babe," Lori said.

Vesper shot a glance back to her brother. "Why *are* you here?"

He set the book aside. "Artemis called. Said you were coming here and that we should catch you."

"That man hates me." Lori frowned, crossing her arms over her chest. "With a passion."

"Hate is a strong word," Marcus replied. "Let's just say he dislikes your kind intensely. I, on the other hand, find it extremely accurate in my estimations." He gave the auburn-haired woman a wry smile. She bristled.

"Well, he tolerates me." Cain piped up, heading back from the door.

"You're only half witch, Cain. Shut up." Lori's irritation vibrated through the room.

Cain leaned against the counter and she watched Decker look him over. As usual, the kid was rocking one serious wardrobe. He forever looked like the doomed offspring of

Billy Idol and Bozo the Clown with his spiky bleached blond hair tipped with every color of the rainbow, his over the top punk rock leathers and steel toed boots. Several heavy silver chains adorned his neck, one of them the same crossed swords as Vesper. Cain caught him staring.

"What's the matter, cop?" he growled at Decker's frank perusal. "We gonna have a problem?" He flashed fangs at Decker and Vesper tensed beside him.

Decker slashed one more quick look at Cain and replied coolly, "Nah. I was thinking, I got drunk once and had sex with a peacock. Just wondering if you were my kid."

Cain's face split wide open in a toothy grin. "I like him," he said to Vesper.

"Enough, Cain." Lori put her hands on the counter. "What is it you need, V?"

"Victor Delacroix has resurfaced," she said quietly. No one spoke, and all eyes turned on her.

"Vesper?" Marcus urged softly.

Vesper reached in her pocket and pulled out the vial and set it on the granite counter top in front of Lori. "He was looking for this. I need to know why."

Lori peered at the unassuming crystal vial for a second, and then her eyes went wide with fear. The air around the vial suddenly rippled and convulsed and a giant black flash burst forth, and Lori held her hands up defensively.

"Holy fuck!" Cain exclaimed, jumping back. "Did you see that?"

Lori moved like lightning to grab a bottle from beneath the counter and poured a massive circle of salt around the smoking vial. She gasped and pointed a finger at the object. "You get that thing out of my shop and don't look back." Her green eyes held a mixture of anger and fear.

"Not until you tell me what it is and why he needs it," Vesper countered.

"It's bad, V. I mean *bad*. I'm serious. I want it out. Now." The witch's tone meant business.

Vesper plucked it from the counter and handed it off to Cain with her keys. "Put it in the glove box and lock it." She looked at Lori. "Fine?"

"Whatever. Get it the hell out of here."

Cain whisked it out the door.

Marcus shifted in the plush chair and called to Vesper. "You're sure about Delacroix?"

She nodded at her brother. "He killed Evan Reardon." Marcus' mouth fell open in a silent 'O'. "And, I'm pretty sure he's involved with a human. That's why he's here." She gestured to Decker. "He's got a serious lock on that guy. I think Victor's been feeding him."

"Guy?" Marcus sat up in surprise. "He's feeding a *male*? A *human* male?"

Vesper shrugged. "I don't have proof as of yet, but yeah, I think so."

The pale-haired vampire blew out a breath and sagged back in the chair. "That's depraved, even for Victor." Vesper locked eyes with her brother for a second at the allusion to events long past. Marcus blinked and looked past her. "Welcome to the Otherworld, cop. Gonna be a hell of ride for you," he said dryly.

"No shit," Decker replied. He turned to Vesper. "You found *that*," he jerked his head in the direction of the door, "at Reardon's, didn't you?" he said, displeasure in his voice. "Anything else you're keeping from me?"

"Probably. But right now, I'm concerned with finding out as much as I can about that thing and not so much with your persecution complex." She sniffed and looked at her friend. "Lori, can you help me or not?"

"With that?" the witch asked as Cain sauntered back in. She shook her head. "No. I don't want to be associated with-" she paused, "that."

"Look," Decker pointed his finger down on the counter and leaned in aggressively. His face knit together in a fierce frown. "We came to you for answers. If you know something that can help, then I suggest-"

Lori's eyes blazed with green fire as a sudden gust of wind erupted in the room, blowing her long auburn locks back with major force. There was a loud hiss, like someone letting the air out of tires, and a sharp ozony scent swirled throughout the room.

Great job, Decker. Let's piss off the elemental witch.

The witch's eyes came down hard on the detective as she yelled, "What do you think this is? This is dark, and I mean dark, magic. This isn't your mammy's dime-store voodoo. You want to read chicken bones and shake some gris-gris? Get your ass down the Quarter with all the tourists."

"Easy, witch," Marcus warned, dropping his fangs.

She turned her anger on him. "Pipe down, you. You don't come into my place with your Doctor Who entourage and start issuing orders and flashing your fangs around." She looked at Vesper. "Sweetie, I like you, I really do. But you don't know what you're asking."

Vesper cast pleading eyes on her friend. "I do know. I'm sorry to put you here. Please, Lori. I wouldn't have come if I didn't think you could help. This is important to me."

Unspoken words passed between them and after a long moment, Lori calmed and sighed.

"Okay, V. For you. That's the only reason. But I will investigate."

Vesper relaxed. "Thank you."

"I'm going to regret this."

"That makes two of us," Marcus added.

The twitter of a cell phone playing "SexyBack" came jingling from Cain's pocket. He fished it out and flipped it open.

"Hey, love. Yeah, I got your text. You're a dirty girl." He laughed. "Yeah, you know that's right. Listen sweet, I got to hit you later. You wait for me okay?" He licked his lips. "Oh baby, you know it. I got you." He shut the phone and found them all staring. "What?"

Vesper and Lori both shot him dirty looks. He smiled at them and held up his hands in mock defense. "Don't hate the player, ladies. Hate the game."

"Why is it you think every woman with a pulse is dying to sleep with you?" Vesper asked.

Cain laughed and shot her a wide grin. "Oh, come on, V. All the ladies love to ride the Cain train," he drawled. He laughed and rolled his hips and drew a hand down the front of his T-shirt to his crotch. "All aboard, baby. All aboard."

Vesper wrinkled her nose. "I think I just threw up in my mouth."

"Get in line," Marcus echoed from the corner.

"All I can say is...Wow," Decker said lightly.

Cain made a small frown at Decker. "I thought you said we weren't gonna have a problem. Change your mind, old man?" He flashed his fangs.

Decker shook his head. "Nah, man. We're cool. Like the tat, by the way."

Cain cocked his head. "It's tight." He tapped the intricate scroll tattoo that ran from above his left eye across his face to his hairline. "Nuns named me because of this bad boy. Said I was 'marked by God'." His chest puffed a little. "Yeah," he sighed, "it's gotta be divine to look this good."

"You probably just passed out at a Paramore concert," Marcus huffed.

The young vampire turned to him, offended. "Seriously, *jefe*, why you hatin'? It's not like you don't get some stares from the chickies." Cain smiled at Decker. "My man's cool, right? He's like something from Lord of the Rings or World of Warcraft or some shit. Legolas has got my fucking back. Awesome, right?" He scoffed, checking his watch. "Shit, I gotta jet. Call me if you need me, V."

"Got one waiting?" Vesper asked.

"Yeah. My ladies always wait for me. Besides," he grinned, "I'm hungry for love and it's feeding time." He laughed again and strolled out the door, but not before pumping a fist into the air and yelling, "Thank you, Alice Cooper!"

Decker looked at Marcus. "Is he always that obnoxious?"

He nodded. "You get used to it."

"How do you put up with that? I just met him and already I want to slap him." Decker stared out the door after the kid.

"Don't underestimate him, cop. He can rip your eyeballs out of your ass and hand them to you before you stop twitching."

Decker smiled, nodding. "Good to know."

Lori came from around the counter and ushered Vesper through the curtains to the back room. All evidence of her previous anger was replaced with girlish glee.

"Okay, spill. What's up with you and Detective Tight Pants out there? He is über hot." She grinned, poking Vesper in the shoulder. "Does Artemis know about this?"

Vesper frowned. "Yes. And nothing's up. You're imaging things again."

"Remember who you're talking to, V. 'Persecution complex'? Really?" she laughed. "Have you slept with him?" A bigger grin.

Vesper gasped, "No!"

"Are you going to?" Now the witch was giggling.

Vesper blushed, "Christ, Lori! This is serious!"

The witch sobered and shook her head. "Yes. It is. Serious." Another giggle. "Seriously hot."

Vesper rolled her eyes. Lori never ceased to bring out the twelve year old girl in her. "It's complicated. It was....unavoidable."

Lori nodded. "I see how hard you're trying to avoid him. I can read you, sister."

"Read what? We've only been here twenty minutes!" Vesper hissed, keeping her voice down.

"Whatever. There's a vibe between you two." Lori waggled her fingers back and forth. "You can't fool me. Witch, remember?"

"As if I could forget. You enjoy trying to convince me of your superiority at every turn."

Lori sniffed. "Yes, well....all I know is that is one rock hard hunk of fine ass man-candy." She pointed to the curtain. "You can't deny that."

"Tell me something I don't know, then." Vesper drawled.

"You've got a sweet tooth."

Vesper groaned. "Just let it go, Lori. Please."

The witch waved her hands in the air. "Fine, fine. Deny it all you want." A devious glint sparkled in her eyes. "Hey, I can whip you up a little-"

"Save it for Cain." Vesper said flatly.

Lori chuckled and shrugged. "I just wanted to put it out there."

"Consider yourself put out. Call me when you hear something." Vesper winked at her walked out.

Decker turned from the counter and went to sit in the chair opposite Marcus. The long-haired vampire considered the human carefully.

"Legolas, huh?" he asked. Marcus glared. "Yeah, I can see it."

Marcus bared his fangs. "You really want to go there?"

Decker shrugged. "Just commenting on the kid's observation."

"Cain's mouth gets him in trouble."

"It seems that way." Decker sat back in the chair, getting comfortable. "You know about this Reardon guy then?"

"I do."

"What do you make of it?"

Marcus tilted his head to the side. "I think you're in way over your head, cop."

"Probably."

The two men stared at each other like lions circling before a fight.

The cop in him couldn't help but pry. "What is it she's not telling me?" Decker asked.

"A lot of things, I would imagine. However, it's not my place to say."

"Really? Because from where I'm sitting, I'm thinking a brother would be pretty willing to help me help his sister."

Marcus inspected his fingernails and laid the detective flat with his gaze. "Let's this straight, *cop*. I don't give a rat's furry ass about you. I don't give a shit about Reardon or this fucking burping black magic. Delacroix is alive and I want to see him dead. Period. If you get lost in the shuffle, so be it."

Decker's nostrils flared. "Likewise. We gonna go a round on this?"

Marcus smiled menacingly, the light gleaming off the points of his fangs. "If you think it's necessary. That would just piss my sister off. Plus, I think it would be a shame to kill you before you've proved to be useful."

"As bait you mean?"

The vampire shrugged. "Semantics. I know Delacroix. He's smart, incredibly devious and even more deadly. Whatever this magic is, whatever's he after, he will kill whoever gets in his way. Vesper's been on the receiving end before. I don't plan on letting it happen again."

Decker stiffened and his gaze raked over Marcus, for the first time noticing the same small pendant of crossed swords. Damn. They were Penitent, all three of them. Vesper, the hulking brother and the smart-mouthed kid.

"What happened between her and Delacroix?" he asked. *Christ, just give me something.*

Marcus shifted in the chair, suddenly looking uncomfortable. "I don't think-"

Decker's hard voice cut him off. "Everyone keeps preaching to me how dangerous this guy is. So tell me what I am dealing with here. What the fuck happened?"

Decker thought he imagined a chill in the room as Marcus' eyes iced over, their depths reflecting a cold hatred. The vampire's hands tightened on the arm of the chair, his knuckles white from the steely grip. He spoke slowly, his tone implying that these words would never pass his lips again.

"He raped and nearly murdered my sister. Delacroix tortured and mutilated her for three days before I could track them down. He left her for dead." Decker's eyes went wide, all the pieces starting to fall together. "A mistake he will not repeat. So you see," he paused, "there is much more to this than just Vesper's failure to kill him."

No shit. Decker swallowed and nodded, unsure of what to say. Marcus returned to his fingernails and Decker knew the subject was closed. Anything else, if it ever came, would have to come from the source.

A bright flash of memory and Miranda's face filled his head. His stomach clenched at the thought of Delacroix and Grainger doing unspeakable things to his wife. She wasn't missing for nearly that long, so maybe....just maybe. He let the thought go, not wanting to follow that grisly trail of speculation. A slow maddening freeze wrapped around his heart and squeezed so tight he couldn't breathe. What *had* they done? The coldness spread and splintered into amazing clarity. Vampire or no, whatever had happened to Miranda and Vesper, Marcus was right. Victor Delacroix was a dead man.

Vesper and Lori burst through the curtains, a secret smile on the witch's face. Vesper eyed the tension between Decker and her brother, but said nothing. Decker's gaze shifted away from hers with an awkward lurch and she blanched.

He knows. Fucking Marcus.

Her blood ran cold. The thought of them discussing things they had no right to speak of cracked her face into an angry frown.

"If you two fat hens have finished your gossiping, there's shit to do."

Decker glanced at Marcus, who wore a resigned expression. Marcus picked up the discarded book and made a show of thumbing through the pages again.

"Evening, Detective. Vesper."

"Fuck you, Marcus." She turned to leave and Decker followed her out the door.

As the door shut behind them, Lori planted her hands on her hips and scowled at the vampire. "You really are one first-class bastard, aren't you?" she sneered.

He set the book down and headed for the door. He stopped in front of her and peered down at her. She didn't budge. "You'd do well to remember that, witch." He walked to the door and smiled as her litany of curses followed him out.

"Where's your place?" Vesper asked him, even though he knew she really just wanted to throw open the door and toss his ass bouncing down the street.

He gave her his address in the Garden District and she pulled the Vantage out onto Magazine and headed for the freeway.

"This is how it's going to play out. You're going to pack a bag; you're going to make a phone call. As of now, you disappear. Take sick time, vacation time, I don't care if you fucking call in dead. You're gone. Poof. You're a ghost." She gripped the steering wheel with white-knuckled hands. "You got me?"

Pissed was an understatement. She was seething. Whatever spark that had passed between them before was gone. He wanted it back. "I'm in the middle of this investigation, Vesper. I'm not going to drop my end of it just because you're hacked off."

He turned to look at her. Her cheeks flushed hot and she growled, "Let me reiterate for you that if you fuck with this, it's your ass. You will do as I say or I will fucking kill you myself. I *own* your ass. Accept it and deal."

The fury in her voice was mirrored in her face but her eyes stared straight ahead on the road. This was for Miranda, he reminded himself. The truth was all that mattered. Maybe. Maybe after this was over, there might be something. It was too much to dwell on for now. He closed his eyes and laid his head back.

"Just take me home. We'll do it your way."

Vesper stood inside the door to Decker's apartment watching his every move with a calculated eye. He'd used the phone in the bedroom and made his call, waking up and subsequently pissing off his captain with the fuzzy details of his sudden departure. Now, he paced the apartment, packing a large black duffel. She decided he was moving at a snail's pace just to irk her. *Mission accomplished.* He passed by once more, giving her a slow, wicked smile that set her blood boiling. The man had a death wish. Her fangs itched and low growls rumbled through her. She was already hot with anger and now pangs of hunger added to her displeasure.

"Would you get your shit?" she snapped. "You're not packing for a trek through the Andes." He rattled a drawer in the bathroom in reply. "Christ, if you need toothpaste, I've got you covered. Let's *go.*"

Decker strolled out of the bathroom. "If you plan on being a total bitch for all of this, it's only going to make things more difficult. Get a grip, chère."

Vesper stalked toward him, ready to strangle him. "The only thing I will be getting a grip on is your throat if you don't get your ass in gear." She pointed to the duffel. "Now."

He turned from her and went back to the bag, settling its contents in place. With his back to her, she took the moment to swallow hard against the well of shame that reared its head. Everyone knew about how Victor had tried to kill her, but only

Lori, Marcus and Artemis knew about the rape. And now Decker, she was sure of it.

How dare they? She couldn't count how many times she'd scrubbed herself raw, trying to peel the sick of it from her skin. Peel away the fear, the anger, and the disgust. Victor had fed from her, tortured and violated her body in ways she still could not bring herself to reconcile. The thought of them discussing it, discussing her, set her teeth on edge. The darkness was moving deep inside her, building, swelling, pushing, barely keeping itself contained.

As if he was reading her mind, Decker stood and said softly, "It's nothing to be ashamed of, Vesper."

The dagger whistled through the air and landed in the wall with a heavy thud, just scraping Decker's ear as her agonized cry of buried rage split the air.

Decker grabbed his nicked ear and wheeled around, grabbing and yanking the blade free of the wall with a hard jerk.

"How dare you!" she hissed. The darkness inside burst through, finally breaching through her defenses, revealing its ugliness to the light of day.

Decker held the knife aloft and the dam broke on anger and pain tightly bottled for what felt like centuries. Her mind fractured under the tide of memory and she was no longer here, her secret self pulled back in time to the core of her degradation. It all came back in one sudden wave and she cracked.

"You can't possibly imagine...." her voice trailed into shuddering gulps of air as she fought through the images. "You don't know..." She saw Decker's mouth move as if to say her name, but her brain couldn't register any sound over her own voice shrieking in her head. "The pain....the blood," she hiccupped. "He touched me...." She sobbed louder, her body breaking down under the strain into convulsive jerks. She pitched forward. "He.....used me....put things....oh God!"

Decker rushed forward, holding out his arms, preparing to catch her. She shrank back, screaming, "Don't touch me!" Victor's face pasted itself over Decker's and all she saw was her tormentor and the blade he held in his hand and she screamed louder in high pitched wails, "No! Don't touch me!" He froze in his tracks.

Decker looked at the knife and cursed, throwing it aside and it slid under his couch out of her sight. "Vesper!" he shouted. "It's all right!"

This time she heard Decker's voice break through the fog.

She stared into his eyes, so wide with fear and wonder and the cold ice blue that haunted her dreams melted into his soothing cerulean depths. The release of emotion was staggering and she felt herself shift back into the now and she held out a hand and closed her eyes.

Decker grabbed her and wrapped his body around hers, muffling the sound of her sobs with his chest as she sagged against him, boneless. He pressed his hand to the back of her head and the raging torrent of fire that seared her soul was suddenly extinguished.

He was whispering in her hair. It was soft and fluttery and the little vibrations kept pushing and pushing until his voice reached her ears.

"Are you okay?" he asked quietly, pulling back to look at her. Her lashes were thick with tears, but she managed to open her eyes.

"I don't know," she confessed, sniffling. "I've never..." She couldn't finish the thought.

He hugged her tightly again. She wanted to melt into him, to fold herself inside the cocoon of his arms and feel safe.

Decker tilted her chin up and looked straight into her eyes. "I'm going to tell you again. You have nothing to be ashamed of." She opened her mouth to speak, but he placed a finger on her lips, hushing her. "Nothing," he repeated.

Her eyes welled again with bright tears. "Marcus," she whispered brokenly. "Marcus found me. Victor was gone and I...." she stuttered, "I...was almost.....he fed me." She closed her eyes at the thought and shook her head violently. "I fed from my.....my brother." The last wave of confession pealed forth, the admission leaving a foul taste in her mouth. "My brother," she whispered again. "Oh, God."

"Shhh." Decker cooed, rocking her in his arms. "You survived. How is not important."

Decker edged them over to the couch and eased her down. She buried her face in his shoulder and he reached up a hand and ran it through the silkiness of her hair. He tucked the chocolate strands behind her ear and grazed his knuckles over her cheekbone and cupped her face. Her eyes were hazy, unfocused with the turbulent remnants of the past. There was also an insistence in them that he couldn't quite reconcile. She felt so good against him and he wanted to pick her up and carry her to the bedroom, wrap himself around her and let her just cry it all out, as long as it took, and shield her from the world until she was ready to return.

His body leaped to life at the thought of tossing her down in the bedroom. Hot, naked images quickly followed. Decker closed his eyes and rested his lips on the top of her head. Not now. Wanting her now was not good. She was reliving the most horrific moments of her life and he wanted to nail her with a hard-on that was swiftly becoming uncomfortably large. *Classy, Price. Real fucking classy.*

She shifted in his arms, no doubt feeling the tension that had crept into him. Or had she noticed the erection? He looked down at her and noticed she was staring at his ear. Her eyes were wide, the violet irises focused intently on the side of his head.

Her voice rasped a little. "You're bleeding."

Decker reached up to touch the still wet cut. Her eyes followed his movement closely. "Yeah, well your aim was off. You clipped me." He smiled. "I'm not going to die of blood loss or anything." She swallowed hard and her breathing quickened. She sat back from him and looked away, smoothing hands down the front of her legs.

Something was off. Her demeanor changed from upset to distracted in a second. He frowned. "What is it?" He put his hand over hers. "It's okay. Tell me."

She shook her head and stood up and strode past him. She was almost to the front door when she stopped and turned back to him. "Thank you for...well, thank you," she sniffed. "I think we should be going, though." She paused. "And, you should do something about that cut." He frowned again. She was cagey, nervous. Had she suspected what he had been thinking? He groaned inwardly. Decker stood up and went to her.

"Look, Vesper, I'm sorry. I'm very attracted to you. Please don't let it..." He trailed off. She wasn't registering his words, but she was staring at his face. She licked her lips and the point of one pearly fang peeked through the fullness of her lips. The gesture was strangely erotic.

She shook her head. "What? No. I....It's nothing. I'm just...Let's go."

"Please, Vesper. Tell me." He was praying to God she wasn't going to out him.

Her voice was soft and her next words sparked a wild, hot rush of fire in his blood.

"I'm hungry. I need to feed." She couldn't have been more seductive if she'd said she wanted to strip him naked and ride him to the floor. But she looked confused and edgy. A very visceral, very male need rocketed through him and the words fell from his lips before he knew it.

"So take me."

Vesper made a choking sound, as if she'd swallowed a gasp and he came toward her. With each step, the idea firmly cemented itself in his mind as undeniably right. The wide, startled stare in her eyes said she would need some persuasion. So be it.

"Vesper."

She shook her head and held out a hand to ward him off. "Please. This is not necessary. Let's just go. I will take care of things once we get back." She looked pale and small there against the door. "The situation is more complicated than you realize."

"What's complicated? You're hungry." His voice dropped low. "And *I* can feed you. Can't I?" The thought once again reared up his primal male instincts and the desire to protect and provide for his woman overrode every neuron firing in his body. *His woman.*

The chocolate waves around her face moved softly as she shook her head. "You don't understand, Decker." His name was a whisper on her lips.

"So make me understand, then." She looked up and away.

"Feeding is...." she paused, her brow knit in frustration, "a difficult thing to explain. First, you're human. It's not forbidden, but it is frowned upon. I've told you why. Second, it's a very, um, powerful urge. And it tends to kick start other....urges as well." She rubbed her hands on her hips as if trying to dry them. "Sexual ones."

Decker's mouth broke into a dry smile. "Really? That sounds god awful."

Her brows furrowed. "It's a lot less complicated if you're not really attracted to whoever is feeding you." Her eyes were soft. "Then, it's easier to deal with those feelings. Or deny them." She sniffed loudly, drawing herself up. "I've never fed from a human, and I don't plan on starting now. Even if-" She stopped herself.

"Even if what?" His eyes narrowed, pleased she had given part of herself away. "Even if you're attracted to me? A human?" Decker waited for her to give voice to it. Right now, he needed to hear her say it; he wanted her to admit to wanting him like he wanted her.

She wiped a hand under her eyes and cast her eyes on the floor for a second. "This can't work. There's too much...it just can't..." Vesper looked up and he could see the emotions warring in her face. She wanted him but she was afraid. *Afraid.*

"Say it, Vesper. Tell me you don't want this. That you don't want me." He was pushing again, but he knew she had to face it. If there was any hope in hell for the two of them, she had to make a stand now and be willing to fight for it.

A tear escaped and ran down her face and her lips trembled. *Be strong, Price. She needs you to be strong. Be the hero.*

Vesper blew out a breath and wiped her face again. Her eyes were clear and calm and she said, "Yes. I want you. But going to bed with you and feeding from you are different things."

"Sounds like they're one and the same, if I take your word for it. You're already taking a big risk being with me in the first place. I think you're strong enough to make a bigger leap into something that could be very good for the both of us. I think you know you won't be able to do one without the other." The flush in her cheeks gave her away. She was coming around. Good. Keep it going. "I'm willing to risk it. I've given in and made concessions, decided to play by your rules. You're one tough woman, Vesper. But you're in no condition to be ordering me around, you know. It's time *you* learned to listen." Decker popped the gun and holster off his jeans and tossed it on the couch and then slowly pulled his shirt off, whisking it over his head. He stalked forward, ready to take what was his.

"Whatever it takes, Vesper, whatever you need, I'll give it to you."

Desire and fear came together until her teeth ached with its force as he came toward her. His eyes held hers in a gaze so piercing she could not look away. He was magnificent. Tall, tanned and muscular, his body exuded a dominance that would not be ignored. Her breath caught hard in her chest. That dark, damning scent was back, rushing around her and breathing life into her skin. He was so vibrantly, undeniably *male*, and she found herself responding to him without question.

She reached out to push him away, but he grabbed her wrists and pinned them next to her shoulders against the door and pressed his naked chest into hers.

"Decker," she gasped.

She felt his erection surge and opened her mouth in a silent cry of pleasure. Her breasts heaved as they were crushed beneath the weight of his chest. The contact was electric and sent a flush of wetness straight to her core. She swallowed hard.

Vesper watch the pulse pound at his throat and her mouth watered. As if sensing her desire, he tilted his neck just a little, causing the vein to tighten and pop out against his skin. She closed her eyes and moaned, "Don't do this to me. Please." The last word was a whisper.

"Look at me, Vesper."

She lifted her lids and met eyes that sparkled with passion. It was so tempting. He was so tempting. His lips parted in a slow, sensuous smile.

"I am offering myself to you on a platter here," he whispered, pressing harder, bringing his neck ever closer to her lips. "And you don't even want a taste." His breath was moist and hot in her ear, and she barely heard him over the blood pounding in her ears. "I thought you were hungry, Vesper," he purred.

His tongue reaching out to trace the curve of her ear was her undoing. She hissed, sucking her lower lip between her teeth, biting down hard, her fangs drawing blood. She should have cried out, but didn't have the strength. The taste of her own blood, the heady spice of his scent, and the feel of his hardness pressed against the juncture of her thighs was overwhelming. She moaned once more, control slipping from her grasp.

"God, that's hot. I don't know why, but God, Vesper..." his voice trailed off. She felt him harden even more and her body responded again. Fear vanished in an instant. This was what she wanted, needed.

She didn't recognize the desperation in her voice as she whispered, "Take me to bed. Take me now."

His head swiveled down to find her eyes and asked, "And the other?"

She opened her mouth to reveal her fangs, fully extended and aching for him. His pupils narrowed to points and she felt his cock jump through the thick denim of his jeans. *He wanted it. Oh God, he really wanted it.*

"Yes."

She had barely uttered the word when he scooped her up and carried her back to the bedroom and began divesting her of weapons and clothes.

She lay naked, waiting, as his hands went to the fly of his jeans. He stepped free of them with a swoosh, revealing himself and she relished the rush of heat that spread through her at the sight.

His arousal was *enormous*. The man had been carved from stone and brought to life, a figure of raw sexual power. He was gorgeous.

"You're beautiful when you blush, Vesper."

She eyed him with approval and watched his body respond to her gaze. "So are you."

He crawled toward her on the bed. "I don't know how to do this, so just tell me where you want me." He knelt beside her.

She shook her head and sat up, placing a hand on his chest. "This is about your pleasure. You are offering me the gift of your vein. We find what's comfortable for you." She came forward and pressed herself to him and put both her hands on his shoulders. She leaned in and felt him tense and smiled as she pressed a soft, biting kiss on the nape of his neck. "I could face you, like this."

"That's nice," he murmured, attempting to pull her closer.

"Or," she continued, moving around behind him, "I could be here, if you prefer."

"Yes," he breathed.

Her body was on fire with hunger and want. There was no turning back. She flattened her breasts against his back and wound her hand against the back of his head, pulling it to the side. The sensation of skin on skin was dizzying and her focus was slipping. She wanted to forgo the feed altogether and beg him to flip her over and take her hard, but the call of his vein taut against his skin dragged her back to her hunger.

Decker's breath was coming harder and faster underneath the touch of her hands. She leaned forward and pressed her mouth to his neck again just below his cut ear. She tasted the blood there and groaned softly. He hissed as she lightly scored her fangs down the column of his neck as it curved to his shoulder.

He shuddered hard and said, "God, Vesper, yes."

She looked down and saw his cock jutting out from his body, hard and straining. *Yes, from behind.*

Her lips curled against his flesh as her hand tightened in the sandy locks of his hair. Her signal gave him a moment to tense before she sank her fangs in with a deep sigh.

Decker cried out sharply and bucked in protest, but she held him tight. He soon relaxed, the rush taking hold, and she drank deeply. He tasted as good as he smelled and she shut her eyes in rapture as his blood flowed over her tongue and into her mouth, washing away the darkness and filling her with light.

His body was responding with breakneck speed, his erection growing larger with each pull of her mouth on his neck. She guided her other hand around to his arm and nudged it forward, urging him to grab his cock.

Decker hesitated, but at her deep growl of approval, he wrapped his hand hard around the pulsing shaft and began to stroke it vigorously.

The erotic sight sent sizzling tendrils of fire straight to her core. Her flesh ached, begging to be touched. Tasting him, watching him, was only adding fuel to the fire of her desire. She reached down between her thighs and parted the slick folds. Her fingers stroked, moving closer to the engorged button of her clitoris, her pleasure rising with each heated pass. She moaned against his neck, the feel of him threatening to drown her in the electric tide of sensation.

Vesper bucked harder against her fingers, rocking into him. The realization of what she was doing made him groan and call her name and move his hand faster along the length of his cock.

Blazing licks of flame burned their way through her body, scorching at every turn. She wanted him now, needed him inside her as her body screamed for a release that could only come at his touch. Vesper pulled free of his shoulder with a wet smack, and ran her tongue along the two puncture marks, sealing them over. They would be gone by morning.

"Vesper?" he groaned.

She lay back on the bed, pulling him around and opening her arms. "Please, Decker, I need you."

He moved forward and positioned himself at her core. "Open for me, baby." He leaned in a little, and she felt the head of him against her, hot and blunt. He moaned, "Yeah, baby, that's it."

Vesper pulled her legs up higher, giving him more access to her aching center. He pushed one of her knees upward and drove in a little farther, easing further inside. Her body surged with the stroke, but she gave in to the pressure. His body shone with a fine mist of sweat as he grimaced against the pleasure he was feeling.

Heaven. The feel of him was pure heaven as he inched forward, stretching her to take all of him. With one last push, he was fully inside her and his breath came in erotic, deep gasps as she felt the walls of her sex mold to his rigid length.

"Are you okay?" he asked through gritted teeth. "You're so damned tight. God, Vesper....it's so good."

She ran her hands up his shoulders and placed kisses on his chest and neck, loving the salty tang. She dropped her head and flicked her tongue out at his nipple and smiled at the hiss of pleasure she elicited.

"Decker," she whispered, breathless. "Do it. Make love to me."

Decker moved forward, rolling his hips in a great wave over her body. She was on fire, hot, wet, and swollen and he was driving deep, pinning her to the mattress with each hard thrust. She grabbed greedily, clutching him to her, urging him on deeper, higher.

He yelled out her name and held on for dear life, his hips pistoning in and out as he threw his head back and bore down upon her. The grinding, undulating rhythm lit the fuse on the fire burning deep inside of her and she clawed at him for more. As he pounded, she felt herself on the edge, ready to fall. He rocked her once more and she went straight over.

Her orgasm slammed into her like a brick wall, her inner muscles clenching and grabbing onto his penetrating shaft. The tight convulsions of her sex must have been enough for Decker, because he shouted, loud, and seized up over her, shuddering his release.

He came in a torrent of spasms, pouring into her body, filling her completely and collapsed to the side of her. She raised a hand to her head, but he pulled her close and tucked her in tightly, burying his face in her hair, letting out a contented sigh.

Good. She felt so good. It had been so long, and certainly never that good.

He rumbled into her hair, "Are you okay? I didn't hurt you, did I?"

Vesper turned toward him and snuggled in, letting out a sigh of her own. "No. It was wonderful. Thank you."

He pulled back to look at her, an unwavering certainty in his dark blue eyes. "I should be thanking you. That was an incredible experience that I will never forget. Sleep." He folded her back into his arms and maneuvered covers over them. "Besides, if you go all bat shit crazy now and I have to kill you, I've got a happy memory to reflect on." He grunted as she elbowed him in the ribs. "I'm just saying."

"Be thankful I'm full and just had an amazing orgasm, or you would have gotten to experience 'bat shit crazy' firsthand." She smiled against his chest. "I'm just saying."

His arms tightening around her as he chuckled were the last thing she remembered before falling into a deep, restful sleep.

CHAPTER SIX

Decker reached across a sleeping Vesper and picked up the phone on the second ring. His voice was thick as he managed, "Price."

"Yo, cop!" the voice on the other end chimed, "Wake up V and get her ass home pronto."

"Cain?" he muttered. "How did you get this number?"

The vampire gave a hearty snort. "Bitch, please. You're a public servant, *jefe*. Man, I Googled your ass." He sniffed. "No, seriously. Enough with the nookie. The Council's convened and some shit's going down. She needs to be here."

"The what?" Decker's brain was trying to shake off the fog.

"Dude. Just tell her. It'll light a fire under her, I promise. You feeling me, cop?"

Decker rubbed a hand over his tired eyes. "Yeah, man. We're on our way." He hung up and shifted his focus to Vesper. She was awake and staring at him with a soft smile on her upturned lips. God, she was beautiful. He dropped a tender kiss on her mouth and she stretched creamy limbs into the air. His body stirred at the sight and he wanted her again.

"Mmmm, who was that?"

"Cain." She stilled, instantly alert. "Something about the Council convening." She was out of bed like a shot and chucked his jeans at him.

"Get dressed." She pulled her clothes on in record time and was strapping on her knives as his feet hit the floor. "Did he say anything else?"

"Nah, that was it." He paused, watching her efficient movement. "This is serious, then?"

She nodded. "You bet." She put on her watch and checked the time. "Five minutes, then we're outta here." She rushed from the room.

So much for post-coital canoodling. He sighed and went to grab a fresh shirt from the closet and put his work boots on. He opened the bottom bureau drawer and took out the metal gun case he kept there. Unlocking it, he retrieved the Colt .38 Super. He grabbed two extra clips and shoved the backup weapon in the waistband of his jeans. He turned back to the closet and pulled out the 12 gauge shotgun from the gun rack and a box of shells. Satisfied he was fully armed for whatever hell had broken loose, he headed to the living room where Vesper stood waiting with his duffel in hand.

She smiled as he entered and said with a mock laugh, "I hope you're wearing a cup, babe. It's going to get rough."

He rested the shotgun against his shoulder. "I have no doubt."

Vesper pulled the Vantage in behind the line of vehicles at the mansion. She recognized Marcus' black Range Rover and Cain's Harley right off the bat, but she didn't know who the three silver Escalades belonged to.

"Christ, it looks like 'Pimps Gone Wild' is parked in your driveway."

She threw it into park and gave him a frown. "I guess we'll find out."

Cain waited for them in the foyer, his face widening into a broad grin as they approached. She noticed the rainbow tips were gone from his hair and it was back to his standard platinum spike.

He caught her gaze and ruffled a hand through the gelled locks. "Yeah, V. It's back to my 'Rude Dude' do. Artemis made me fix it. Can't go before Council looking like Rainbow Brite's bitch, he said. Well," he shrugged, "I could be paraphrasing."

"Sage advice," Decker murmured.

"They waiting for us, Cain?"

The kid shifted on his feet and nodded. "Yeah, and Lori's here with some of the warlocks from her coven." Vesper's eyes widened. "I know. 'Locks, right? It's pretty intense in there. And Dulcinea's got a bug the size of New Jersey up her ass, so be careful."

Vesper smiled at Cain. "Will do, thanks." She turned to Decker. "You ready?"

"As I'll ever be," he replied.

They started up the stairs and he asked, "Who's Dulcinea?"

Vesper wrinkled her nose in distaste. "The High Elder's daughter. She's also a ranking Council member. We don't get along. The woman hates me."

Cain snorted from the bottom of the stairs. "If she hates you, then I don't think there's word to describe how she feels about me. 'Loathe' doesn't *even* begin to cover it."

"She sounds delightful," Decker drawled.

"Dulcie's a bit of- I guess you would call her an aggressive go-getter."

Cain barked out a sharp laugh. "She's a fucking bitch." He gave Decker a mock salute. "Good luck, cop."

"Thanks." The pair made their way up the rest of the stairs.

The Archive Council kept their chambers on the second floor in a converted ballroom. Vesper took a deep breath, threw open the double doors and stepped into the room. Twelve sets of eyes raked over them from behind the rectangular conference table and she steeled herself, leading Decker inside.

She bowed formally. "High Elder."

Artemis stood from the middle of the table, his expression tense but placid. "Vesper," he nodded in greeting. "Detective Price, I presume?"

Decker inclined his head in respectful return.

"Please, come in," Artemis continued.

Her brother and the raven-haired Dulcinea sat on either side of Artemis, Marcus looking grim while Dulcinea's face could barely contain the contempt in her cat green eyes.

Artemis gestured to the two empty chairs beside Lori, who sat the right of Marcus. On Dulcinea's left sat Gideon, the Penitent master-at-arms and Keane, the Archive historian. Down from them sat four men, one woman and a girl she couldn't place, all of them eying her with veiled scorn. Warlocks.

Braeden Masters, head warlock of their coven, was a gray-haired gentleman who resembled Artemis in his carriage. He was also Lorelei's estranged uncle. "Do you have it, girl?" His tone was as imperious as his gaze.

Vesper bristled at the insult but kept her cool. "I do," she said, taking the crystal vial from her jacket and placing it on the table.

The girl, who couldn't have been more than twelve if she was a day, gasped and waved her hand quickly in response. A thick, perfect circle of salt appeared around the vial and questioning murmurs swept the other end of the table.

"Well," Artemis deadpanned, "wasn't that exciting? Now what the hell is it?"

The female folded her hands primly and leaned forward, daggers in her eyes for the High Elder. "That, vampire, is piece of dark magic that you never should have meddled with."

His expression didn't change, but Vesper felt his anger as if he'd shouted. "Thank you for your cryptic and useless commentary as always, Renata. But you still didn't answer my question. If you planned on coming here to waste my time, I would tread carefully, *witch*." His voice was edged with steel.

"Are you threatening me, Artemis?" she huffed.

No smile, just a calm stare. "Yes, I believe I am."

"Enough!" The elder warlock warned. "Curb your spiteful tongue, Renata. This concerns all of us."

"Glad to see you finally making some sense, Braeden. Maybe now we can get somewhere." Artemis met the warlock's gaze. "I'm assuming you know what it is and how it wound up in our hands."

"It's a shielding charm. A very powerful one," Braeden replied.

Artemis frowned. "Shielding? From what?"

Vesper's eyes grew large and she murmured, "From you, Artemis. From your sight."

The High Elder sat stock still in comprehension and Braeden opened his hands. "It could certainly be used for that, old boy. If that's the case, someone went to a great deal of trouble to hide from you. A great deal. This kind of dark magic is not easy to come by. There aren't many of us powerful enough to control a magic like this."

Artemis blew out a breath and sat back in his chair, a little more relaxed. "That should narrow our field a bit, then."

The little girl piped up. "Not necessarily, sir. There are a few among us who are able to channel a magic such as this. Fewer still, are those who would admit to it." It was hard to reconcile the formality coming from the child who was sporting a Hannah Montana t-shirt and sparkly pink lip gloss. Vesper resisted the urge to roll her eyes. Warlocks.

"You assured us cooperation, Braeden. Is that not the case?" Dulcinea's voice was smooth. The slick tone made Vesper's hair stand on end. If there was an angle here, Dulcinea would find it and exploit it. Crafty bitch.

"And you shall have it, Dulcinea. *I* am a man of my word." Vesper smiled to herself as Braeden's tone implied he knew that she was not a woman of hers. "Like you, I am very much interested in who is practicing this kind of magic without my knowledge or permission."

A flutter of movement caught her eye and Vesper noticed Lori shift slightly in her seat. Marcus noticed too, and she watched her brother's eyes cut over her friend in silent interest.

Braeden sniffed and stood, the rest of the warlocks following suit. "I think we've indulged your curiosity enough for one evening. It appears we each have our crosses to bear. I leave you to find your Judas. I assure you we will find ours."

The parade of warlocks started toward the doors and the rest of the table stood as a group. Lori made a move to squeeze past Marcus, but Vesper noticed the staying hold he had on Lori's wrist, obscured from the view of her elder. Braeden paused at the double doors and turned to the witch.

"Lorelei?"

Vesper watched Lori's face pink up and she said, "I'll stay, Braeden. If you don't mind."

He gave her a hard glare. "I mind."

The witch stiffened and she swallowed hard.

"That's an awfully short leash you've got there, Braeden. Careful, too tight and she'll hang herself." Marcus' voice was low as he moved Lori slightly behind him.

There was a collective hiss from the warlocks and Braeden growled at him, "Remember yourself, leech." He turned back to Lori. "This is a dangerous path you walk with them, niece. Do not forget where your loyalties lie." He didn't wait for a response and disappeared through the open doors.

Lori jerked her hand from Marcus' grasp and hissed, "Let go of me!" Her irritation sparked and the chair next to her burst into flames, causing him to jump back suddenly. "How dare you!"

The chair burned and crackled and Marcus pulled her back. "Douse it, you phoenix! You'll set the whole room on fire!"

Her eyes blazed as she waved her hand and the fire died, the chair black and smoking. "You grab me again and I'll-"

"Enough!" Artemis roared. Lori fell silent and he turned to Gideon and Keane, who both wore looks of displeasure. "Call the others to order. They have one hour. I will go before the full Council then." Both men inclined their heads in understanding and left without a word. Artemis turned to his daughter, who watched the spectacle with obvious contempt. "Dulcinea, get Cain before we convene. I want him with Vesper and Marcus on this." She opened her mouth to protest, but shut it at her father's stare and headed downstairs.

The room was silent and Vesper could feel the tension in the room as if it was a wet blanket wrapped around her shoulders. Marcus stood glaring at Lori and she returned the look tenfold. Decker stood calmly next to her and placed a reassuring hand on the small of her back. She gave into the slight pressure and relaxed against it. A moment later, the double doors opened and Cain and Dulcinea appeared.

"Little late in the season for a barbecue, isn't it?" Cain sniffed as he arched an eyebrow at the smoldering chair. No one returned his smile and he quickly gave Dulcinea a wide berth as he stepped around her to stand on the other side of Vesper. "Tough crowd," he murmured.

Artemis ignored him and pulled out a cell phone from his pocket and dialed. His voice was terse as he spoke into the phone, "Council chambers. It's time." He replaced the phone and looked up to the group. "One more piece of the puzzle," he sighed. "I'm hoping this will lead you in the right direction."

The door at the back of the room opened and Vesper's breath caught in her throat. A tall, blond man with close cropped hair and ice blue eyes strolled casually into the room.

Decker let out a strangled gasp and tried to shove Vesper behind him with one hand while the other automatically reached for the weapon concealed at his waist.

"No!" Vesper cried, reaching for his arm, understanding his gut reaction. The description she'd provided earlier now appeared in the flesh. She stopped him from pulling the SIG as the doppelganger walked further into the room, right toward them. The rest of the room, save Artemis, laid wide, startled eyes on him as he stopped next to the High Elder.

"Varian," she whispered. The sight of Victor's twin clenched her heart in an icy fist.

Varian Delacroix's face was serene as he smiled and said smoothly, "Hello, Vesper. It's been a long time."

Howard closed his eyes and thought of Victor as the guard pumped steadily from behind with a series of soft grunts. It was only a matter of time and then all of this would be over. He would be free and he and Victor would be able to go on as they did before, but this time with no opposition. He would be one of them, Victor promised him as much, and together not even The Archive, its Council, or the fucking Penitent could stop them.

The Penitent. Yes, the little brunette vision in leather that came to see him the other day with Price, she was one of them. He could smell it on her. He bit his lip and the scent memory came to him and he grew harder in response. He sucked in a deep breath and reached down to stroke himself, the move causing Harper, the guard, to moan in satisfaction at the sight.

Two more long thrusts and Harper groaned out his release. He moved away from Howard off the cot and adjusted himself back into his pants. He tossed Howard's jumpsuit to him and cocked his head back to look through the small window in the door and check the hallway.

His voice was raspy and he said to Howard, "I managed to get you on the work detail in the fields. I pulled some strings to make it happen."

"You fuck somebody else or is that where I come in?" Howard asked bitterly, tugging on the suit.

Harper frowned. "You forget I'm doing this for you. You could be a little grateful." The anger in Howard's face disappeared and he did his best to look meek. He snapped the front of the jumpsuit and went to Harper, putting their faces close. Harper's quick intake of breath made him want to smile. The naive young guard had been so easy to wrap around his finger, not to mention his cock. A closet homosexual in a prison full of loud, overbearing, fag-hating rednecks, he'd stood out to Howard like fireworks at a funeral.

He let his gaze drift to Harper's mouth slowly, amused by the excited glint in the guard's eyes. "I am grateful," he said softly, fisting his hand into Harper's shirt. "I know it's risky. I'm just...excited, that's all."

Harper licked his lips nervously. "You'll have to wear the ankle bracelet, but I'll get that off you when you get to the van. I've also taken care of the radios for the chase team. You'll have only a couple of minutes before they let dogs go and start using cell phones." Howard nodded, still staring at Harper's lips. "The last thing you'll have to manage is getting over the razor wire. You'll be searched at least twice before you get out to the cotton fields, so I can't give you a weapon."

Howard looked up at Harper and smiled. "I understand. But," he paused, looking hopeful, "you'll be waiting for me?"

"Yeah, if you skirt the field past the fence line and the trees, I'll have a white van waiting about a half mile down. I'll meet you there. If you can make it. You'll have ten minutes, maybe less." Harper's breathing grew shallow as Howard tightened his hand on his shirt.

"If not?"

Harper's face hardened. "Then I can't help you."

"I understand." Howard leaned in and kissed him tenderly.

Harper returned the brief kiss and sighed. "Give me twenty and I'll be back to take you down."

Howard stepped back and let him leave. Shaking his head, he snorted a little. So stupid. So trusting. Just like a woman. He closed his eyes and thought of Victor.

It was too easy. Howard snorted to himself and disappeared into the line of trees at the far edge of the cotton field. The jumpsuit came off quickly, revealing the black tank and jeans Harper had slipped him earlier. He balled it as best he could, holding it in front of him to hide the orange and made for the fence at breakneck speed.

It was a long run, about three minutes, and he whipped between the trees in a zig zag fashion. Suddenly, a sound drifted past the rustling leaves to reach his ears. Fucking dogs. They were already onto him. The barking was getting closer, but so was the fence. He unfurled the jumpsuit and used it to climb up and over fence and the imposing coil of razor wire. It shredded the damn thing, but once over the top, he kicked off and dropped to the ground with a couple of nasty cuts, but nothing serious.

He kicked his run into high gear and made the half mile in five when he spotted the white van with government exempt plates parked in a little clearing. Harper jumped out of the driver's side and went around and opened the back doors. Howard climbed in and Harper reached down to cut the ankle bracelet from Howard's leg, tossing it aside. He slammed the doors shut and the van took off down the road.

Howard leaned back and took in great gulps of air, the reality of the situation just now washing over him. He was free. Completely and totally free. The thought was dizzying and he closed his eyes in satisfaction. There was only one thing left standing between him and Victor. Howard's eyes opened and the stormy depths gleamed with a sinister calm. He smiled to himself. God, this was too fucking easy.

They drove for about a half hour when he felt the van turn, slow and come to a stop. The back doors opened and Harper climbed in, shutting them behind him.

"There's an APB out for you, but road blocks haven't gone out yet. They still think you're in the vicinity of the prison. We've got time to get to New Orleans. We should make it out before the blocks go up and even if they do, nobody's going to stop me. I'm cleared to be out." He paused a moment before chuckling. "We did it." He smiled brightly, his breath coming quicker with excitement as he moved closer.

"Yes," Howard nodded. "It's done." His gaze dropped to Harper's mouth. "And we have time." He tilted his face up and met Harper's kiss, the young man so engrossed in his passion, he didn't notice Howard's hand creeping toward the gun at his hip.

Harper pulled back. "I've got a place on the-"

Howard's hand found the grip and pulled it from the holster. "That won't be necessary," he sighed, bringing the gun level to Harper's astonished face. "I already have a place to crash. And a roommate. He doesn't like to share."

Harper's mouth opened to emit a yell, but he was quickly silenced as Howard brought the butt of the gun down on his head, knocking him to the floor of the van. Howard pulled the cuffs from the guard's belt and handcuffed him to the grate separating the front from the cargo area. Harper moaned as a stream of blood trickled from the head wound and Howard made quick work of his uniform, stripping him naked. He hung limply from the cuffs and shook his head as Howard forced a sock into his mouth. His head dropped to his chest and he began to shake in muffled sobs.

Howard pulled the nightstick from the utility belt and brought the end underneath Harper's chin, forcing his face up to meet the malevolent gaze of his captor.

"On your knees," Howard bit out. Harper's fingers clutched the grate and he shuffled his legs until his knees came up underneath him. "Good," Howard replied. "I must say, you were quite endearing in your own little way." He trailed the end of the nightstick down the length of Harper's back until it reached the crack of his buttocks. "A bit stupid, perhaps, but much more trusting than I ever expected. It was refreshing." He laughed softly and shook his head.

Harper let out a violent, muffled scream as Howard shoved the nightstick roughly into his anus, the flesh tearing, burning and bleeding. Harper's body bucked wildly and he thrashed about in chaos, the metal cuffs scraping loudly on the grate. His eyes were wide with pain and disbelief and sobs racked his body. Howard watched with a delicious satisfaction and pushed harder, the tormented cries sounding delightful to his ears.

Howard let go of the nightstick and left it, moving up to whisper in Harper's ear. "You really didn't see this coming, did you?" He sniffed and chuckled. "How sublime." Victor's face filled his mind and he smiled in anticipation, reaching up and fisting a hand in Harper's hair. He pulled back slowly and exposed Harper's neck. Howard laughed as he ran a tongue across the top row of his teeth. "I want to thank you for making this so terribly easy for me. I could have done it without you, but somehow, this just seems fitting, don't you think?" His lips curled back in a monstrous sneer, revealing canines that had been sharpened to points. Howard gave a short, baleful growl and sank his teeth into Harper's neck.

Victor. I'm coming home.

"Well, well. Look what the cat dragged in," Dulcinea sniffed. "You here to help clean up Vesper's mess?" Her green eyes cast a sidelong glance at Vesper. "Again?"

All eyes turned to her and Cain frowned. "You been smoking crack with Satan again, Dulcie?'Cause it's making you a little pissy."

Marcus and Decker suppressed a chuckle as Dulcinea's eyes narrowed before turning back to Vesper. "This is just a bad dream for you, isn't it? Your sins have returned to bite us all in the ass. If you knew you were going to fuck it up so badly, you should have at least had the decency to die."

The air in the room went cold and Marcus let out a low growl.

Cain cut in. "Dream or no, Dulcie, when you wake up, you'll still be a whore. Leave Vesper alone."

Dulcinea looked at him pointedly. Her gaze raked over him, taking in the spiky blond hair, the eerie scroll tattoo, the leather and jewelry, all the way down to his black steel toes. "You are a bad mating." She didn't even try to veil her disdain.

Cain's expression hardened. "Yeah, you're not at the top of my 'to do' list either, sweetheart. Never have been one for a mercy fuck."

"Cain!" Artemis' voice echoed like thunder off the walls. Cain lowered his gaze and let it go. "Come, Dulcinea. You are not needed here." He held his hand out to his daughter and they turned and left.

The tension in the room dissipated only slightly as Cain blew out a deep breath and watched Dulcinea glide out behind her father.

He wrinkled his nose at the door. "I'd hit that," he muttered.

Marcus gave him a sardonic glare. "I know you're not picky, but I'm starting to question your apparent lack of taste."

Cain's face broke into a cocky grin, revealing his fangs. "Dude, by 'hit that', I meant with a baseball bat. I can't fucking stand that bitch."

Varian stepped forward and gave the kid a wry smile and clapped a hand on his shoulder. "Nice. Good to see some things are still the same around here."

"Yep," Cain shrugged. "Dulcie's still as cantankerous as ever. I'm convinced she eats kittens for breakfast."

Varian let out a chuckle and sat down at the table and stared at Vesper. "My homecoming is bittersweet, no?"

Vesper's face was ashen, and she stiffened beneath Decker's hand on her back. "What are you doing here, Varian?" she asked quietly.

"Who the fuck is this guy?" Decker growled.

Varian smiled at Decker. "Varian Delacroix," he said. "And you are?"

"Delacroix? As in?" Decker's brows furrowed.

Vesper nodded.

Decker pointed to the vampire. "Twins?" His voice broke. "Jesus Fucking Christ."

Varian turned his smile to Vesper. "The human catches on quick, doesn't he?" he said dryly.

"What *are* you doing here, Varian? I thought you were in Prague. Hiding." Varian's eyes were so clear and blue, the openness in them so strikingly different than that of his brother. The realization should have been a small measure of comfort, but she couldn't shake the shiver of dread that rolled up her spine.

"I was content in Prague. However, I've been informed my brother has resurfaced in his usual disturbing fashion. Artemis called and so," Varian spread his hands, "here I am."

"You weren't much help the first time around, so why should now be any different? Last I recall, you were more interested in saving your own ass and getting a free pass to sip cappuccino in the heart of the Czech Republic." Marcus' smile was snide and he waved a hand at Varian. "Are you here to play homing pigeon?"

Varian's smile vanished and his face creased into a cold mask as he turned his head to face Vesper's brother. "Not exactly. You know I haven't been connected to Victor since our," he paused, swallowing hard, "falling out."

Decker's arm came around to pull Vesper against him protectively. "Falling out? What, you don't share his penchant for murder and mayhem?"

Varian leaned forward and placed a hand on the table, spreading his fingers wide and locked hard eyes with the detective. "Once upon a time, my brother and I shared a very special bond." He drummed his fingers on the table. "Among other things." Varian's voice was low and pained as he continued, "The deep connection we shared was severed when my brother lost his mind and attempted to kill me. It has yet to be restored. I don't think it ever will."

Decker was unmoved. "Spare me the circle time stories, Uncle Remus. You know where he is? I suggest you start talking." Vesper felt Decker's fingers dig into the flesh of her hip, biting angrily for a moment and then relaxing. The sensation was oddly reassuring.

"Are you aware that your brother has involved a human in his games? Feeding him? Possibly even killing with him?" Vesper asked. She stared into his eyes, hoping to gauge a flicker of recognition. "I think they're lovers as well. Does that surprise you?"

Varian closed his eyes for a moment and shook his head, a tired sigh escaping his lips. When he finally looked up at Vesper, she could see the sadness at the edges of his gaze. "No. It doesn't. Victor loves control. He needs it. It was only a matter of time before he became bored and sought out someone who was more like him. If that's the case and he is involved with this human, I can tell you, they have a bond as well. And it won't be easily broken." Varian's eyes shadowed. "It doesn't surprise me at all. This man, I take it he's like my brother?"

Decker nodded. "Howard Grainger is one sick fuck. He's locked away at Angola for the time being."

"That's good news at least," Varian said.

Cain shifted on his feet and shook his head at the floor. "Dude, that is supremely craptastic. Who do you think is the meat in that man sandwich?" He let out a shiver. "Gives me the willies thinking about what date night is like for those two." Varian shot him a menacing frown and Cain put his hands up defensively, yet continued to run his mouth. "I'm just sayin'. Man, your bro is rolling with one serious Anne Rice routine. Anything that tortured should be dragged out into the swamp and shot. Hell, I've got a hard-on for Brad Pitt right about now. Anybody else creeped out by this?"

"Cain, shut it," Marcus growled. The kid shrugged.

"Just sayin'."

Lori cleared her throat and stepped away from Marcus. "Wow, the angst in this room just shot from after-school special to emo in a heartbeat. If I have to stand here and listen to much more, I think I might be forced to get a bad haircut and slit my wrists. Can we just figure out what his next move is? Some of us have lives, you know."

Marcus whirled on her. "And just where do you propose we start, firecracker?"

She ignored the remark and looked past him to Vesper. "Realistically hon, if he's still in the market for the black magic, there's only one place he'll go."

Vesper's eyes brightened. "Absynthe."

The witch nodded. "Bingo."

"She's right, Marcus," Vesper said, turning to her brother. "Let's go. We'll see if anyone's been digging around over there."

The tall vampire's expression was resolute. "Fine. Vesper, you and Decker head on over. Cain, take Varian down and wait for me in the Rover." Cain caught the keys Marcus chucked in the air with an easy hand as he turned to Lori and glared. "I want to have a quick word with the phoenix."

Lori swallowed hard under Marcus' stare as the two vampires followed Vesper and Decker out the door.

"Phoenix?" Lori bristled at the door shut behind Varian.

"Cut your shit, witch." Marcus' pale blue eyes bore into her face. "You were very quick to distance yourself from Reardon's little charm and you were awfully nervous while the mystics were here." He arched an eyebrow. "What are you hiding from them? More importantly, what are you hiding from Vesper?" He moved so fast that as she blinked, he was right on top of her, peering down at her with controlled ire, so close their bodies almost touched.

She drew herself up to her full height but Marcus still towered over her. Irritated, she snapped, "Don't think you can use your sister against me. She's my friend."

"Then act like one."

She jabbed a pointy finger in his chest and the air started to ripple around her hair as she spoke. "Don't you fucking tell me I'm not her friend. I was there for her when-" her voice trailed at the look of furious warning that flared in his eyes. "I was there for her," she finished. "How I interact with my people is my business, not yours. Don't presume otherwise."

He frowned down at her small hand. "You can kill the hurricane, Lorelei. I'm not moving."

He stood firm among the increasing winds, his white hair ruffling around him. Damn right he wasn't moving. The man was a brick wall. She blinked and the air subsided. "You can back the fuck up then, mosquito. Don't make me swat you down."

Her threat didn't faze him and he didn't move. "One way or another, I will find out what you're hiding. I excel at secrets. Remember that. Now move." He pointed to the door.

Lori swept past him and he followed her to the door. She could feel the anger in his gaze as it moved over her back. He was one touchy son of a bitch. Clever, too. So, he had noticed her earlier discomfort. Figures. Looks like she would have to wait until the Victor thing was firmly resolved before she let the cranky vampire see all her cards. She didn't like pissing him off mainly because she didn't want to upset her friend. But being an elemental witch, she just couldn't help but play with fire. She stopped mid-stride and kept facing the doorway.

"You know," she said lightly, looking over her shoulder, "my ass is a lot like birthday cake. Stare at it all you want, but you can't have a piece unless I invite you to the party."

She heard him snort, "It's not your birthday. And I hate cake." His hand shot out and smacked her smartly on the rear as he sidestepped her and beat her out the door. "Get in the fucking truck."

She rubbed the stinging spot on her backside and stuck her tongue out at him as she followed. "I swear, you ticks have no sense of humor."

CHAPTER SEVEN

Vesper pulled the Vantage in behind Marcus' Range Rover and threw it into park. Figured he got here first. Her brother drove like a bat out of hell.

The converted warehouse stood four stories tall, with no indication of its business other than the thumping of the house music drifting out into the alley.

"So what is this place?" Decker asked as he came around to her.

"Absynthe? First floor is dance club and bar. Second floor is referred to as 'The Cafeteria'." She paused for a moment and watched his face. "We feed here." She smiled at his wide-eyed expression.

"Feed? You mean?"

She nodded. "It's consensual. There are some of us here who are willing to serve in that respect. Despite the nickname, we take it very seriously. It's sort of like a public service to our race."

"I take it you've eaten here before?" His eyes sparkled in the lamplight and she reached up to touch the faint marks at his neck.

"Yes. Does that bother you?" she asked, her heart pounding.

"Sure as shit does." He pulled her close and backed her up roughly against the side of the car. Her body flared in response as his gaze lowered to her lips. "But you won't be anymore." His hand brushed her cheek. "Understand?"

Her knees would have buckled beneath her if he wasn't holding her so tightly. "You sure about that? That's an awfully big promise you're making."

"Do I strike you as a man who makes promises easily?" His breath was hot on her face. No, no he wasn't. "I told you, Vesper. Whatever you need. Whatever it takes."

He brooked no protest as his lips came down on hers, sealing her fate. The kiss was searing in its intensity, his mouth branding her in silent claim.

He pulled back slowly and smiled down at her. "Maybe when we get home, I can interest you in a tray lunch?"

She chuckled. "Yeah, I'd like that. I'd like that a lot."

He dropped a quick kiss on her forehead. "Third floor?"

She continued, "Third floor is a sex club. It picks up where The Cafeteria leaves off, if you catch my drift," she said, arching an eyebrow at him. "I told you there was a lot about my world you would have to understand."

"Sex clubs aren't anything mysterious, Vesper. I've seen a few," he replied. "As long as it's all legal."

We keep it that way." She smiled again. "For the most part. Our tastes are a little less vanilla than yours."

"We'll see about that. Fourth floor?" he asked, nonplussed by her comment.

"Just offices."

They made their way inside and started pushing through the bodies to get to the bar where the others were all waiting.

Vesper's eyes locked with her brother. The firm set of his jaw and resolute glare set off a sisterly response in her body. He was angry about something. She frowned at him in question, but he ignored the look and turned his eyes on the group.

"Cain and I will hit The Cafeteria. Vesper, you take Price and the witch and see what you find down here. Varian, I assume you will take the third floor?" Marcus asked.

"You into the kinky shit, my man?" Cain smiled at Varian and nodded appreciatively. "Awesome." The young vamp readjusted his jacket. "Maybe I'll just tag along with you, bro. See what kinds of nasty I can get myself into," he laughed.

Marcus laid a staying hand on Cain and frowned sourly. "Not tonight, Romeo. Keep it in your pants and remember why we're here."

Cain shrugged off the hand and adjusted again. "Don't make me stake you, bro."

"You know that's an urban myth," Marcus ground out.

"Yeah," he sniffed, "but it would annoy the fuck out of you and that would be hilarious."

Marcus glowered at him.

"What?" Cain raised his hands. "I'm just feelin' my stereotype. Man, I swear, you're the reason I am soooo Team Jacob. And why are we assuming V-man gets the fun floor? No offense dude," he said to Varian, "but I think I could work some seriously hot voodoo up there. I'm just two chicks short of a threesome." He waggled his fingers and smiled wide.

Varian suppressed a chuckle. "I'm sure. However," he paused, "Victor and I played here together before things went awry. I may still have a contact or two."

Cain's eyes widened in rapt surprise. "No shit?" He turned to Marcus. "Dude, you know you're my towering inferno of two-fisted cool, but man, that's fucking awesome. I might have a new hero."

Marcus' eyes narrowed and he shoved Cain toward the stairs. "Come on, there's more important things to do here than figuring out how you can get involved in a three-way."

"Man, I did *not* expect the cock block," Cain scoffed. "Dirty pool, Legolas. Dirty, dirty pool."

"One more time, mouth. Call me that just one more time."

The young vampire's hands shot up as Marcus grabbed Cain's jacket by the shoulder, moving him bodily up the stairs with a series of hard shoves. "Aw right, Marcus! Fucking Christ on the cross! Don't get your pointy ears all in a twist! Ouch! Dude, watch the leathers! I-talian cows, man, I-talian!" he yelled as they disappeared.

The hollow, nauseous feeling in the pit of her stomach kept growing, threatening to eat its way through her belly all the way back to her spine. Lori swallowed hard and put her hand on the edge of the bar, blinking her eyes against the brightness of the neon. Marcus' angry face kept swimming in her head, bringing her back to Vesper. The haunted look she'd seen on her friend's face multiplied the guilt she was feeling in her soul a hundred times over. She took a deep, shuddering breath. The time for secrets was over. Even if it meant she had to lose Vesper, she had to come clean.

Suddenly, the tiny hairs on the back of her neck stood eerily at attention and she turned slowly.

"Looking for someone, little Lorelei? Found me."

Victor.

The bastard was smiling. She opened her mouth but hissed instead as his fingers bit cruelly into the flesh of her upper arm as he dragged her into a dark corner near the rear of the building.

He chuckled, "You look like someone just walked over your grave, witch." Her eyes darted back over his shoulder nervously and he laughed again. "Don't worry. We haven't been spotted. Yet." The dark smile vanished. "You lied to me, Lorelei. Where is it?"

"I didn't lie to you," she managed to growl. "You're just a shitty burglar." She forced herself to stand straight under the evil scrutiny of his gaze. "Reardon still had it. If you hadn't been so intent on killing him right off the bat, you probably would have found it." She shook her head. "Either way, it's moot now. Vesper's found it and turned it over to your Council. And to my coven." Her blood ran cold as she watched the mask on his face harden further.

"Then we have a problem, you and I," Victor said between clenched teeth. "We had a deal."

She stood her ground. "Deal's off. Find someone else."

Before she knew it, his hand clawed at her arm again and he muscled her back into the open door of a storeroom off to the right. She struggled beneath his grasp and wrenched her arm free.

The fury in his face was terrifying as his fangs dropped and he bit out, "Do not play with me, witch."

Her heart pounded furiously in her chest and the acrid taste of fear crept into her mouth.

"If you cannot recover the vial, then you will fashion a new one." His voice lowered an octave and she could feel the hate in his voice slide across her skin as he rasped, "I will strip the flesh from your bones if you think you can play me."

Fear gave way to terror and instinctively she began to call forth her power, preparing to fight. He grabbed her chin and forced her eyes to his, breaking her concentration.

"I would be careful about what you unleash here. You know most of my kind don't appreciate your antics. And I don't think there's enough of your coven here to save your ass. A fireworks display might get you killed."

Lori's eyes flashed with green fire and she choked down the fear just enough to become irritated. Pulling her face from his hand she snapped, "I can't get it back. And a new one is out of the question." She stiffened. "If you kill me, your chances of finding someone who can control that kind of magic are slim to none. So I suggest you just back off and slip back into whatever sewage you came from before you're the one who gets royally fucked."

A dead calm spread over Victor. "You will give me what I want or witch, you will pay in ways that you can only dream about. You know about what I did to Vesper." She stepped back a little. "I've become so much more imaginative since then."

149

Lori's eyes widened in surprise and she gasped. Suddenly, Decker's face filled the doorway and she opened her mouth to warn him.

"Hey Varian, have you-" He tapped Varian on the shoulder but his voice stopped short as cold blue eyes that should have been Varian's turned to meet his gaze.

"It looks like you have the wrong brother." Victor's face broke into an evil grin and the vampire moved like lightning, grabbing him by the throat and reaching out with the other hand to backhand Lori into unconsciousness and she tumbled to the floor with a soft grunt. Decker went for the SIG at his waist, but he was unable to put a hand on it as Victor rammed forward with a solid head butt. There was a loud crack as pain splintered in his head and everything went blurry as his head snapped back.

Dazed, he felt himself being pulled out the back door into the alley. Victor shoved him hard across the way into the brick wall and the breath whooshed out of his lungs. His teeth rattled so hard he thought they would fall out, but he remained standing. This time, his hand found the weapon and he pulled it fast, pointing the barrel straight at Victor's heart.

"Don't move. Put your hands up." Decker ground out, blinking hard to focus. The four Victors melded into one.

Victor let out a rich, musical laugh. "How original." He raised his hands in mock surrender. "Really, Detective, is this how you want to play it? I think Vesper would have been much cleverer." Victor started forward.

"You move and I will lay you the fuck down. Count on it."

The vampire froze and shrugged his shoulders. "I thought we had things to discuss, you and I. Let's be civil, shall we? We don't have much time before the witch comes to and the rest of your merry gang saunters out. Along with my traitorous brother too, I see. Makes things so much more interesting."

The mocking tone lit Decker on fire. Miranda filled his mind and his brain went red with the idea of Victor being involved in any way. And then there was Vesper. *Vesper.*

"You're over thinking, Detective. Tick, tick. Time is of the essence."

Decker's arm stiffened and he clicked off the safety. "You seem awfully sure I'm not going to shoot you. You a betting man?"

"Yes, well, I had hoped we could carry on like gentlemen," Victor sniffed.

"Gentlemen? I think your definition differs slightly from mine." Decker ticked off the seconds in his head, knowing he had little time to stall or make a move.

"One can kill people and still be a gentleman, Detective. The two are not mutually exclusive," Victor smiled. "It's all a matter of the little things, of," he paused, "the pleasantries, if you will."

Decker's eyes narrowed. "Then you'll excuse me if I don't say 'please' when I tell you to suck the end of my SIG."

"Temper, temper. Let's talk about...your wife."

Flares went off in Decker's head and he raised the gun higher, locking on to the head shot. "Do. Not. Go. There."

Victor chuckled. "A sore subject, I know, but it focused your attention, I see. Howard says you two were quite the love story." He paused with a wicked smile. "She called for you, you know."

The vampire didn't flinch as the bullet buzzed by his temple and Decker's arm shifted back to center.

"It was really quite charming to watch, I must say. His best work to date." Decker's stomach knotted in disgust as Victor's eyes glazed over in wistful remembrance. "He took such joy in her." Decker started to shake and his arm wavered, but he sniffed hard and steeled his elbow. "I know he gave you a choice. Save her or catch him. But you really didn't have one. Her fate was sealed by the time he decided to play." Another chuckle. "A slight misdirection, of course. And you played into it beautifully. I don't think I could have done it better." He shook his head slowly. "You couldn't have saved her. But it was amusing to watch you try." He looked down and shuffled his foot.

Decker's arm moved left and the next shot speared across the other side of Victor's face.

"She was angelic, your Miranda. Not at all like our Vesper." He lifted his gaze and an arrogant smirk swept across his face.

Rage boiled within him and Decker growled, "Shut your trap or the next one will be dead on."

"Do you honestly think you can have a relationship with her?" Victor asked casually as he folded his arms and leaned back, propping one foot against the wall. "How long do you think it will be before her darkness consumes you? Before you aspire to more than you can possibly be? You are human, and she...well, she is not." He shook his head again and the vampire's cold stare froze Decker solid. "You cannot sustain her. It will eat you alive." Victor dropped his fangs and licked his lips. "She is one delicious little morsel, I will admit. Ah, but look who I'm talking to, you've already had a taste."

Vesper's admissions rolled back over him and Decker's mind reeled with tortures he could only imagine. His finger itched to pull the trigger, to end it now, but the vision of Miranda's face stayed his hand, willing him to focus.

"And the witch? The charm? Isn't that what you're really after?" he choked out. "All this drama so you can have secret sex with your boyfriend? You and Howie could've just gone to a bath house and you guys could pillow bite like crazy. I think there's one or two left in the city."

Victor's arms fell to his side and the smile vanished, leaving behind a mask of pure hatred. *Jackpot.*

"You think you know so much, Detective. It is so far beyond your simple comprehension." Victor's eyes glittered icily in the lamplight as he shook his head. "We will not be controlled. Howard and I will dictate the terms of our existence. *We* will not be forced into living on their terms. *I* will not be forced." His voice was gritty. "Not by The Council, Artemis, or my brother. But yes, I'm not through with the witch. Or with the dark princess, either."

Decker's resolve returned. "If you want to get to them, looks like you'll have to go through me. Still feeling like a gentleman?"

"Not hardly," Victor snarled and launched himself from the wall toward Decker.

Lori groaned and rolled to her side and reached up to touch her burning cheek. She probed the swollen flesh gingerly, wincing. It was going to be one hell of bruise. *Serves me right.* Victor's face flashed before her and she blanched, rising to her feet and hitting the door in one swift motion. The club was packed and she muscled through the sea of gyrating bodies, forcing her vision to focus and scan. The rapid file of images as her eyes searched the floor made her dizzy and her stomach turn. She swallowed against the bile that rose up in her throat when suddenly, she spotted him. He wasn't hard to miss, tall and imposing with his long shock of silver hair, at the far end of the bar across the dance floor.

"Marcus!" she yelled. Moving closer, she saw Cain's spiky head parked next to him. "Marcus! Cain!" she yelled again, getting her voice to cut over the din of the thumping house music.

She met Cain's eyes, which widened as he noticed her frantic waving. He tapped Marcus and jerked his head in her direction and started toward her. Marcus turned and as their eyes met, his face paled and he followed hot on Cain's heels.

Lori fell into Cain's open arms and she gasped, "Victor! He's here! Took Decker out back!" She regained her footing and Cain pushed past her. "Go! Go!" Cain broke off at a run and Marcus' fingers bit into her arm as he jerked her to him and lifted her face to his, turning her bruised cheek into the glare of the pulsing strobe lights. His eyes darkened to points as she winced at the touch to her face.

"I'm okay!" she yelled. "Just go! I don't know how long I was out. Decker, he thought Victor was Varian. He knocked me out and hauled Decker outside."

Marcus stilled. "What were you doing with Victor?"

She shook her head, "There's no time. I'll explain later." She shoved at him. "Just go!" she cried.

His fingers tightened around her upper arm and his face went hard with rage and she knew he was putting two and two together and coming up with her ass on four. "Stay here and don't fucking move!" he ground out. He pushed her to the bar and started after Cain.

The vampire was unbelievably fast as he grabbed Decker's wrist and forced it up, the shot firing high into the air.

Decker howled as Victor's fingers crushed his wrist and he felt the bones snap and the gun fall from his grasp. His left arm came up and he delivered a solid blow to Victor's midsection and the vampire hissed in pain. He didn't let go, hanging on and muscling Decker to the wall.

The blade came from nowhere as Victor whisked it up, slashing him diagonally across the chest. The cut was deep and it burned like fire, but he managed another body blow with his fist, this one hard enough to push Victor back. Shutting his mind off from the fire at his chest, he brought his foot up and kicked Victor hard, sending him flying back and to the left into the steel wall of a nearby dumpster.

There was a loud clang as Victor's body connected and he slumped to the ground. Decker's eyes roved the concrete for the fallen SIG. He locked eyes on it and dove with his good hand, but Victor moved forward and tackled him, the two men crumbling to the ground in a flurry of blows. Decker grunted and rolled, moving away from the snapping of Victor's fangs as the vampire came in close for a bite. Pain flared as he closed the injured hand into a fist and brought it up solid, knocking into Victor's face with a loud crack as he connected with jawbone.

His fingers groped for the SIG, but it was too far away. Victor snarled as Decker's knee smashed into his groin and he pushed him aside, reaching down for the snub nose .38 in his ankle holster. Decker's arm came up with the piece, but Victor delivered an elbow to his nose and his vision went black while his nostrils filled with blood.

Blinded, Victor plucked the revolver from his grasp and shuffled off of him. He heard the cock of the gun as his vision came back to focus in on Victor standing over him. He braced for the shot that was coming when the door burst open behind them and Cain came barreling into the alley.

Victor's eyes widened in surprise and Cain yelled, coming up in a roundhouse to knock the .38 out of Victor's hand, snapping his arm wide to the side.

Victor bent and lunged for Cain. The hard grunt gave him away and Cain turned, raising one hand. The air around his hand rippled and Victor slammed face first into the invisible wall, the force hard enough to send him hurtling back to smack into the brick wall. Cain reached for Decker and shoved him toward Marcus' waiting hands.

"Ah, so you're the halfling. I'll bet they've got you thinking you're something special. Save the Jedi parlor tricks for Artemis and his cronies." Victor sneered, wiping the blood from his mouth and nose.

Cain lowered his head and pulled his two Desert Eagles and watched the twisted grin slide from Victor's face at the sight of the fifty-caliber cannons with the seven inch barrels. He bared his fangs with a dark smile and countered, "Bad ass I am. Fuck with me you will not."

He fired but Victor was faster, the two shots just missing as he lurched to the right and rolled, pulling his own piece and taking a shot at the spiky-haired vamp. The shot went wide and Victor dove behind the dumpster. Cain moved for a better angle but before his boot hit the ground, the dumpster came barreling through the air right for him. The guns clattered to the concrete and Cain's hands came up quick, the air around him suddenly coalescing thickly, almost stopping the dumpster mid-air. It kept moving slowly, threatening to give way and crush him at any moment as he fought to keep it aloft.

"Marcus!" he yelled. "Fuck! *Marcus!*"

Marcus' head snapped up and he shoved Decker in the Range Rover and slammed the door. "Stay here, cop."

Cain stood in the alley, his body nearly bent back in half, arms folded at the elbow as his hands kept the dumpster at bay. It moved scant inches through the thickness of the air and Cain's voice was gritty and strained as his knees threatened to buckle beneath him.

"This is not as fucking easy at it looks, man! I can't hold it much longer!" It slipped even further toward him and he lurched back even more. "Get this shit off me!"

Marcus hit a dead run alongside the alley wall and as he got even with Cain, vaulted himself sideways off the brick and tackled Cain across to the other side. They hit the wall with a hard thud and a second later, the dumpster fell to the ground in a colossal heap of groaning and creaking metal.

"I'm not in the mood to cuddle, bro. You wanna get off me?" Cain pushed against Marcus and the pale vampire helped him to his feet, looking down the alley.

"He's gone. Damn." Marcus scooped up the dropped .38 and the SIG and started back to the SUV. "Come on, let's see if the cop's still in one piece."

Lori took a tentative step into the alley, careful to keep her presence undetected by flattening against the brick wall and peeking around a pile of stacked crates. She could see from her hiding place that Vesper's face was ashen as she emerged from the building and watched Marcus and Cain inspect the bleeding detective. Bright crimson bloomed across his shirt and even from her distance; she could see the cut on his chest was deep. Her stomach knotted. She closed her eyes and swallowed, offering up a quick prayer for Decker. She forced herself to look again at her friend.

Concern etched Vesper's face as Marcus and Cain helped Decker into the back of the Rover. Vesper climbed in and folded her arms around him and Marcus shut the door. Lori watched as he spoke and gestured to Cain, whose head popped up, scanning the alley in her direction. *He was looking for her.* After all, they had driven out here together. There was no way in hell she was going back with them. Not now. She couldn't face Vesper. Remembering the fury in Marcus' face when he connected her with Victor, yeah, she definitely couldn't face him either.

She cursed herself for the cowardice, but for the moment, self-preservation was beating out loyalty to her friend and she tried to focus, forcing her mind to concentrate. One stray thought and she could end up miles from where she wanted to be. Or worse, stuck somewhere in another dimension, floating in oblivion forever. There was always a slight drawback in dealing with the dark arts. Very powerful, but awfully finicky. Lesser witches tried teleporting and just disappeared. Concentration was key. She emptied her mind, focused on home and chanted softly. In the next breath, before Cain could find her, she was gone.

CHAPTER EIGHT

"Why do I feel like I've been hit by a truck? Several trucks," Decker groaned.

Cain paused with his hands over the detective's midsection, the soft white glow of his heal emanating from them and chuckled, "Because you got a spectacular ass-kicking, cop. They're supposed to hurt." He brought his hands together and then spread them out once more over Decker's body as the glow dissipated.

"Did I at least win?"

"You bet your ass. You're still alive, aren't you?" Cain stepped back. "Now, let that do its thing and you should be feeling a lot less pain."

"Christ, Cain! Feels like someone dipped my whole body in a tube of Ben-Gay." Decker's eyes were slightly glazed, but his face held a smile.

Cain shook his head and smiled back at the cop. "Man, if we're gonna be buds, I'm gonna have to ask you to not use my name and 'gay' in the same sentence. I got a rep, you know."

Decker lifted a weak arm to the young vampire. "Done. Thanks, man."

They clasped hands and Cain shook it gently. "No sweat. Anything for V. And you're okay, too." He winked at Decker and let out a wide yawn. "Fuck, I'm beat. Nighty night, folks." He waved a hand in goodbye and disappeared out the door.

Gideon, the tall, dark-haired behemoth he remembered from earlier, turned from the sink, drying his hands on a clean, white towel. "He's going to be sore for a few days, but he'll be fine. Keep the sutures clean and dry. I should be able to take those out in a day or two."

Vesper nodded.

Decker lifted the arm with the injured wrist. "And this? What about this? I can't even feel it right now."

Gideon's eyes narrowed, making him look even more dangerous. "Delacroix got you good. You're lucky the kid got a hold of you."

"Thanks." The detective's voice was quiet.

Gideon laid the towel down. "Cain's right. Anything for Vesper." The big man walked over and gave Vesper a brusque hug and set her back on her feet. "Now, he needs to sleep, and so do you. Get some rest. I mean it."

She nodded again as he left and then turned her attention to Decker.

"And I thought your brother was heavy." Decker managed a weak smile. "That guy is hardcore. Quietly hardcore."

"Still waters run deep. And if you had his job, inscrutable would be your stock and trade." She reached out and placed a hand on his forehead. "You sure you're okay? Cain's spells usually make me a little queasy." His head bobbed in a light nod.

"Yeah, I'll be fine. Besides your guy there said I'd be up and running again in no time."

"My guy? The Penitent master-at-arms and Artemis' personal bodyguard is hardly 'my guy'. He's over three hundred years old. That would be like dating," she paused, shaking her head. "Ew. No. Ew." She looked back at Decker. "I'm a Penitent. That's our bond. Nothing else." Her fingers automatically went to the silver necklace.

"Why do I feel like you've got every man here eating out of the palm of your hand? Cain, Artemis," he tilted his head to the door, "that guy." Decker gave her a tired smile. "And why does that irritate the hell out of me?"

She leaned down to his face, savoring the scent of him, and swiped her mouth across his with slow calculation. She smiled as his lips opened under hers without reserve and met the kiss. "Because you want me," she murmured against him. "Bad."

He groaned. "Yes." Decker slanted his head and deepened the kiss with marked fervor. His hands found their way from his sides up to tangle in hair, pulling her closer. Her weight shifted as she was caught off guard and her body came down on his.

"Your stitches!" she gasped, pulling back. "You'll hurt yourself!"

The fire in his eyes was unmistakable. Deep within those depths she saw desire and a need that would not wait. The playful kiss had sparked something. Something carnal. She backed off of him as he rose from the gurney with a grimace. He was all heat and determination as he grabbed her hand and shoved her toward the door. "Now."

The detective in him knew he should be scanning the dark interior of her room for hidden danger, but the animal male that was bursting forth was only looking for a surface. A bed, a chair, something, anything on which he could throw her down to sate the burgeoning need. The black inside was so thick his eyes couldn't pierce through, so instead, he went by instinct. By feel. And it felt good.

The heavy door was loud as he slammed it shut and he found her in the dark by her cry of surprise. His hand snaked out and grabbed her by the arm, whipping her around to face him. Her skin was warm beneath his touch and he swore he could hear the frantic beating of her heart in his head.

"Decker." Her breathy voice was a plea.

He jerked her into the circle of his arms and ran seeking hands up her back to hold her closer as his mouth crushed down on hers. The rich taste of her filled his mouth and he wanted more, so much more. The heated need she had sparked inside him with that one soft kiss raged and his fingers clenched tight in possession.

Decker's hands found the leather of the holster she wore and his fingers curled at will and ripped the thing from her body in a quick, fierce motion. His palm came down hard on the edge of one of them as it fell to the floor, slicing it open. He growled at the offense, the sharp sting an annoyance. The holster hit the floor with a soft thump as it hit the plush of the rug under their feet.

She moaned into his mouth and he brought his hand up to her face. The smell of his blood made her turn and she grabbed his wrist, staring into the darkness at his hand.

"Be careful," she whispered, taking a breath, "they're extremely sharp." He felt the wetness of her tongue dart out and slide over his palm, sealing the cut. The erotic gesture make him rock hard.

"Get rid of them. All of them. Now." His voice sounded rough, but he didn't care.

Several more thumps followed and when he reached for her again his hands greedily stripped the shirt from her body. She pressed her breasts into his hands and covered his mouth with hers. He squeezed hard and thrust his tongue inside her mouth, tasting the darkness within.

He wanted her. Wanted to feel her writhing beneath him. Decker took two steps forward, his hands still stroking and teasing, forcing her back. He kicked the holster to the side as he went, tumbling them to the floor, the only sure surface he knew in the room, popping the fly on her jeans and shoving them roughly to her ankles.

Her hard gasp was rough feminine pleasure. His cock swelled in response, rigid with the knowledge that she knew going slow and easy here was not an option. His hands grazed the mound of her sex as he tore the soft scrap of lace off her hips. She was bare. An erotic fact he had not appreciated at their previous encounter. She bucked briefly, kicking off her boots and ridding herself completely of her jeans. His hands splayed wide across her and his thumb stroked the slick folds. She gasped and arched and he smiled at her pleasure. He didn't recognize the deep, lustful growl that escaped him as he hands pushed her thighs apart and plunged his tongue into her core.

The hot scream she gave split the air but he did not stop the assault. She tasted dark and sweet and his mouth watered for more with each pass of his tongue. Her back arched up off the floor and her hands clutched tight in his hair, her nails digging sharply into his scalp. The twinge of pain spurred him on as she tried to hold him in place. His lips curled into a feral smile at the ragged mewling sounds coming from her throat. She was breathless and wanton under his mouth, right where he wanted her. He snarled in satisfaction as his lips wrapped around the sensitive nub that hardened to life and he sucked hard. She screamed again and he felt her move as her head thrashed from side to side in ecstasy.

His hands clamped down on her shaking thighs to still her but she was tense, her body quaking as it readied for the release that was soon to come. He sucked harder to hear one more delicious cry then relented, selfish in his desire to taste her some more. He traced each sweet fold, each crevice of heaven, until he gave in. His hold on her thighs eased and he swiped his tongue in a sensuous rhythm, feeling her topple over the edge of her orgasm. She broke apart under his mouth with a throaty cry of passion and her body shuddered in a series of hard spasms.

Decker panted hard as he lifted his head and looked at her in the shadows. She was so beautiful. The need for his own satisfaction would not wait any longer, not now after the erotic spectacle he'd witnessed. He was beyond hard, beyond ready. He chucked off his jeans and shoes and reached out to crawl up her body. The stitches in his chest tightened in a massive contraction of pain and he cried out suddenly. Cain's spell was wearing off. His cock pulsed and throbbed despite the agony and the need. He groaned through the pain and grabbed her, covering her with his body. He let out a loud grunt as he rolled them over, reversing their positions on the rug.

Vesper didn't miss a beat as she went with him, positioning herself perfectly and took the lead. It was her turn to growl this time as she came down on him, encasing his hard length. His world shifted in perspective, all his focus centered on the hot, wet feel of her wrapped around his cock. She took him to the hilt and drove him mad as she began to move.

His hands shot out and grabbed her hips, urging her harder and faster as his teeth gritted together with each thrust of her body. Decker's eyes slammed shut as she played the same teasing game, giving and giving without relent. Wave after wave of blazing heat spiraled through him and he hissed as the tightness in his chest blossomed and he felt stitches pop and rip in a painful symphony. Warmth covered his torso. He was bleeding. He didn't care. The pounding of her body against his had him mindless to the rest of the world.

"Decker! You're bleeding!" she cried. Her motion stilled as her hand reached out to inspect the damage.

He tightened his hold on her hips and his jaw clenched as he threw his head back. "Don't. Fucking. Stop." he managed. She braced herself and bore down, honoring the request, and rode him hard to the last.

His body drew tight, moving beyond the pain, sliding into a blinding vortex of pleasure. Vesper gave one last thrust and his cock erupted in volcanic release. Flashes of light strobed behind his eyes as he sucked in a deep, guttural breath. He opened them and focused, finding the glittering emeralds of her gaze in the dark.

She was panting and flushed. Well-loved. He could see the concern there, peeking out from behind a myriad of other emotions. His chest tightened again, but this time not in pain. She was so beautiful. God, he loved her. What in the hell was he going to do now?

The door to Cain's room rattled on its hinges and then swung open, victim of a heavy kick. Marcus stood in the opening, glaring daggers at the young vampire.

Cain set down the book he was reading, cracked his knuckles and folded his hands behind his head while a cocky grin turned up the corners of his mouth.

"Dude, polite society dictates a 'knock knock' and a 'come in' before you come busting in here like a Stormtrooper."

"Where the fuck is she?"

"Last I saw, she holed up with the cop after Gideon stitched him up and set his wrist."

Marcus flexed his jaw in irritation. "You know what I'm talking about, mouth. Where's the witch?"

The kid shrugged. "Dunno."

He was in the room in a flash, fisting a hand in Cain's shirt and hauling him to his feet. "Don't. Fuck. With. Me." Marcus snarled, baring his fangs.

The grin vanished and Cain grabbed the offending hand, knocking Marcus back. Anger flared in his eyes and he sucked in a hard breath, the points of his own fangs revealing themselves. "We're tight, bro, but I'm no pushmonkey and you know it. Keep your fucking hands to yourself. I *said* I don't know."

"Bullshit," Marcus growled. "Now tell me how to find her."

Cain rolled his eyes and sighed heavily. "Man," he drawled, "I don't want to do this with you. This is a big fucking rock and a hard fucking place I'm in. I-"

"Don't give me your shit, Cain!" he roared. "You tell me where she is, or I swear I will go to the coven and tear it down brick by brick until I find her." His voice dropped low. "And you'll be to blame. How do you think that will sit?" Marcus shook his head. "Halfling or no, Braeden's asshole will pucker so tight there will be no room for your lips. They will freeze you out. No more magic for you."

The light in Cain's eyes died and for a brief second, he felt a pang of guilt at the threat. Not that he was bluffing, but that he would do it in a heartbeat.

"Marcus, please. Don't ask me to do this. It's her place, man," he pleaded. "Her haven. I violate that and-"

"She's involved, you idiot! Can't you see that?" Marcus took a deep breath. "Choose. Choose now. Prove to me where your loyalties lie. Show me which side of you is stronger. I'm not asking for me. For Vesper. Do this for Vesper."

Cain turned sad eyes away and collapsed back in the chair and ran a resolute hand over his face. "I can't believe you're doing this. I just can't believe it," he sighed.

Marcus felt his heart tighten. "Where, Cain?"

The young vampire's face was pale as he swallowed hard and closed his eyes. "She's got a little cabin off the Northshore. Back in the woods up near Covington." He reached over to the table and picked up his cell. "The GPS coordinates should still be in there. It's fucking hard as hell to find," he said, tossing him the phone.

Marcus slipped the phone inside his jacket and turned for the door.

"Dude," Cain said softly.

Marcus looked back at him.

"Tell her I'm sorry."

The tall vampire said nothing and was gone.

You really fucked the dog on this one, didn't you, Lorelei? She grimaced, blowing out the candles. *Shit.*

She rose from the tiny altar and slipped a robe over her naked form. She stepped into waiting slippers and cinched the silken robe tight around herself and rubbed her arms in an effort to shake an invisible chill. She walked softly into the front room of the little shotgun cottage, her feet making whispered noises on the hardwood floor. The room was totally dark except for slivers of moonlight that filtered in through the closed shutters. She bent over a small table in the corner, lifted the glass from the kerosene lamp and snapped her fingers. A thin tendril of orange flame shot upward, dancing on the edges of her fingertips, casting a flickering glow in the shadows of the dark room. She stretched out her hand and placed the flame on the wick of the lamp, watching it light. She replaced the glass and turned up the flame, illuminating the room.

She let out a bloodcurdling scream, almost knocking over the little lamp. Marcus' large frame filled one of the oversized chairs in the opposite corner of the room. He sat serenely, with one hand resting firmly on the arm of the chair and the other idly stroking her cat Spectre's traitorous feline head. With the soft light from the lamp swirling with the shadows around his mane of silver-white hair, he looked like a king on his throne.

"How...how in the hell did you get in here?" she screamed, clutching the edges of the robes together. "Get out! Get out now!" She jabbed a finger at the front door. She started sputtering and came toward him. "I don't know how you...I mean, this place is warded. I should've known," she frowned, angry and confused. "How the hell did you get in here?" she yelled again.

"Front door. Open." His voice was cool.

"The front door was not-" She stopped, closed her eyes for a second and reached out with her mind. The wards she erected around the property earlier were still holding strong. Since she'd started this little experimentation, she'd been careful to keep herself protected from prying eyes. Everything was tight. Which didn't explain how Marcus had been able to get through undetected. If a gnat so much as farted near her place, she would know. But the broody vampire had slipped past. Disturbing. Very disturbing.

The feline under Marcus' hand stretched and let out a loud, comfortable yawn. Lori frowned at the gray cat. "Turncoat," she muttered. Spectre blinked sleepy green eyes at her, unmoved.

Marcus gave her the once over with a cool stare. "You've got some explaining to do."

She clutched the lapels of the robe tight and turned her sour frown to the interloper. "I don't think so." She pointed to the door again. "Get the hell out of my house." She turned her back on him and took a step back toward her altar. "Lock it on your way out. If you're not gone when I come back, I'm calling down the thunder. It's *not* just an expression."

"I'm not leaving." His strong hand slashed through the air. "Period. Blow the fucking place down. I'll still be here and I'll still want an explanation."

Lori's hair whipped around her face as she wheeled on him, "I don't care what you want, Marcus. Get out." Moisture in the humid air crackled and the flame in the lamp danced wildly as she raised a hand, power swirling in her eyes. The shutters began to rattle under the force of the winds she was calling forth and Marcus' hair began to tangle around his face, but he did not move. Spectre hopped down from his lap, seeking shelter further inside the little house.

The ice in his eyes focused on her through the silver locks blowing around him. The steel in his voice set her even further on edge as he said, "The tornado is a distraction, Lorelei. It will not deter me. I am here for one reason and one reason only." His lips curved into a smile that wrapped coldly around her heart. "To find out if you're a good witch or," his voice hardened, "a bad witch."

Her fingers closed into a small fist and dropped to her side as the shutters burst into flames. "Click your heels three times and go fuck yourself."

He laughed. The bastard actually laughed.

"Calm down before you set this place on fire." He was still smiling. "You have some control issues you need to work on. Tone it down."

She waved a hand and fire died with a soft hiss.

He went to the front door and flung it wide, glaring back at her. "Christ, open a window before the smoke chokes us both."

"Get out."

He swung the door back and forth on its hinges, drawing the smoke out the open doorway and into the night. "You're a broken record, witch. How about you sing a new tune? One about Victor Delacroix." He shut the door and turned back to her. "Now."

Short of setting the house on fire she knew he wasn't going to let it go. Damn him and his one-track mind. He needed to take his tall, angry ass home and let her take her time in talking to Vesper. An unlikely occurrence, but a girl could hope, right?

She watched him carefully as he crossed the floor to stand in front of her, impaling her on that direct, stony stare. Lori lifted her chin and challenged his gaze.

"This is not my fault."

"The hell it isn't," he snarled. "What did you do, Lorelei?"

He was so close. The heat in his breath was a sharp contrast to the cold in his eyes and the tension was coiled so tight in his body she stepped back instinctively, afraid he could snap at any moment. She forced herself to keep looking at him.

"It's none of your concern, Marcus. I'm handling it."

His hands clenched into white-knuckled fists and she knew he was resisting a very powerful urge to reach out and throttle her. A cold wave of realization hit her. Marcus wasn't just her best friend's older brother. He was dangerous. Raw, angry and very dangerous. Pushing him too far suddenly lost its appeal.

"Handling it?" he ground out. "What the fuck have you done, woman?"

"I made the charm for Reardon and Victor knows it, alright!" she shouted, blurting out the words before she could stop herself. His face twisted from anger to full-on rage in a split second and his hands came up like a shot to bite hard into the still tender flesh of her upper arms. She winced at the stab of pain and continued, "He wants me to make another one for him to replace the one Vesper found." She gasped for a quick breath. "I told him – Marcus, you're hurting me!" she yelled, yanking away.

The thin fabric of the robe gave way, tearing under the force of his grasp as she pulled back. Green silk pooled at her feet, leaving her naked, wide-eyed and trembling.

Marcus' hands opened in release and face registered a quick look of surprise at her bare body. They stood there in shock as seconds ticked by before his eyes went from frank perusal to cold once again as he calmed.

She opened her mouth to speak but no words came forth. His breathing evened and the hard mask returned. "Cover yourself."

Her voice broke on a gasp and she turned heel and ran for the safety of her bedroom, slamming the door behind her. The wood was cool against the flushed skin of her back as she sagged against it. She pressed a hand over her heart and felt the hammering within. Fear was one powerful emotion. She swallowed against the bitter wave rising in her throat. Tasted like shit, too. Lori closed her eyes and willed the wildness in her heart to still. She shook her head in frustration. This was not happening. This was not how it was supposed to go. She was supposed to call Vesper, meet her for a latte, chat about shoes and the hot firefighter she'd been off and on with. Talk about how great the 'on' was and have a laugh or two. Then she would tell her about Victor and the charm.

Tall, silver and scary out there had shot her plan all to hell and back in the blink of his baby blues. Damn. Damn, damn, damn. And if that weren't enough, the wretched man had seen her naked.

"Don't think I won't come in there." His low voice was right outside the door and it sent a delicate shiver up her spine. He meant it.

She flew off the door and managed to pull on some jeans and was shoving into an oversized t-shirt when he flung open the door and breached the doorway.

Her head popped out of the gaping neck of the shirt, her eyes giving him the go-to-hell look that always worked on Cain. Nothing.

She fluffed her hair and settled the open neck over a bare shoulder. "If you don't mind." She gestured to the door. "I didn't invite you into my bedroom."

"I wasn't waiting for an invitation."

The bulk of him filled the small bedroom, making all of her furnishings and trinkets feel small and fragile. It was irritating.

He just kept staring. "What?" she huffed.

"I'm waiting. My patience is wearing thin."

She took a step back and sat down on the foot of the bed and curled fingers into the softness of the quilt she had folded there. A sigh of resignation escaped her and she lifted her eyes.

"I'm telling you this was not how things were supposed to be." He crossed his arms over his chest, waiting for her to continue. "When I started all of this, it was just for me. I was pushing my boundaries and opening up to my power. No one was going to know, and certainly no one was ever supposed to get hurt." The words tasted awful in her mouth.

"Wrong on both counts. What exactly were you doing?"

She sighed again. "Just...well, I was experimenting." She paused. "With dark magic." His eyebrow arched and she frowned. "Don't give me that look. I can control it. You don't understand."

"So explain it to me."

"It isn't that simple, you know. The things I was trying, the spells, were all very advanced." A shadow crossed her heart. "Forbidden." She paused again. "I could get in some serious trouble if this gets out, Marcus."

"Too late. What happened?"

Her fingers tightened in the quilt. "Everything was fine in the beginning. It was all working perfectly and I was progressing, but somehow Reardon found me out and wanted a piece of it." She raised a hand. "I know, I know. I told him to get lost. I knew all about what he was into. The drugs, the girls and all that. And I did not want to get involved." He was glaring again. "Look, vampire issues are not my thing. You know our races get along best with a 'live and let live' policy. But I had no choice. He was going to go to Braeden if I didn't help him. He wanted the charm to hide from Artemis and the Penitent, so he could get as dirty as he needed to make his money."

Marcus' face was stone and his gaze shot through her gut like a rock. "You could have said no. You could have come to Vesper." His voice lowered. "You could have come to me."

"I *said* no, dammit!" she exclaimed, shaking her head in frustration. "But once it was out there was no way to guarantee the coven wouldn't find out! And if he went to them, to my uncle, they would have killed me!" she hissed. "Killed me! I was scared, damn you, can't you understand?" Tears welled in her eyes. "There was nothing I could do, so I did it. I made the fucking thing and was eager to be rid of the bastard."

"Surely you realized that was not going to be the case?" he said snidely.

"Don't mock me!" she shouted, rising from the bed in a flash. "I know it was a mistake!" She flung a hand out in desperation. "But everything was fine. I never heard from him again." Coldness crept into her bones at her next words. "But Victor found me." Her head shook in disbelief. "I-I wasn't expecting to see him. Not after-" she stopped short and sniffed. "He didn't want to deal with me at first, he just wanted Reardon." She sat back down, her heart heavy. "You know the rest." There, it was out in the open. She should've felt a little better at the very least, but she didn't. She wanted to vomit. She felt sick, dirty. Guilty.

"And that's it?" he asked quietly. "He didn't mention anything about Vesper and you haven't done anything for him?"

She shook her head. "Just talk. That's all, I promise."

"Pardon me if I don't believe you."

"Whatever," she frowned, sniffling. "It's the truth."

"And Vesper?" His voice was strained. "You were planning on keeping this from her even after she realized Victor returned and she came to you for help?" He snorted loudly. "You know what this is doing to her, Lorelei. You know the hell she experienced. And you would take her back there without a single word to the contrary? Some friend."

Guilt washed over her and the tears fell. "No...I-" she hiccupped, "I was going to tell her. I swear I was. I realized it at Absynthe. And then I saw Decker and her face, I just-I just needed to find the right time." Her voice trailed. Shame. This was shame, pure and simple. *Dear Goddess, what I wouldn't give to turn back time.*

He leaned forward into her face and flashed his fangs. "You're a fucking coward," he growled. Tension sprang back into his body; it radiated from him in waves. "You have no fucking clue what you're doing, screwing with people's lives, playing around with this shit because it amuses you!" he thundered. "You're dealing with forces you can't control, and you want us to sit back while you try to figure out how get your ass out of the frying pan!"

"Control?" she barked, sudden heat flashing in her eyes. "How dare you? You cannot imagine the power I possess!"

She felt the room get hot as sweat beaded at her temples and her hand came up to smack him solidly in the middle of his chest. She felt the raw tick of power surge through her veins and opened herself to the delicious rush. Lori stared back at him with daggers, reading the startled look that crossed his face. She smiled inwardly. *Good. You do not want to screw with me. Control? I will show you control.*

Baleful voices whispered at the edge of her consciousness and her palm began to heat. Her fingers splayed wide against his shirt and she felt the hard plane of muscle beneath. The little voices grew louder in her ears, beckoning her to feel the power. *Burn. Burn him. Show him.*

She pushed with her mind, calling forth rolling waves of flame and almost sighed as she felt his blood begin to rise.

Shadows crossed her vision as she sent the tendrils of flame outward, feeling the hot rush seep through him. She waited to feel his pain, waited to feel it dance across her palm and into her soul. But there was no pain. Something else passed between them, even darker and more addictive. Her eyes shot to his, expecting to see the cold glare of anger. Her confusion spiked as she watched the icy blue darken to sapphire, the depths veiled with – desire?

What the hell?

His blood boiled beneath her hand and his gaze dropped to her lips, followed a split second later by his mouth. He captured her in the searing kiss, sending the whispers of the dark voices screaming in retreat. The heat in his body consumed her in a rush and unbidden, her mouth opened in traitorous invitation. For a moment, they were both lost in the heat and power and he claimed her lips with a vengeance, rubbing hard, tasting every corner. There was pleasure, so hot and sweet, and then a sudden sting. Blood coated her bottom lip and she pulled back sharply from the metallic taste with a hiss.

The points of his fangs peeked out from beneath his lips and his expression was hungry and shadowed. She could still feel the fire in his blood underneath her hand and she jerked it away. The flesh sizzled like she'd been branded.

Marcus took a ragged breath and swiped his tongue across his lips, removing all traces of her blood. "What in the hell was that?" he rasped. His eyes narrowed in accusation. "What are you doing to me, witch?" The ice returned.

"Get out." Her voice was low and dangerous. "Get the hell out."

He went to the door. "Belle Ombre. Tomorrow. Artemis will be expecting you. I haven't decided whether or not to involve your uncle. I'll leave that to the High Elder. If you don't show," he spoke over his shoulder, "I will come for you. And then God help you." The veiled threat hung in her ears.

She closed her eyes to steel herself against whatever else he might pitch her way. She waited for a second, and then heard the front door. He was gone. She opened her eyes and a giant sob welled out as she collapsed on the bed. Sweet Mother, what had she unleashed?

Decker smiled as he smoothed back a wayward strand of chocolate silk from her face. She was breathing softly, deep and even. The edge was gone as sleep rounded the angles of her beautiful face, leaving her with a peaceful expression. He closed his eyes and leaned his head back against the pillow, trying to make sense of the disturbing emotions that were creeping in the back of his mind.

What was happening to him? Never had a woman so expertly demolished his entire outlook on the world with such little effort. A world he thought he knew. He sucked in a tight breath and felt the sutures stretch and itch. He grimaced and ran a hand over his face. Vesper uttered a few soft, sleepy words and shifted, her eyes still tightly closed. Miranda talked in her sleep, too.

Decker swallowed. He should be feeling guilty, right? But he wasn't and that was the trouble. He was opening to Vesper in ways he couldn't understand and certainly never thought possible. His heart was making promises to her without consulting the rest of him. The darkness of her world was pulling him in with each passing hour and he wasn't putting up much of a fight, rushing headlong into a set of feelings that had not existed between him and his wife. How could any good possibly come of that? No, he had already been ass deep in pain for a long time and he sure as hell didn't need to volunteer for any more.

He sniffed again and looked over one more time to make sure she was still asleep. He slipped out of bed and quietly rummaged through his duffel to pull on a pair of sweats before going to the window and drawing open the heavy drapes.

Moonlight poured in and he basked, bare-chested, in its glow. He looked down at the red slash on his chest and noted the puffiness was going down and the itch had eased, even from a minute ago. Whatever the punk kid and his dark juggernaut of a friend did, he was healing up at an alarmingly supernatural rate. One more reason to get and go.

He had to disappear, she said. No contact with his world, the Council dictated. Decker frowned and retrieved his cell phone from the duffel. Without another thought, he flipped it open and dialed his partner. He'd told her he'd never been any good at following orders.

He wasn't surprised to find that C.C. wasn't asleep. The woman kept strange hours and had even stranger vices. He'd half-expected to find her at Absynthe, sneaking in among the non-humans to feed a particular darkness of her own. She answered on the third ring.

"Decker? Are you alright? Where the hell are you?" she cried.

No stranger to secrets, he knew C.C. would keep her mouth shut. And right now the vampires and their Council be damned. He took the phone into the bathroom, leaving the door open a crack and proceeded to catch her up, unaware of Vesper's violet gaze following him the whole way.

The metal door burst open with a hard clang, jolting Victor awake. He jumped to his feet from the tiny cot and pointed the nine he grabbed from under the pillow at the silhouette in the open door frame. Howard ambled inside out of the steamy rain, his arms full with a bundle of wet blankets. Victor's eyes widened in surprise and his arm lowered to the floor.

"Really, Victor, I thought you would be happier to see me after all this time. And ahead of schedule to boot." Howard's eyes sparkled in the low light and he shook the water out of his hair. His mouth curved in a smile while his eyes raked openly over Victor. "It's been a long time, hasn't it?" he rasped.

Victor's eyes flicked to the blankets. Howard looked down at his massive parcel and smirked. "This? Yes, well, Mother would never forgive me if I came to the party without a hostess gift." He whipped his arms out from under the blankets and the body of unconscious woman fell to the floor and rolled out to a stop at Victor's bare feet.

Victor stared at her still form, her chest rising and falling so slowly he could barely see it. His heart caught in his throat. So many things were finally coming together; it was almost like a dream. The fight with the witch and with the human, and now, Howard. Howard was here. It was no dream. It was thrilling. He raised his eyes back to Howard, the words swirling around his brain, but nothing would emerge.

"Here I am." Howard smiled. "In the flesh."

Victor stepped over the woman and grabbed Howard by the shirt with his free hand and pulled him close. Their eyes locked in a heated stare, both men breathing deeply. Victor broke the gaze and his eyes darted over the planes of Howard's face, etching it into his memory.

Suddenly, he brought his mouth down hard over Howard's in a rough, fevered kiss. It lasted a few hot, ragged seconds before he pulled back and touched his forehead to Howard's. Victor blew out a slow breath and savored the hungry look in Howard's eyes.

"Welcome home."

Howard's gray eyes stormed over and a sly smile played on his bruised lips. "I missed you, too." He brushed a soft kiss across Victor's mouth and then his eyelids fluttered closed and he tilted his head in open invitation. Victor's breath came in greater waves, the force of it burning his lungs. It had been so long. His fangs dropped out quick like switchblades and a throaty growl erupted from him as he opened his mouth and sank his teeth into Howard's waiting neck.

Howard hissed loudly, reaching up to grab him. Victor felt the bite of his fingers as they dug into his upper arms. Both men moaned in low rumbles of pleasure as they clung to each other. The tart, rich taste of Howard washed over him in a great tide of sensation and his mouth molded even harder over Howard's neck in remembrance.

It was too much for both of them and in unison they fell to their knees, still clutching handfuls of each other wherever they could to keep the connection between them alive and pulsing. In an instant it went from too much to not enough and Victor broke free, roughly ending the exchange, grabbing Howard to him for pleasures long forgotten. Rain pounded on the tin roof of the building, echoing like thunder in the small space of the warehouse, its booming cadence mirroring the pounding in Victor's heart. They rolled onto the dirty, wet blankets with greedy hands and mouths, tangling limbs and tearing clothes, seeking, touching, and tasting in such a blind fervor that the woman was forgotten. For now.

Two short raps on the door woke Decker from the sleep of the dead. He untangled heavy limbs from Vesper's still sleeping form and padded to the door, careful not to disturb her.

"Cain, this is becoming a disturbing habit," he began on a yawn, opening the door. His words stopped short as Marcus' face filled the doorway. The somber vampire's expression quickly turned vicious as he laid eyes on the detective.

Marcus arched a tight eyebrow. "You don't look like a man who's slept on the couch."

The big guy wanted to go a round? Fine.

"That's because I'm not." Decker gave him a cool smile and leaned casually against the door frame, crossing his arms over the now-pink slash of sutures on his chest. "You got a problem with that Marcus? Either way, I don't really care, because it's none of your goddamn business."

Marcus' lips pulled back in an angry sneer as he swept past him into the room. "Vesper?" he called. "Get out here."

Decker shut the door and followed him.

Vesper looked up from tying the knot on her robe as he entered the bedroom, three strides behind her brother.

The vampire's voice was strained as he glared at his sister. "What the hell is this, Vesper?"

She frowned. "I'm pretty sure I heard Decker tell you it was none of your business." She cinched the knot hard. "And I'm inclined to agree with him."

"Vesper," he warned.

"Butt out, Marcus. My love life has never been a concern of yours. Decker shouldn't change that."

Marcus ran an angry hand over his face and groaned softly. "Save me from the idiocy of the female mind. It's blazing like wildfire these days."

"What the hell does that mean?" she snapped.

"Nothing," he muttered. "I hope you know what in the hell you're doing, little sister. You've already put him in harm's way. This," he gestured, "is only going to complicate matters further. You know what can happen. You know the danger."

Her eyes went hard and she lifted her chin. "I do."

"Have you fed from him?"

She hissed sharply. "That too, is none of your business." Vesper's arms crossed angrily over her chest.

The vampire looked back to Decker.

The brother knows. Screw him.

"I see," Marcus sniffed. "And?"

He didn't like the tone in her brother's voice and he really didn't like the scrutiny he was giving Vesper. The tall vampire was right when he said things were complicated, yet here he was, adding fuel to the fire.

"I thought she covered that when she said it was none of your fucking business. I suggest you leave it at that," Decker said through gritted teeth. He drew himself to full height for emphasis. "I'm getting tired of having to repeat myself, or are you stupid as well as deaf, vampire?"

Pissing Marcus off was probably not the best idea at the moment, but he was damn sure he wasn't backing down.

Marcus' eyes narrowed as he crossed the floor to Decker, lowering his head so their eyes met, lips pulling back slowly to reveal pointed fangs. Neither man moved an inch and Decker stood his ground as he matched the vampire stare for stare, their stony gazes locked in a silent game of visual chicken. The vampire's broad shoulders and imposing height blocked out his surroundings and Decker could only hear Vesper's hiss of indrawn breath as she watched the tense confrontation unfold. Maybe it was going to come to blows. Might be tough. He could hold his own, but man, Marcus was huge.

"You gonna kiss me, Legolas?" Decker's voice was low and teasing.

"I don't like this."

"Spare me the over-protective big brother crap. I don't answer to you. Vesper's the only one I have to deal with." Decker's blue eyes darkened as he said her name, the involuntary gesture revealing the detective's intentions. Marcus scanned his face and frowned.

"Just so we're clear."

"Crystal. And dreamboat, you get those fangs up in my face one more time, and you and me, we're gonna rumble. Don't think I won't go toe to toe with you and hurt you bad before it's all over. Got me?" Decker arched an eyebrow in question.

Marcus took a small step back and the tension in the air dissipated as if someone cracked a window. He turned to his sister. "Just don't get him killed."

Vesper looked to Decker, her eyes sparkling. "I'll try, but he doesn't listen too well."

"I'm beginning to see that."

Decker snorted, "Yeah, well, I see that stubbornness is an inherited family trait." He went to Vesper and curled his arm tight around her waist.

The vampire gave Decker a wry smile as he moved past them to the door. "It sure as hell beats a messiah complex."

Decker pulled her closer into his arms and bent his head to her lips, smiling in spite of himself. "Then this must be our 'come to Jesus' moment." Decker's lips came down hard and fast, moving across her mouth in a hot kiss. His lips rubbed against hers once more, softly this time, and he broke contact. He smiled at the pink flush of her cheeks and slid his arm around to her hip, pulling her around to face Marcus. "Now that we've gotten this crap out the way, is there anything to eat around here? I'm starved."

"What did you come up for in the first place?" Vesper asked her brother.

Decker watched as the vampire's face flinched. "The witch is downstairs. She has...information."

Vesper perked beside him. "Information? After last night? Has she found him?"

"Just get dressed. We're meeting her in Artemis' office," he replied, turning to leave.

They dressed in a seconds. Decker was strapping his holster to his belt as she shrugged her jacket on over her knives and fluffed her hair. She was still waiting for an answer from Marcus.

"Well?" she huffed.

Marcus sighed and gave him a long look. He frowned back at him in question, but the vampire just blinked once and turned his attention to Vesper.

"You're going to have to hear it from her. That's what I know."

CHAPTER NINE

"You're royally pissed, I know," Lori said, blowing out a soft breath as she looked at her hands.

Vesper saw the guilt etched in Lori's delicate features and her heart felt heavy. They had been friends for so long; whatever the reason, Vesper knew hurting anyone was never in Lori's plan. But that didn't mean she wouldn't have to answer for her sins. Vesper forced an edge into her voice. "That's putting it mildly."

Lori nodded and Vesper heard her bite back a sob as the dark auburn curls shook up and down.

"I'm a horrible friend," Lori whispered, sniffing.

She laid a gentle hand on the witch and sighed. "This won't get you 'Friend of the Year', no. I won't lie to you, I'm hurt, but I'll get over it. You could have told me. You could have come to me."

More sniffing and nodding. "I know." Lori lifted her tear-streaked face. The witch's green eyes were full of remorse. "I'll understand if-" Lori's voice trailed and her breath caught on words she couldn't speak as she wiped a hand across her eyes. Lori didn't want to lose her friendship.

Vesper was drawn to her eyes. They brimmed with apology, bright around the edges, but the longer she looked into Lori's eyes, a spreading emerald void spiraled back into their depths. A tiny shiver hit her skin and for a passing second she thought the dark green stars belonged to someone else.

Vesper blinked and waved her hand. "I said I'll get over it. End of story. Besides, I know you. Outright malice is not in your bag of tricks. I'm the least of your problems at the moment, sister."

"Your brother?" she asked.

Vesper gave her a questioning look, but her reply was cut off by the opening of the study doors as Marcus and Decker strode into the room, followed by Artemis.

The High Elder was silent as he made his way around the desk and sat down, folding his hands on the mahogany desktop.

"I take it you ladies have caught up?" he asked in a low rumble. Both women nodded as Decker came to stand behind Vesper's chair. Marcus shut the door and remained there, leaning against the adjacent bookshelf.

Artemis' focus was all on Lori as he spoke again. "Ms. Masters, I presume you have an excellent explanation as to why this was not brought to my attention the last time you were here?"

Lori held herself straight under the High Elder's scrutiny. "I believe Marcus has already brought you up to speed."

The definite tension between the elder vampire and the witch had Vesper's nails curling into the leather arm of the club chair. She cast a quick glance at Lori and noted the green darkness still lingered.

Artemis' jaw twitched as he replied in a tone that made Vesper's hair stand on end, "You are on the wrong side of the table here, Ms. Masters. Let's not make matters worse."

The witch shifted in the chair, but kept Artemis' gaze. "I didn't want the coven to know."

"What makes you think I haven't told them?"

"Simple. I would be dead."

"True." Artemis tilted his head and steepled his hands. "So, how do we resolve this without your uncle and the coven poking around?"

Vesper let out a relieved breath and Lori relaxed. She had expected a much more volatile response from the High Elder, given the severity of the situation.

Lori shook her head, the auburn waves floating around her face. "I don't know," she said quietly. "But I will do whatever I can to repair the damage."

"Damn straight," Marcus growled from the door.

Artemis held up his hand, silencing him, his gaze never wavering from Lori. "How hard would it be to give him what he wants?"

"No!" Vesper gasped suddenly. It was unthinkable. "You can't let him loose with something that gives him a license to kill our kind! He will disappear and we'll never find him!" She shook off Decker's staying hand on her shoulder. "We wouldn't have found him in the first place if it wasn't for his connection with the human! I can't just let him walk away again!"

"Enough, Vesper!" It wasn't a shout exactly, but the steel in her Elder's voice stopped her.

She sat back, defeated. "You can't do this, Artemis. You can't," she said quietly.

The elder vampire ignored her and turned to Lori. "If you create another, can you track it?"

"Magically?" Lori's brows furrowed.

Decker's hand returned to her shoulder, giving it a gentle squeeze as he cut in, "Track him by the charm instead of by your sight? Is that what you're getting at?"

Artemis nodded. "Exactly."

"It's possible," Lori conceded, "but I'm not sure. Dark magic doesn't like to be confined...or controlled. Creating the first one almost killed me. That's part of the reason I wasn't too hot to repeat the experience for Delacroix in the first place. Tagging a tracker on at the back door might make it unstable. If something goes wrong, there's no telling what might happen."

"Can you do it or not?" Marcus snarled at her. He started to come off the bookshelf and reach for her, but she whipped around to glare at him.

"Look, this isn't 'Conjuring 101'. I was stupid enough to go in blind on the first go-round and it took me two weeks to fully recover! I can't just snap my fingers and make it so. Reardon was hard enough. You're talking about going from getting inside the head of a low-life thug to fucking around with someone like Victor. And if I try to make nice with him now, he'll see right through it." She paused, looking back at Artemis. "Vesper's right. If you spook him now, he's gone, and for who knows how long."

Artemis sat back and sighed. "So, you need him."

"Yeah," she sniffed, "I do. This is personal. You're crafting for someone. You're tailoring the magic to their needs.

I have to have some idea of what's rolling around his sick head."

Dirty flashes of memory began playing in Vesper's mind at Lori's words. She swallowed hard as a painful tingling spread its way through her body. Victor's bloody face filled her field of vision. *Her blood.* He was covered in her blood, a sadistic grin of triumph on his lips. His laughter echoed through her brain with each peal setting fire to nerves already sizzling in pain. She felt his victory with each labored breath, her lifeblood draining away. She knew his mind. Intimately.

"What about me?" she whispered brokenly. "Can you use me and my memories in his place?"

Lori turned slowly to look at her. "What?"

Her nails dug deeper into the chair as the ugliness receded. "What he did to me. It-it went on for a long time. Days," she paused. "It's still real sometimes. If you get inside me, can you get to him that way?"

The confusion faded from Lori's eyes and they darkened again as her friend stared intently, searching.

Vesper suddenly went cold underneath the piercing gaze and found herself caught inside it. She could not look away. The emerald darkness held her fast, probing deep. She was trapped.

Finally, the dark bubble burst and she heard Lori's voice, or at least she thought it was Lori's, low and husky, as the witch said, "Yes. Oh, yes."

As quickly as it came, the darkness in Lori's eyes receded, leaving Vesper with a lingering chill. "Are you sure you're up to this?" she asked. "If-"

"Yes," Lori blurted, cutting Vesper off, "I'm strong enough. I do want Cain with me, though," she sniffed. "In case anything does happen, he can heal."

"Then it's settled," Artemis said, rising from the desk. "Bring it back when it's finished. Then we'll decide how to get to Delacroix." He inclined his head toward the door. "Take Marcus as well." At Lori's scowl, he smiled, "He goes. Period." At Marcus' scowl, the High Elder frowned, "You're going. Period."

Lori reached over and grabbed a pen from the bronze desk cup and began scribbling on a notepad. She ripped off the white sheet, pressing it into Vesper's hand as she stood. "This is where I will perform the ritual." She checked her watch. "I can't start until after dark, so you've got some time to kill." Lori's fingers gave her hand a tight squeeze. "I wish I could say this was going to be easy, but it's not. For either of us. So, prepare yourself for that."

Vesper swallowed the lump in her throat and stood up, nodding silently. "I will." Her arms came around to enfold Lori in a quick hug. Lori's embrace was a little tighter and Vesper closed her eyes and sighed.

"'Kay," the witch sniffed, pulling back. "You and Decker grab my pain in the ass apprentice and meet me about nine. I should be ready by then." She turned to Marcus, who was still scowling in the witch's direction. "You going to stand there frowning all day, or are you going to drive me home, Jeeves?"

The scowl on Marcus' face deepened, but he remained silent as he opened the door and stepped back, waiting for Lori to exit.

"Selective mutism?" she asked, gliding past him. "I can make that permanent, you know." Her chuckle faded as she walked out the door with Marcus, still frowning, on her heels.

Artemis closed his office door behind him and watched the four pair off. Vesper and Decker headed back toward the kitchen, while Marcus and Lori headed out the front entrance. The situation was becoming more complex. If the witch didn't come through, he was prepared to gather the Penitent and raze the city in an all-out manhunt for Delacroix and the human. With or without Council approval. And then there was the witch herself. He wasn't so sure how he felt about the redhead getting so involved in Archive affairs. She seemed to be popping up all over the place. First Reardon, then Delacroix. Her heart was in the right place, he was fairly certain, but there was something about her that made him cautious at the same time. Marcus noticed it, too. That much was obvious from his seemingly arrogant fixation with her. A fixation which made him nervous.

Varian stepped into the foyer from a side alcove. "So, what now Artemis?"

He looked at the Delacroix brother with a pointed glare. "After they return, I want you to follow the witch. I still don't trust her. And I don't want her doing anything without my knowledge."

"I thought Marcus-" Varian frowned.

"I want new eyes on her. Eyes that don't see what he sees," The High Elder finished. He handed Varian a business card. "That's my private line. Keep it that way. And keep me informed. Housekeeping has you a room ready in the guest house on the south lawn. You'll be able to come and go as you please. Everything you need is in your quarters."

Varian pocketed the card and nodded. "Thank you, Artemis. I didn't expect this." He held out his hand. "Thank you again."

Artemis clasped his hand firmly. "It was only a matter of time before you came back, Varian. Prague could only keep you for so long."

Varian's face was ashen. "I didn't want to come back. Ever."

"What happened between you and your brother cannot be changed. Neither can the reason he was Condemned in the first place. You did the right thing. Never question that," Artemis said quietly.

Varian's eyes went wide. "Then you know...everything?"

Artemis nodded. "Why do you think I let you stay in Prague as long as you did? You were never in any danger. I told you that in the beginning when you came forward."

"I didn't believe you," Varian whispered. "Victor…"

"Is a liar and a murderer. Despite the depths of your filial bond, you are not the same person," Artemis intoned. "If leaving gave you clarity, I am glad for you. If not, then I'm afraid you're right back where you started. Only now, you've lost time."

The Delacroix brother nodded silently and turned and left, the weight of the world perched on his shoulders.

The inside pocket of his jacket vibrated softly and he pulled out the cell.

"Go ahead," he answered. There was a brief pause, then, "Let her through." He ended the call and headed to the entry. Two steps from the double doors, the door chime sounded.

As he opened one large oak door, his gaze settled on the very tall, very pretty, dark-haired woman in front of him. Her red lips parted in a wide smile, and she wasted no time in flashing a polished metal badge in his face.

"Detective C.C. Anderson, N.O.P.D.," she said briskly with a distinctive Southern drawl. "There are a few things I think we need to discuss."

He didn't look like a man who kept secrets, but she knew better. Vesper watched him push around the last few bites of lunch on his plate with his fork and wondered if confrontation was the best option. Would he lie and deny he called his partner or would he be straight up if asked? Would it start a fight? If it did, would she even care? Vesper's heart clenched. Yes. She would care deeply. Decker laid his fork on the plate, wiped his mouth with his napkin, placed it on the table and regarded her with the same cool expression she was giving him.

"You're awfully quiet. You barely spoke to me, chére." The half-smile was somewhere between smug and sweet and the sparkle in his sapphire eyes only added to the unreadable expression.

She smiled back. "Didn't want to disturb your lunch. You missed breakfast and I didn't want you getting all hypoglycemic on me. I know I'm hell to be around when I'm hungry."

He patted his stomach appreciatively. "No worries there. Lunch was good. Too good, in fact. If you turned off the lights, I might be forced to nap here under the table," he chuckled. The rumble in his voice rolled up her spine like thunder. She drew in a deep breath as she sat back in the carved wood dining chair and contemplated how to broach the subject. A hint of spice and chocolate hit her palate as the air wafted over her tongue. Damn the man and damn the scent.

Decker pushed the chair back from the table and headed out of the kitchen to the back stairs. She darted after him.

"Where do you think you're going?" she asked.

He paused on the second floor landing and looked back at her, the hard line across his brow moving his expression from unreadable to mightily annoyed in a flash. "Back to the room. If that's okay with you, chère?" He turned and continued upward, not waiting for a response. He flung the door to her room open and strode inside, not bothering to close it behind him. She stepped inside and kicked it shut.

Decker began rifling though his bag and fished out a clean set of clothes, a few toiletries, and the box of shotgun shells.

"What are you going to do with those?" She crossed her arms over her chest and frowned at him. What in the hell was he up to?

"Presently, I'm going to go take a shower," he said, taking off his shirt, "since 'your guy' was kind enough to remove the staples this morning." He looked down at the pink ridge of tissue and kicked off his boots.

"I meant the shells."

"There's enough time for a trip to town before tonight, so I thought I'd bring along Betsy for insurance." His hands dropped to the fly on his jeans. Vesper's mouth went dry.

"Insurance?" she croaked.

Decker's face froze into a tight mask. "Yeah." Those blue eyes locked onto her face. "I'm not letting that bastard get the drop on me again."

She dropped the bomb. "Is that why you called C.C.? Because you think he's got the drop on us?"

He stiffened. "Are you spying on me?" he asked quietly.

"It's not really spying when you stand in the bathroom with the door halfway open. Spying would be getting up out of bed to peek at you through the keyhole like a nine-year old girl at a slumber party. Overhearing the conversation because you're yakking it up in a tiled echo chamber, not so much. Were you trying to hide it from me?" she asked sarcastically.

"No." His tone was flat.

"Then you don't need to be defensive, do you?" she finished. The determination in his eyes started to make a few things clear. He was going to find Howard and Victor. And if that meant going behind her back and defying her, he was fine with it. Definitely a departure from his earlier stance. She wondered what other risks he was willing to take for Miranda's memory.

He strode past her with the change of clothes and shut the bathroom door. She couldn't help but think the hard slam of the door meant something.

Miranda. The woman was an enigma. Vesper knew virtually nothing about her. She was beautiful; that much she knew from the photo she'd glanced at on his desk what seemed like ages ago. What kind of woman was she? What kind of woman held so much sway over a man even after her death? And it wasn't just her death. It was everything about her that Decker was clinging to. Just who was she? She thought about the faint line on his ring finger, a line that shouldn't exist after so long. The pale circle on his tanned skin was proof it hadn't been that long since he'd stopped wearing the ring. Vesper closed her eyes. The answer was simple. Miranda was a woman who was still deeply loved.

The muffled sound of the shower spray brought her eyes to the door and she sat down on the edge of her bed, her thoughts drifting from the wife to the widower in her bathroom. Everything was happening so fast and she had fallen into his arms with a swiftness that startled her. Him, too. Maybe it was too much too soon, but they were both on a course to exorcise demons that had long lay buried. Now they were coming to the surface and Vesper was suddenly afraid that what brought them together would ultimately lead them apart.

The blood rushed in her veins and quickened her pulse. This is what I get for dealing with them, she thought. Humans. Their ties to life and death were convoluted and messy. It just wasn't that way with her kind. She was used to survival and propagation. Lust and desire by-products of a function that kept her species enduring for thousands of years. And here she was, a warrior by any number of standards, revered among her kind, bemoaning over a man who couldn't let go of the memory of a dead woman. The knot in her belly twisted some more and she put her heavy head in her hands. Warrior or not, how do you compete with a ghost?

The rush of the water hit her ears again and she swallowed back a harsh sob. Decker was no more than ten feet away, but it felt like he was already gone.

Night fell on the Northshore, the waves of humid fog rolling in over the Vantage as Vesper pulled the car off the dirt road into the clearing behind the Rover and the Harley and Lori's little Mini. No more had been mentioned of his conversation with C.C. and their drive through the city earlier had come up with zip. She threw it into park and placed her hands on the wheel with a deep intake of breath. There was no other choice. She had to face this again.

"Are you ready for this?" Decker's low voice broke through her reflection.

"It has to be done," she said flatly and got out of the car.

Lori, Marcus and Cain were waiting about twenty yards into the little clearing between a circle of mighty oaks. Hanging Spanish moss wafted lazily in the night breeze, bringing the sounds of the Louisiana woods at night to her ears.

Lori was piling handfuls of dead leaves and moss onto a small stone brazier. There were three other structures, each one equidistant from the other, all four creating a square. Decker broke from behind her and went to stand with Marcus beneath one of the massive oaks.

She stepped across the barrier of salt that ringed the area and entered the center of the square, facing off with her friend. It was nine on the dot.

Lori's face was focused and it dawned on her that she'd never actually seen her perform any kind of ritual before, dark or light. The unease of what to expect was setting in.

"Where do you need me?" she asked.

"In the center. I'm just about ready," Lori replied.

The witch pulled out a small red velvet pouch and headed to one of the empty braziers near the men. Vesper watched silently as she opened the ties and poured out a mound of dark earth on its top. Two braziers still stood empty at the north end of the space. Lori motioned for Cain and as they came back across the middle, Vesper's eyes locked with Decker's.

He stood next to Marcus, stiff as a board, all his attention focused on her. If Marcus even twitched, he'd probably jump out of his skin. A sentiment they shared at the moment. Whatever was lying ahead of her, right now, she was glad he was here. She turned back to Lori and Cain.

They had separated, one at each of the final structures to be prepared. Lori pulled a silver chalice from beneath the folds of her robe and placed it atop the brazier. A gleaming knife suddenly appeared in her hand and the witch made a quick slash across her palm and held the dripping cut over the cup. Crimson flowed from her hand, the ruby river filling the chalice. She made no sound; only a glimpse of pain crossed her face.

She laid the knife down next to the chalice and came toward her. They stood almost nose to nose, Lori's green eyes sparkling in the moonlight. Not breaking the gaze, the witch motioned to Cain, who raised his hand to his altar. A burst of wind erupted near their feet, rising from the earth to swirl rapidly around both women. She lost Lori's face for a moment in the wild tangle of her hair as it blew around her face. The wind shifted and changed course, barreling across the ground toward Cain. He raised his hand higher in the air and the rush of wind swirled tighter into a spiral, coming up to rest on the brazier. It stayed there, the small cyclone spinning into infinity.

Her hair settled and once again she met Lori's stare. The witch's face was darker, more intense, and the same dark expanse was creeping into her eyes.

"We're almost there. You ready?" Lori whispered.

She couldn't choke down the lump in her throat to speak so she just nodded.

The pile of leaves and moss on the first brazier burst into flames. Decker's cry of surprise startled her, but she didn't turn to look at him. She couldn't tear her eyes from Lori's.

All noise, save for the crackling of the burning leaves, ceased at the completion of the square. A thick wave of dread passed over her as Lori blinked her eyes long and slow. When she opened them in the dim firelight, all traces of green were gone, the darkness spreading through her irises to envelop the whites of her eyes.

She couldn't be sure if the rumble came from beneath her feet or from the woman in front of her. What in the hell was Lori going to do to her?

A malevolent smile slid across Lori's face. "This is going to hurt."

A dawning horror made her blood run cold as she realized whoever this was staring back at her, it was not Lori. Then there was nothing but pain.

She roused to the taste of blood in her mouth. The sharp tang cut through the hazy fog of lingering pain and she opened her mouth to take in several gulps. Just as her focus was about to return, the source of the healing liquid was wrenched free.

"Ah, ah, ah. Not too much. Just enough to keep you lucid, I'm afraid." Victor's voice was laced with sinister amusement. "I was starting to think you were giving up on me. And just when things were getting interesting."

She shifted and the burn in her shoulders became an inferno. Vesper turned her head to discover the cause. She was trussed up, her arms shackled over her head, chained to a large metal frame. Her legs were free to support her weight, but her body ached like she'd been this way for ages. Her skin crackled as she moved and she looked down to see the dried trails of blood that covered her body. He'd been bleeding her.

The realization had only a moment to set in before he stepped in front her, holding his wrist to his mouth, sealing over the punctures her fangs had made. Oh God, he'd been feeding her.

Her stomach turned over in one large roll and she pitched forward despite the protest from her aching limbs to vomit at his feet. The hard slap connected with her jaw and snapped her head back with a jerk.

"That," he looked down at the pile at his feet, "is insulting. And after I've been so accommodating by keeping you alive," he chuckled.

"Fuck. You." She could barely croak out the expletive.

Another slap and this time her mouth filled with the taste of her own blood.

"Such a foul mouth on so pretty a woman," he chided. "Careful, or I'll have to cut out your shrewish tongue." He chuckled again. "Then again, I might have to go ahead and do it on principle. One step closer to perfection, eh?"

The tart reply she had died on her lips at the sight of the wickedly curved blade he held up. Her blade. Her stomach rolled again but nothing came forth.

He came forward and brushed his lips across her ear. She flinched, but couldn't get away from the raspy whisper.

"You're so beautiful, Vesper. You really are," he breathed. "What a shame it has come to this. Perhaps in another time-"

"No," she groaned. "Never."

The kiss was soft on her cheek.

"Ah, well, have it your way." He sniffed suddenly, as if regaining focus, and pulled back. *"No matter. This is proving to be immensely pleasurable in its own right."*

Her knees screamed in agony and she shifted to try to ease the burden. It didn't help.

The blade winked in the light and then she howled in pain as it slashed across her torso.

"Screaming so soon? We've barely started this round, pet."

The blade slashed again and her anguished cries soon drowned his hysterical laughter.

Decker watched in horror as Vesper fell to her knees in front of the witch, her screams pounding in his ears. The air whooshed out of his lungs like he'd been sucker punched and he barely noticed that Cain had taken his own watchful stance next to Marcus.

Both vampires looked on with grim expressions as Lori stood over Vesper with her arms outstretched, dark power radiating from her. How could they stand this? With each hoarse cry ripped from Vesper's throat, the knot in his gut tightened painfully. Was she actually in pain or just remembering? The wake of helplessness spread through him and he hated it. He could do nothing but stand back and watch.

His hands clenched into fists, a stark terror growing in his heart. *Miranda.* Her sweet face filled his mind. Did she scream like this? He swallowed the rising bile. Delacroix said he had watched. Did he direct as well, teaching and guiding Grainger in the torture of his wife? Did they do to Miranda what Victor had done to Vesper? Sweet Christ Almighty. *Miranda.* Broken, bleeding, calling his name. Calling for him to save her. *Save her.* And just like now, he could do nothing but let it happen.

He fell back against the tree, the sharpness of the trunk digging into his back. He watched as Vesper collapsed at Lori's feet, the witch's eyes black as twilight and twice as deadly. Vesper twitched and writhed in convulsive starts, her screams breaking the thick night air.

He did not belong here. This world, her world of blood and death and pain was more than he was used to and so much more than he could handle. He did not belong here. He could not belong here. He closed his eyes against Vesper's voice and sought the comfort of Miranda's face again, praying for peace.

Her doe eyes stared back at him, wide with fear and anguish, streaks of blood rolling down her alabaster cheeks. His chest burned as he gulped in deep lungfuls of air, but he could not slow the frantic beating of his heart. He couldn't live like this, deal with this on a daily basis. The sorcery. The torment. In her world, it happened every day, like brushing your teeth or taking a shit. Here, the pain and the blood lived and breathed every second of every damn day. Forever.

He dedicated his life to ending suffering like this. But Vesper and her kind served it up on a silver platter with a smile. He drew in a determined breath, unsure if he was dealing with clarity or cowardice. Either way, it didn't matter. He had his fill. It ends here. He would see it through with Grainger and his vampire lover because he owed it to Miranda, but then he was gone. Because he knew if he stopped to look back, he wouldn't survive. Delacroix was right. It would eat him alive.

She gasped, the searing breath burning through her lungs. And then she felt him behind her, naked and aroused. Victor buried his face in her hair, his ragged breath hot and moist on her neck. His hand caressed its way down her spine, over the roundness of her buttock, around to the curve of her hip.

She cried out harshly as his fingers bit cruelly into her flesh. She thought she would be numb to the pain by now, but Victor carefully crafted his tortures with a precise ebb and flow meticulously designed to keep the agony ever-present on her psyche.

He rubbed the rigid length of his erection against her, holding her to him tightly with the hand on her hip. She had lost the feeling in her thighs hours ago and was unable to move away from the abomination of his touch.

His breath came in hard, disjointed puffs and then she stilled at the scrape of his fangs.

"Yes," he rasped, fingers digging harder. "So perfect. So beautiful."

He squeezed her hip once more, and then his fingers trailed back around and dipped lower to forcibly stroke between her legs. She gave a wild start and tried to thrash away, but her weakness held her fast.

Victor blew out hard through his nose in a vicious snort as his lips molded to her neck.

A muffled sob burst from her chest at the rough penetration of his fingers and she felt the smile bloom across his mouth. His cock jutted menacingly against her and he pushed hard. She whimpered.

Vesper felt the cold slide of the steel as his left hand came around to place the flat of the blade between her breasts.

His chest heaved against her back and he raised his lips away from her neck for a moment to purr, "Go ahead and scream, Penitent. It's so much better when you scream."

Victor's fangs sank into her neck as he kicked her legs apart and impaled her. Her ear-splitting wail echoed throughout the room as her world went red for the last time.

"She's killing her, Cain! We have to do something!" Decker yelled.

Vesper's body jerked on the ground, her screeching voice hoarse from the strain. Heat waves now rippled around the witch, her attention completely concentrated on the thrashing Penitent.

Lori's hair whipped around her in wild abandon, the folds of her robe kicked up by the harsh winds of power she had in her control.

"I can't interfere, man!" Cain yelled back. "I can't! If I jack with her it will screw the ritual!"

Marcus grabbed Cain's jacket and began shoving him toward the circle. "Fuck the ritual! You get in there and fucking stop this! Look at her! Lori's going to fucking kill her!"

Terror washed over Decker. *I can't save them. I can't save her.*

Lori's voice began to rumble from deep inside the circle, the thundering cadence vibrating in his chest. Her arms opened wider and flames shot from her hands, setting all four braziers ablaze. Tall, orange spires flared upward into the sky, streaking into the night.

Decker could only stare at Vesper's face, twisted in agony. Blood streamed from her eyes like tears as she moved on the ground, lost in the torture.

Cain shoved Marcus off him and slammed him into the side of the oak as Lori's voice grew louder and more chilling in the night. Marcus grunted as he connected with the tree and then launched himself full-force at the young vampire.

"Do something, you little fuck!" he yelled, smashing his fist into Cain's face.

Cain staggered back and spit out a wad of blood, glaring contemptuously at Vesper's brother.

Marcus pulled out his .45 and shoved it in Cain's face. "Call her off or I swear I will pump you so fucking full of lead they'll be picking slugs out of your punk ass from now until Armageddon!"

Cain wiped the blood from his face, a dark sneer appearing in the wake of his hand. "Marcus, don't fuck-"

Marcus clicked off the safety. "Now, bitch!"

Cain turned without another protest and went to the edge of the ritual space, careful not to disturb the wide circle of salt.

"Lori!" he yelled. "Enough! Lori! *Lori!*" The witch ignored him, pouring her energy into Vesper's torment. He looked back over his shoulder, "If she kills Vesper and comes for me, the two of you cut and fucking run, got it?" He turned to his mentor. "Come on now!" he called out to her, "Hey! Hot potato! Hot potato, babe! Come on, look at me now, Lori! You gotta back off, Obi-Wan, you're-"

The witch's head whipped up to focus on him with her black stare. Suddenly, Cain's body was hurled backward into the tree trunk with a resounding thud. He crashed to the grass with a hard grunt, but scrambled to his feet to yell more frantically this time, "Hot fucking potato, Lorelei! HOT FUCKING-"

His shout was drowned out as white-hot flames erupted around the witch, engulfing her and Vesper. Vesper's screams hit an all-time high as Marcus and Decker came up behind Cain, flanking him.

"You dare interfere?" The loud, penetrating rumble that shook the very earth did not belong to Lori. "You will pay! *You will burn!*"

The circle of salt burst into a hissing geyser of orange flames, the blast wave knocking all three men to the ground in a smoking heap.

"Shit!" Cain shouted, slapping at the burning sleeve of his leather jacket. He stood up, still patting, and faced the wall of fire that separated them from the girls. "She's gone, man!" he called out. "She's channeling some deep shit! I can't break through to pull her out! I'm not strong enough!" He blanched. "Oh Christ, I think she's really going to kill her."

Marcus and Decker struggled to their feet. Decker couldn't see through the flames, the heat warping the air around them. A nagging feeling swept through him. He had to at least give it a shot. He pulled the SIG.

"I'm going in!" he announced. "I'll put one in her if I have to!" He muscled past Marcus, who narrowly missed clutching at him.

"No!" Cain yelled over the roar of the fire. The young vamp moved quick to get between him and the inferno. "The second you cross the salt, you're toast. Literally. You won't make it a foot inside before she roasts you like a marshmallow."

"Then do something, Cain, before she sets us all on fire!" Marcus roared.

Cain's face turned to stone and his body stiffened. "Stand back!" Neither man moved, their attention focused on the witch and Vesper.

Cain turned to the fire and held his arms out, bringing his palms together. "I said get the fuck back!" he barked. The two men immediately sought shelter behind the oak, peeking out from opposite sides, waiting to see what sorcery Cain had up his sleeve.

Heavy winds soon sprang up around Cain as he began to chant in another language, loud and low. He spread his arms wide like Moses parting the Red Sea, and instantly, Marcus and Decker fell to their knees, gasping as the air was violently sucked from their lungs.

The vortex of winds swirled and rushed at Cain, bringing with it precious oxygen. Deprived of fuel, the wall of flame snuffed out with a hiss and Lori hit the ground hard next to Vesper. Both women struggled to breathe.

Cain stood fast under the torrent of air, his mouth agape as he drew the howling winds into his body, swallowing them. He took in the last rush of air and his eyes rolled back in his head and he collapsed to the ground without a sound.

"Cain!" Decker cried as air once again circulated in his lungs and he and Marcus rushed to the young vampire's side.

"Girls," he huffed, "Get the girls."

They ran in across the now smoking circle and retrieved the limp bodies of the two women and brought them back to rest at the base of the oak tree.

Vesper's face was cold and pale and Decker wiped the blood from her eyes. She took in a soft breath and opened them.

"Did we get it?" she asked.

He smoothed the silky locks from her face without thought. "Don't know yet."

She managed a weak smile that made him feel like a complete ass. "I hope so." Her voice was raspy. "'Cause there's no way in hell I'm doing that again."

He raised his head to check on the others. Cain seemed to be holding up fine, just breathing heavy and muttering curses as he inspected the damage to his jacket with a serious frown. Lori had pulled away from Marcus and was checking the folds of her robe. She pulled out a small crystal vial and held it up to the moonlight.

She nodded to herself and placed it between some folds of silk and tucked it away. She cast now-emerald eyes on Vesper and Decker. "It's done," she managed.

Cain took a long look at the billows of black smoke rising from the scorched circle of salt and the charred remains of the ritual space and shook his head at his mentor. "Lori?"

"Yeah," she coughed.

"You know I how bug the fuck out of you to teach me new and impossibly cool new things?" he asked.

"Yeah."

"Well, let me just tell you...that," he gestured to the smoke and the charred braziers, "you can keep that shit to yourself."

Vesper watched as Lori gave him a pointed look, but said nothing. The young vampire managed to look thoroughly chastised and ambled over to her, eking out a dry cough as he moved. He slowed as he neared, as if waiting for an invitation to get closer to the witch. Lori's face softened to him and she wordlessly opened the circle of her arms. He rushed forward and gathered her up in a fierce hug and buried his face in her wild auburn waves. Cain's body shook for a few, brief seconds and Vesper felt her heart clench in sisterly love. He was as much a brother to her as Marcus, but she knew Cain loved the witch like a mother ever since she took him under her magical wing. Even Marcus's normally grim facade melted a little at the sight of the witch and the young vampire.

Cain pulled back from Lori and wiped a hand across his face to rid himself of the tears and sniffed, "I'm sorry, Lorelei." He cast a glance back to Marcus. "I didn't want to tell him how to find you. I know you need your sanctuary. But this, with Vesper and Delacroix-" he stopped short and fixed his gaze on her, "He was right. I had to make a choice. I hope you can forgive me."

Lori smiled softly at him, tolerance and wisdom shining in her eyes. "I know," she said quietly. "I've told you over and over again, you have to find balance. I, too, am finding it a hard battle to wage." Her hand cupped his cheek. "Your mind and body are trying to exist in two different places, fighting over what world is right for you. You have to listen to your heart, feel with your body. You have to embrace your duality. Once you do that, it will all become clear." Her fingers trailed over his brow and skimmed the scroll tattoo. At her touch, the ink glittered in the moonlight and glowed with an otherworldly aura. Her smile widened. "Just wait Cain, just wait. You will figure out who you are and what you were meant to do. I have a feeling power is your destiny. Learn to balance it and the world will be yours."

Cain nodded to the smoke. "So then, what exactly was *that*?" he asked.

Lori's eyes hardened as she looked past him to lock gazes with Marcus. "A momentary tip of the scales. Nothing more."

With tired hands, Vesper unstrapped her knives and let the holster fall into the chair. She kicked off her boots next and stripped off her tank top. She could feel him standing in the doorway to the bedroom, watching her.

"You look pale."

They were the first words he'd spoken since he'd driven them home. Whatever he had going on in his head, he wasn't sharing. Which, for right now, was just fine. Her head was spinning six ways from Sunday and her body hurt like hell. She knew it was a shock, the ritual, the magic, and all the uncertainty afterward. It was a lot for even her to choke down, but it was done and she was thankful for that. One step closer to getting Victor.

"I'm always pale," she said. "Most men find my alabaster skin alluring." She managed a weak smile for him.

He didn't return it.

"You don't look good."

"Well, that's always what a girl wants to hear," she sighed, pulling off her jeans and chucking them to the side, nearly falling over in the process. She steadied herself on the arm of the chair.

"You're weak. You can barely stand." He didn't move from the door.

Her head whipped up angrily. "Are you going to call me fat next? Because you're batting a thousand with the complements, lover."

He stiffened at the endearment and frowned, "I just meant you look tired, that's all."

"I am tired," she snapped. "Having Lori stick her fingers in my brain and root around through my pain wasn't exactly a picnic for me, you know."

"It wasn't easy to watch, either," he said flatly.

"Well, I'm sorry you were put out. You learn anything?"

"Yeah," he huffed. "Several things became clear."

Her hands went to the snap on her bra. "Such as?"

He slowly walked into the room. "Why I'm here."

"And what's that, then?" The scrap of black lace fell to the floor and she brazenly turned to face him, clad in only her black satin panties. She thrust her chin in the air in satisfaction as his sapphire eyes roved her nakedness.

"Miranda."

It couldn't have hurt worse if he'd ripped out her heart and handed it to her.

"Miranda?" she asked, hoping her voice sounded as hard as she meant.

Decker's shoulders slumped. "It was never like this with her."

His eyes shadowed over as he moved closer and she felt a lump beginning to form in her throat. That he could mention her, be thinking about her now, after the hell she just put herself through, standing here half-naked in front of him was like a slap in the face.

"Everything was simple with her. It was light, soft," he whispered. "Effortless. Natural."

"And I'm not?"

"No...yes," he stammered. He ran a hand through his hair in frustration and turned sad eyes on her. "I just mean that this-" he gestured between them, "this doesn't feel the same. It-"

"What makes you think it would?" Her knees threatened to buckle and she pushed the knives aside to sit down.

"I don't know, Vesper," he exhaled, coming over to sit on the edge of the bed, facing her. "Look, you're tired, I know you are. You've got to be exhausted. You just went through some serious hell." He looked at his hands and then back to her face. "Maybe this isn't the right time for this-"

"I'm hungry," she blurted. "I am weak. I need to feed." *And I need to be somewhere, anywhere other than here.* She reached down for her jeans. "I'll go. You stay here and figure out...whatever the hell you need to figure out," she huffed, beginning to dress hastily.

"No!" He was on her in a second, staying her arm. She dropped the jeans to the floor.

There was turmoil and confusion in his face and just beneath it a glimmer of something she thought she recognized.

"That's not necessary," he said, pulling her slowly to her feet. His scent was coming at her headfirst, wafting into her nostrils, damning her desires to life. She tried to pull away.

"You don't have to do this," she said firmly.

"I know."

"Do you?" she asked. "Because right now, I don't think you do. You can't use me to drive away her memory. You can't have it both ways. You can't want me and not want this. It won't work."

His mouth tightened. "That's not what I'm doing."

"Isn't it?" she shot back. "I think that's exactly what you're trying to do. You're scared of the things you've seen, scared of the things you feel because they're not wrapped up in some sweet little bow like it was with you and Miranda." She pulled her arm away and this time he let go. "And I can respect that, Decker, I really can. I'm not trying to diminish what you feel for her. You should love her." Her heart clenched. "But she's gone. And you should let her go. It won't ever be like that again. Not with me or with anyone. Face it or not, but don't ask me to pretend it's anything but what it is so you can feel better. I know how I feel and so do you."

She tried to turn away from the circle of his arms, scared the tears she felt inside would betray her and fall right in front of him, but he grabbed her and held her still. Their gazes locked in silence.

"I-" He stopped and let out a low breath, the hardness in his eyes melting away as he held up his wrist to her lips. "Go ahead."

She narrowed her eyes on him. "You know where this is going."

"Yes."

Her mind screamed in protest, the very essence of her knowing that this was the last single thread between them, holding them together above an ever-widening chasm. And if this couldn't hold them together, nothing would.

Her fangs itched and her body hungered for what he offered despite the danger it presented. As she grabbed his wrist and bit down hard, she hoped it was enough.

The taste of him, tart and rich, hit her tongue and she groaned as the blood slid down her throat. Decker fell back on the bed and she sank to her knees in front of him with her mouth still wrapped around him.

Desire and hunger hit her full throttle and she drew deeply, letting his flavor roll over her. She released him and swiped the two points with her tongue and let her hands work in a frenzy to get him naked.

He moaned loudly as her hands roamed over his bare skin and she relished the hot slide of skin on skin as her head lowered again and she pushed him down flat on the bed.

Kneeling in front of him on the floor, she pushed the corded muscles of his thighs apart, tangling her fingers in the dusting of hair on his legs, delighting in the sensuous rasp. His erection was instant and it stabbed out greedily in front of her.

He was hot and hard and he hissed as her hand brushed the base of his cock to push it aside for what she really sought.

"Vesper!"

He cried out as her fangs sank into the hollow of his leg, right where it met his body, finding the strong source of nourishment in the most erotic of places. He undulated against her, trying in vain to get the swollen length closer to the pull of her lips. She smiled against his flesh as she drank and trailed a hand over to capture the straining appendage.

Decker growled in satisfaction as she pumped the hardness of his shaft in time with each draw of her mouth. Her body hummed with desire and her blood heated, sending a rush of wetness to flood her core.

Each draw was deeper than the last and his breathy gasps of pleasure spurred her on. Her skin prickled with heat as the hunger abated and the desperate need for his touch took over. She wrenched her mouth free and sealed the area, pulling back to look at Decker's face.

His eyes were closed and his head was thrown back as he moved against her hand. The rough pull of lust urged her even more and she replaced the hand on his cock with her mouth.

He nearly came off the bed with a hoarse shout as he threaded his fingers through her hair. Vesper growled in agreement and continued the erotic slide of her tongue on his hard length.

"Vesper, please!" he moaned, "I can't-I need to be inside you."

Her body lurched in response and she let go. Strong hands gripped her arms and threw her face down onto the bed. He slid in easily from behind and she thought she would die from the delicious feeling of fullness.

She cried out at the first powerful stroke and grabbed fistfuls of the bedspread as she hung on, bracing for each pounding thrust. His hands held her hips steady as he drove into her, keeping her pulled back tight against him.

"Please," she panted, "Harder! I want more!"

She felt his hand slide up her spine and tangle in the hair at the base of her neck. He held her fast in every direction, not letting her move by even an inch. It was so good, so hot, so hard. He pulled her head back, firmly but gently, and deepened the length of his thrusts, the maddening rhythm turning her bones liquid with fire. The sweet coils of burning tension inside her were winding to a fever pitch and there was nothing she could do but ride the delicious crest of the wave as she came.

Vesper's tight sheath clamped down on his cock as she came and the high-pitched cry of her orgasm sounded like thunder in his ears.

He snorted, gasping for air as the last of her spasms rippled through her and down his shaft. He felt a wide roll of darkness up his back and the pull of his own hunger kept him moving within her, unable to stop. The desire was so raw, so fierce, so binding; he needed to see its reflection.

He withdrew and flipped her over onto her back, settling her into the comfort of the now-rumpled bedspread. He shoved her thighs apart and sank back inside her as deep as he could possibly go, sliding forever into sweet oblivion. She closed her eyes and moaned his name.

"Open your eyes, Vesper," he grunted. "Look at me."

Her lids snapped open and he could see the desire ringing the violet depths. He thrust harder and was rewarded as her pupils dilated further, turning from deep amethyst to black. He groaned. She was so beautiful. Dark. Luscious. Beautiful. She was everything.

He could see the throb of her pulse beating rapidly at her neck as her body strained to meet each hard thrust. It called to him. Her blood ran wild in her veins, he felt it. Her blood. His blood.

Primal need swept through him as he pumped steadily, soliciting breathy grunts of pleasure. Everywhere his hands touched, he felt it, the blood coursing through her, making her hotter than ever. He wanted it. He needed it.

The dark tide of orgasm welled within him and he thrust harder, each pound of his body possessing her, claiming her. It wasn't enough. He needed to be closer, needed to feel the very core of her.

Mindless, his lips pulled back in a feral snarl as his mouth watered for the taste of her. Vesper's eyes were liquid pools of twilight and he rocked against her, ready to take the final, desperate plunge.

His sac tightened in painful bliss and he gathered her up in his arms and sank his teeth into the luscious curve of her neck as his release raged through him in a hot blaze.

Fireworks erupted in his brain at the taste of her blood on his lips and he groaned, drinking deeply. She was hot and sweet and tasted of all things dark and desirous. He shuddered at the last hard pang of his orgasm and collapsed upon her, his mouth breaking free.

His breath slowed from hard gasps to shallow puffs and he swiped his tongue across his lips, wiping away the wetness. He stiffened as the fog of pleasure receded. Blood.

He rolled off her quickly and got to his feet, his surprised eyes darting everywhere but in her direction.

She stood up and looked at him. "Decker?"

He was pale and his brows furrowed in confusion. He shook his head softly and finally pulled his head up to meet her gaze.

She wanted to go to him, to hold him, kiss him, but the look on his face kept her still.

His mouth opened, but he closed it as his gaze focused on her shoulder and his blue eyes widened in shock. She looked down to see the tiny trail of blood roll from her neck and down her chest, between the valley of breasts he'd worshiped only moments ago.

"Decker, it's okay. I-"

His eyes watched the slide of the blood and then he turned a pallid shade of green. His stomach lurched visibly and he clapped a hand over his mouth, running past her to the bathroom.

Her heart went cold at the sound of vomiting.

Silent tears filled her eyes as she watched him sink to his knees on the tile floor, retching loud enough to wake the dead. She suddenly felt very naked and very alone. Pulling open the closet, she retrieved a robe and covered herself, but it was no use. The gap she felt between them surged wider in an instant and she stared at him from the other side. She turned and went to sit on the bed.

She heard the toilet flush and the rush of water from the tap as he washed his face. Finally he emerged, pale and hollow. She tucked her feet beneath her and tried to think of something comforting, but she knew there was nothing to say.

The look in his eyes said it all.

Revulsion. Regret.

He opened his mouth to speak, but he closed it halfway and sighed. He took in a deep breath and laid hard eyes on her.

"I'll sleep on the couch."

Without another word, he disappeared into the other room and the distance between them widened into forever.

CHAPTER TEN

Vesper and Decker sat on the cushioned bench across the expansive marble-floored foyer directly across from Artemis' study. Two large stone-faced Penitents stood sentry outside the door looking every inch the armed enforcers in black turtlenecks, fatigues and combat boots. Both men wore shoulder holsters loaded down with .45s. They meant business. *Gideon's personal picks, no doubt.* She wondered what else was going on behind the Elder's closed doors to warrant this kind of individual protection inside the mansion. Any number of disturbing scenarios came to mind, all of them involving Victor. She shuddered to elaborate on just one of them. Hopefully soon, Artemis would be able to give the go-ahead for this all to be over. She was ready.

"You okay this morning?" Decker asked.

She frowned. *As if you're interested?* She opened her mouth to tell him she was fine, that last night was fine, that it was all fucking fine, when Cain, Lori and Marcus appeared from the nearby corridor.

"Chief ready for us yet?" the young vampire asked, plopping down beside Vesper. "Scooch over, will ya?" he chided, "Sit in his lap or something."

Vesper scooted to make room and found herself wedged between a punk and a statue. At the touch of her body, she felt Decker stiffen up like a corpse.

Her head turned to the study door as she heard it open and her eyes focused on the tall dark-haired woman who emerged.

C.C. Anderson walked purposefully from the room in a crisp black blazer and skirt and left the door open behind her, the smart click of her impossibly high crocodile stilettos echoing off the marble floor. Her raven hair swayed smoothly as she walked and the high-gloss of her red lips slid into a smile as she spotted Decker. Before Vesper could speak, Decker did it for her, standing up and meeting the woman halfway.

"C?" Decker's face was shocked. "What are you doing here? I thought I told you..." his voice trailed and he looked back over his shoulder at Vesper. She arched an eyebrow at him but said nothing. Decker lowered his voice, "I thought I told you not to do anything."

C.C. patted him on the shoulder. "I hadn't planned on coming, really," she said, holding up a hand. "But," her brown eyes turned hard. "There's been an unsettling development since we spoke."

Vesper got up and made her way over. "What kind of development?"

C.C.'s head darted up to look at Vesper and she smiled at her as she approached. "Good to see you again, Vesper. I hope you can forgive the intrusion, but this...well, this couldn't wait." She sighed and pushed back the sides of her blazer to rest her hands on her hips. The twinkly shine of a police badge winked from her waist and the butt of a large pistol appeared on her right hip. "It appears Howard Grainger has escaped from Angola and is in the city. So far, he's left us a trail of three bodies. One is a prison guard we think helped facilitate the escape and the other two were prostitutes, both dumped in the Quarter. All three share the calling card, but something doesn't add up."

"He's out?" was all Decker could manage. Vesper looked at his face, now pale and tight. Miranda's killer was roaming free. She could all but see the knife twisting in his gut.

C.C. nodded. "We're certain of it. And by 'we', that's why I'm here. Brass is an uproar and the governor's been foaming at the mouth since it all happened. There's not a cop in the city that's not looking for Grainger and if what you told me is true, then there's a good chance that if they find him, they find your boy, too." She looked at Vesper. "And I know that's bad for you. So I came to see your Elder and catch him up to speed and see if we can't find them before the department blows everything all to hell."

Vesper saw a spark flare in the other woman's eye and watched C.C. lean to the side, her glance peeking over Vesper's shoulder. C.C.'s glossy crimson lips parted on a breath and her eyes were wide with misty recognition.

"Lorelei?" she called. "Lorelei, is that you?"

Vesper turned to see Lori's face pop up from her conversation with Cain to lay eyes on the woman detective. The witch's face broke into a disbelieving smile and she rushed forward with Cain and Marcus trailing behind her in avid interest.

"Kitten?" Lori exclaimed. "Sweet Mother, Kitten, it is you!"

The two women embraced warmly, both of them all smiles.

"Kitten?" Decker repeated.

C.C. waved her hand. "It's a nickname." She gave Lori another quick hug. "My granny had cats all over her place and I was forever with a kitten in my possession somewhere. Overall pocket, basket-"

"Her good silver bowl, the one our great-grandmother used for scrying!" Lori finished, laughing. "I will never forget how you tromped around with Mr. Pigglepuss in that thing like some kind of royal litter! And how she switched you good when you lost it in the creek trying to teach that cat to swim." Lori clasped her hands together in earnest and shook them lightly in a pleading gesture. "'Come on, Lorelei! Just one spell so the kitty can go swimming with us? Pleeease?'" she mimicked in a high-pitched little girl voice.

C.C. snorted good-naturedly. "And how was I supposed to know that silver doesn't float? I was seven, for crying out loud!"

The two women erupted in peals of laughter.

C.C. caught her breath and stepped back, linking her arm in Lori's. "Our grandmothers were sisters. Lori's my first cousin."

Quizzical looks sprouted all around as Vesper, Decker, Cain and Marcus looked back and forth between the two women. Decker was the first to speak as he nodded in vague comprehension.

"This should explain a lot, but it just raises more questions," he said. "Are you telling me you're a witch?"

"No, I'm not. All the magicalness has been bred right out of me, I'm afraid. My grandmother was only half-witch and she and her daughter married normal, boring, non-magical men," C.C. explained. "I can't even do a proper nose twitch," she laughed. "Like most good stories, it's a long, complicated and sordid tale of lust, adultery and magic in the Old South. A story for another time, though." She cast her eyes back to the open study door.

Vesper followed her gaze to see Varian and Artemis having a heated discussion near the threshold.

"My grammy always spoke highly of your High Elder, despite the race enmity. I think they were friends, once upon a time. Which is why when our captain filled me in on Grainger's escape, I knew I had to come," C.C. finished. "Apparently, the brother is having some issues," she remarked, nodding her head at Varian. "He bolted in on us."

"They're twins," Vesper said.

"And his brother is Grainger's partner?" Her brown eyes flickered in disbelief. "Scary."

"It gets better!" Cain piped up. "They're lovers." He grinned and nodded vigorously. "How's that for creep you out, baby?" His bling jingled as he rocked in his boots.

"Shut up, mouth," Marcus droned.

C.C. just smiled at the young vampire's toothy smile, the points of his pearly white fangs clearly visible in the width of his grin. She pulled her car keys from somewhere within the confines of the tight black skirt.

She was all business as she said, "Killers don't scare me. Gay, straight, or otherwise."

Cain shifted on his feet and gave the detective a hot once over. "How about me, sugar? I could scare you in all sorts of fun ways."

"Cain!" all four shouted at once.

"What?" he exclaimed. "She's hot! How could I not hit on that?" He waved a hand at C.C.'s tall, curvy figure.

She gave Cain a slow, sly smile. "That's really sweet of you, sunshine," she said in a rich, sugary tone. "You're cute," she said, lowering her lashes, "but I would snap you like a twig. And all those pretty girls at the club would just be heartbroken. I need a man who won't break quite as easily. Get a couple of years on you like your friend here," she said, casting her gaze to Marcus, who looked uncomfortable under the woman's brazen perusal, "then maybe we could talk."

"C.C.," Decker chastened, "Don't encourage him. Please."

Cain took it in stride, leaning over and popping Decker on the shoulder, "I like her."

"You can't do this, Artemis! He's *my* brother!" Varian's loud protest turned them all his way.

Artemis stood in the doorway of his study, flanked by the two brutish Penitents, with his hands in his pockets. "That's how it's going to be, Varian. Deal with it."

Varian's face was red with rage. He tried to step closer to Artemis, but both Penitents made a silent move. Varian froze.

"You will not be a part of this. Council and I will determine how to deal with your brother and the human. You will only be in the way. You are confined to grounds until further notice." Artemis looked at the Penitents, who nodded in understanding. "Do not think to defy me, Varian," he warned. "It will not go well."

The tension ebbed from Varian but the jumble of volatile emotion remained firmly on his face. He bowed formally. "Yes, Your Excellency."

Artemis' head snapped up to regard them deliberately. "That goes for the rest of you as well. Until Council makes a decision, you are all confined to grounds. Understood?" The command in his voice echoed with finality. They understood.

"Detective Anderson?" The High Elder's tone was clipped.

She turned. "Yes?"

"I thought we were done here."

"I was just leaving," she said respectfully.

Artemis turned and shut the study door.

"I guess that's my cue," C.C. said, turning back to the group, a small smile on her face. "I'll be in touch if I hear anything," she said to Decker, leaning in for a hug.

He returned the embrace. "You be careful, C," he warned. "They'll be watching you," he said, his eyes flicking to the Penitents.

C.C. gave her partner a wide smile and patted his arm. "Don't worry about me, Deck. Got my big girl panties on and everything. Besides," she said, casting a covert glance at Varian, "depends on who's doing the watching."

"I don't like this," Vesper frowned. "He's been in with the Council all damned day. You'd think they would have come up with something by now." The waiting was beyond irritating. It was killing her.

Lori shifted in the chair and gave her friend a wry smile. "You'd think, but try to be patient. They're probably deciding what to do with your man as well."

"He's not-"

Lori held up a hand. "Oh yes, he is. Whether you choose to acknowledge it or not." The witch plucked at the voluminous folds of her broomstick skirt and crossed her sandaled feet. "You know I'm right, sister."

Vesper shook her head. "I don't know," she sighed, "I thought there was something. But he's slipping away. Maybe it's not right after all. Maybe Marcus-"

At the mention of her brother's name, Lori's smile went sour. "Maybe Marcus should mind his own fucking business. To be so freaking aloof, the man is way too nosy." She sniffed. "So what is it then?"

Vesper absentmindedly twirled a non-existent ring on her left hand. Lori's nose twitched knowingly.

"Right. The wife."

"Yeah."

"Is he still in love with her?" Lori asked quietly.

Vesper shrugged lightly. "I'm not sure. No. Well...maybe." She blew out a long breath and threw up her hands. "Shit, I can't tell. I mean, being willing to come here and face things like Victor and Howard all because he thinks he's failed her somehow...I guess you would have to love somebody. Even if they were gone."

"Uh-huh." Lori tilted her head and focused her gaze. "And what about you? Do you love him?"

Vesper's eyes perked. What about her? This uncertainty she was feeling, was it love? Her brows furrowed as she gave it serious thought. She was irritated, unnerved, unprepared. His blue eyes and strong face filled her mind and she felt her pulse begin to pound. She could smell him. She could taste him. Her mouth watered.

Lori chuckled. "Okay," she drawled. "If it's taking you this long to give me an answer, then I'm going to go with yes. You love him. And wipe your mouth. You're practically drooling."

Vesper shot her friend a dirty look.

"More to the point," Lori continued, "what are you going to do about it?"

"Right now? Nothing," she answered. She got up from the adjoining chair and began to pace the floor in front of the fireplace. "What I want to do is find Delacroix and gut him from stem to stern and flush every last ash down my toilet."

Lori fluffed the skirt again. "Well babe, looks like you're going to have to wait. At least until Council makes a decision."

Why? Why did she have to wait? She'd been given the task once to dispatch him; this time shouldn't be any different. This is what she did. This is what she was. Her eyes narrowed as the plan cemented in her mind and she bolted past Lori from the sitting area to the wooden wardrobe in her bedroom. The witch got to her feet and trailed after her.

"What do you think you're doing, Vesper?" she asked as Vesper threw open the double doors, revealing a large cache of wicked-looking knives within.

Vesper reached inside and grabbed the holster hanging on the inside of one door. "What I should have done a long time ago. Get my ass in gear and do my damn job," she said angrily, shoving knife after knife into its respective place. Satisfied everything was secure, she shrugged it on and grabbed her leather jacket from the bed. "I'm going after him. Give me the vial." She held her hand out.

Lori's eyes widened in surprise. "Vesper, I-"

"Don't lecture me, Lori. Just give me the vial. I need to make this all go away." Her mind was made up. She would find him. Find him and kill him.

Lori held up her hands and shook her head. "Think this through. This is not a good idea. What about Decker? What about this Howard guy Victor's shacked up with? You don't think they see this coming? I mean, if they're willing to get involved and start playing with dark magic, who knows what other lengths they've gone to?"

It made sense, but she didn't care. The old pain was back, fresher than ever.

Vesper's eyes narrowed coldly on the woman standing between her and the service of justice. "I suppose I could ask the same of you, Lorelei. Now give it to me. I want him to see it before I kill him. I want him to know he has failed."

"Now that's not fair!" the witch snapped. "You're being unreasonable. And quite the bitch, I might add. Stop and think about this. Wait for Artemis. Please."

Vesper's heart seized and turned to stone. "I'm tired of waiting. Give."

Lori stood her ground and crossed her arms over her chest, silently reminding her friend that she was a woman not to be trifled with.

"No. I will not aid you in your attempt to commit suicide."

"Then get out of my way."

Lori stood firm. "I won't let you do this, Vesper."

Vesper began moving, determined to blow past her. "You don't have a choice."

Lori's arms dropped to her side and her fingers began to twitch rapidly. Her green eyes softened for a second before they turned hard. "I'm sorry," she whispered.

Vesper opened her mouth to reply, but Lori's open palm flashed in front of her face, a blinding white light searing her vision. Stars exploded behind her eyes and pain erupted in her head as her body met the invisible brick wall. Her mind went black as she lost consciousness and fell to the floor, Lori's soft apology ringing in her ears.

Lori snapped the phone shut and shoved it back in her bag. It was done. No going back now.

She cast a glance at Vesper, still laid out on the floor at the foot of her bed in an unconscious heap. The small twinge of regret made her sigh.

Vesper would have one hell of a headache when she came to, but it was nothing serious. She'd be out long enough for her to leave the mansion and get back to town before anyone else could interfere.

As much as she knew Vesper felt responsible, this part was her mess to clean up. She couldn't let her friend go off half-cocked to confront the vampire and his lover. She could see it in Vesper's eyes. While she had faith in Vesper's ability to be one hardcore bad ass, she didn't have the same luxuries at her disposal. Namely the help of dark and deadly otherworldly forces. Her friend was running on pure emotion and that was an extreme liability. Lori checked the security of the vial in its little black pouch in the side of her bag and swung it over her shoulder.

She left quietly out Belle Ombre's massive front doors and got in her car. Pulling out onto the highway, she knew she was taking one hell of a risk herself, but that didn't seem to matter now. She reached over to the passenger seat and touched the bag, relishing the dark energy that hummed inside. She was confident the power she wielded would keep her safe. She could handle it. A sinister glee began creeping through her body and her lips curled into an ugly sneer. The vampire and his bitch were going to pay in spades. She lost herself to the dark whispers in her head and drove on as the sun began its descent in the west, failing to notice the black Mercedes sedan making her every turn.

Howard put his hand on Victor's shoulder and gave it a soft squeeze. "What is it? You've been over here for a while."

Victor tossed his phone onto the table next to the surgeon's bag and grunted, "The witch wants to meet. She's done it."

"Well, isn't that a touch convenient?" Howard snorted. "It's a trap."

"Of course," Victor sighed. "That's why I'm not going to meet her."

Howard frowned. "I think that would be a mistake. She's motivated. Her fear of the coven may influence her to keep her word. It's worth the risk." His eyes sparkled at the thought.

Anger slashed across Victor's face. "Who are you to decide that?" he snarled. His hands came up and pushed against Howard's bare chest, shoving him back several feet. "*I* will make that determination. I am-"

"What? In control?" Howard taunted. Victor's jaw snapped shut and his gaze turned deadly. "You do, don't you?" He paused. "Yes," he said, nodding, peering at the tight line of his lover's jaw, "you really do. How interesting," he chuckled as he came forward. "Tell me, are you sure you want to have this argument? Because we both know how it will end." His eyes shot to the rumpled tangle of sheets on the cot.

Victor stalked forward to meet Howard, his face still a mask of rage. "You're full of yourself tonight, aren't you? Perhaps you should remember your place," he hissed, the emotion barely in check.

Howard's eyes twinkled. "No more so than any other. I think you're having some trouble defining what this is...," he laid a palm on Victor's naked chest, "between us."

Victor's eyes narrowed. "And what is that?"

"A partnership. The one you've always wanted. Like the one you couldn't have with your brother."

Howard's eyes bulged as Victor's hand shot up and tightened around his throat, cutting off his air. "How dare-" The reply was cut off as the scalpel in Howard's hand whisked up to slash a shallow cut into Victor's abdomen. Victor's hand released him and he staggered back with a small hiss. The humor in Howard's eyes was gone and he leveled them on Victor.

"I dare because deep down you want me to. You want me to push your buttons and call your bluff. Because you know I won't let you control me. Because I am not weaker than you. And you like that. You like that a lot." Both men were breathing in hard gasps. "Varian was weak, wasn't he? Wasn't able to deal with the need. He couldn't handle it. Couldn't handle you. And when you looked into his eyes, that's what you saw. Your weakness staring back at you in his perfect face. Your perfect face. Did you think you were weak, too? What do you see when you look at me, Victor? A submissive?" He shook his head. "No...because that's not what you want, is it? Someone who blindly obeys?" He snorted. "I thought I wanted that, too. Until I found you. Then I realized what I wanted," he moved closer to Victor, "what I needed, was someone just like me. Someone who needed the blood, the pain, the sex. Someone who could give and take. Like we do. A partner." Their faces were inches apart and Victor's eyes were glowing with intense hunger, his body quaking with tremors of rage and desire. "Which means sometimes," he sneered, shoving Victor back hard against the wall, "you do what *I* fucking tell you. And I'm telling you to meet with the witch and finish this fucking thing, because *I* have waited too goddamned long for this. And *my* patience is wearing thin. And we both know that if I have to, I will handle *you*."

The emotion on Victor's face exploded as he grabbed Howard and spun him around to reverse their positions. "*Don't* make me hurt you!" Victor growled, his fist crashing into the wall a breath from Howard's cheek. Victor's body pressed against his, eliminating all space between them. The vampire's face flushed pink as their bare chests touched and he moved to grind his sudden hardness into Howard's pelvis. Howard fixed his lover with a heated stare as his lip curled upward into a wry smile. Finally, the reaction he wanted.

"But that's just it," he said roughly. "You know I want you to." Howard's nostrils flared as he ground out, "How's that for control, my sweet?" His tongue darted out to wet his lips and he smiled as the desire flared in Victor's eyes. "Your turn."

The scalpel in Howard's hand clattered to the floor as Victor's mouth came down on his in an angry, biting crush of lips and teeth. The scent of blood filled the room as they dropped to the concrete floor.

She felt strong, warm hands lift her and then she felt the cool softness of a pillow slide gingerly beneath her aching head.

"Lori?" she croaked.

"No, it's me," Decker said gently. "Are you okay? What happened?"

She struggled to sit up, but fell back against the pillow as pain exploded behind her eyes. She wanted to vomit.

"Don't try to get up," he urged. "Just lay back."

Christ, her head ached. She lay still and tried to will the pain away, focusing her mind using the Penitent meditation techniques. It was no use. Whatever Lori had socked her with was potent. She couldn't get her mind around it. She winced and turned on her side and realized he had laid her on the bed.

He sat beside her and placed his hand on her shoulder. She felt the slide of skin on her bare arm and wanted to sigh at the feel of his touch. He must have taken off her jacket and knives before putting her on the bed. The sudden sense of vulnerability was startling. She might as well be naked. She tucked her knees up slowly, curling herself into a ball. She swallowed hard. She didn't want him to see her like this. Open. Helpless.

The soft question in his voice only made it worse.

"What happened, Vesper?"

As if she couldn't take care of herself. As if she was a child.

"Just go," she groaned. "Leave me." *You're going to do it anyway.*

"At least let me get Cain," he urged, "Maybe he-"

"No!" she barked. The shout sent her sizzling nerves over the edge and she grabbed her head with both hands to stop the throbbing. "Ah!" she cried, squeezing her hands into her hair. "I don't need him."

She felt him get up from the bed and heard his labored sigh.

"Then tell me what happened."

She groaned. If it would get him to drop it, fine. "Lori sideswiped me with one serious spell. Knocked me out flat. Didn't see it coming. Happy?" she sneered, turning to peek at him.

His eyes were hard as he asked, "Why would she do that?"

This time, she braced herself carefully before sitting upright and placing her feet on the floor. She blinked to focus and met his stare.

"Because she didn't care for my plan, I suppose."

"Plan?" He didn't seem swayed.

"Yeah. My plan to go after Victor and kill him until he is very dead and very dusty. Not to mention his boyfriend."

He sniffed. "I can see how she would be concerned. Especially if you were going alone. I have to agree with her." His eyes darted to the chair and her discarded jacket and knives.

So, he already had it figured out, did he?

"Good thing you weren't here for the conversation, then. It didn't go well." He needed to wipe that disapproving look off his face.

"I see that."

She got to her feet and swayed, the movement blurring her vision and wreaking havoc on her brain. She steadied and went slowly to the chair and picked up the holster, turning her head to the window as she strapped it on. No light seeped in from the curtains' edge, which meant it was well after dark. Fuck. She had been out for a good while. Several hours at least. Long enough for Lori to completely screw her over. Anger blossomed and she felt her blood beginning to heat as some of the fogginess drifted away in the red wake of hard emotion.

She cinched up the straps at the shoulders, frowning.

"What do you think you're doing? Sit down before you fall down," he snapped.

"Why does everyone keep asking me that?" she growled. "I'm not a child, Decker. Stop treating me like one." God, she did not want to argue with him. Not now. His mere presence was creating tiny cracks in her armor.

"Then stop acting like one." He grabbed her arm and spun her around, amplifying her dizziness and she fell into his arms like a ton of bricks.

His dark scent filled her nostrils and she struggled to breathe beneath the weight of it. There was no way she could completely regain her faculties with him hovering over her, slowly chipping away at what pride she had left. Against better judgment, she lifted her eyes to his.

They were firm and clear, so blue they were breathtaking and she lost her voice for a moment, her body relishing the feel of him pressed so close.

"Vesper," he whispered.

She put an unsteady hand against his chest, her heart breaking in time with the steady thump-thump she felt there.

He held her back from his chest and stepped away. "This is a mistake. Lori's right. You shouldn't go alone. Artemis and your Council-"

"Screw the goddamned Council!" she screeched. "This is my-"

"You're not alone in this, Vesper!" he shot back, cutting her off. "You're not the only one with something to prove here!" The break in his voice brought her up short.

He ran a hand through his hair and pointed a finger at her.

"Howard Grainger killed *my* wife and this Victor, *your* Victor, was there! They killed my wife! Murdered her! Did Christ only knows what to her!" Pain and rage cut a hard path across his face as he continued, "And I have to live with that! Do you have any idea what that does to me? Knowing that they're out there and not being able to do a fucking thing about it except trail along after you like a goddamned dog! Waiting to see what crumbs you throw my way! I feel like I handed you my balls when I walked through the fucking door!" he snorted. "And you're pissed because you can't run off on some witch hunt with revenge riding your ass! I don't fucking think so," he growled.

"Go to hell," she snarled.

He sniffed in disdain. "If I'm going to hell, you're riding shotgun, sister."

"Then I guess we're both fucked, huh?" she spat. "What a pair. The avenging assassin and the maligned hero with his hard-on for a ghost."

His blue eyes darkened to black and narrowed dangerously on her. "Don't."

"Don't what?" she taunted. "This getting a little too real for you, Decker? A little too dark? I'm sorry it can't be all clouds and kittens for you, hero."

A cold mask of steel froze itself in place across Decker's face.

His voice was low and icy. "Yeah, I gotta be the hero. That's what she used to say to me. And you know what, Vesper?" His eyes flashed dangerously as their gazes locked. "She was right. And that's what's real. You," he sneered, "are anything but."

A slash of rage burned its way into her belly and she dropped her fangs in warning. How dare he?

"Look around you, Decker. This is no fairy tale. You are not the hero. There is no ivory tower, and I'm no fucking princess. I'm *not* Miranda."

Decker stiffened as if she slapped him.

"You don't know how right you are. You have no fucking clue." He started toward her, menace radiating from him. He got in her face and his eyes roved over her, unfazed by the sight of her bared fangs. "Now it's my turn to warn you. If you ruin this for me, I will make sure someone lays you down.

Whether it's N.O.P.D. or your precious Council, I don't give a fuck. You can count on it, because we're through."

He shoved past her and left her quarters, slamming the door behind him. She stood silent, still as stone, holding back hot tears. From outside in the distance, she heard the loud thud of a fist against the wall and Decker's hoarse cry of outrage. She melted onto the foot of the bed and let the floodgate of tears fall. It was over.

CHAPTER ELEVEN

The sense of unease that had been plaguing her since she hit the city limits was getting stronger and she felt the unmistakable pull of darkness whisper in her mind. Lori let conscious thought go as she rolled the Mini to a stop in the empty parking lot.

Leave the machine. Leave the machine.

She grabbed her bag and continued on foot, traversing the New Orleans city streets at a supernatural pace, letting the instinct guide her. She could smell the tang of saltwater and steel as she made her way among the warehouse corridors on the riverfront. As she moved, her focus shifted in perspective and her thoughts converged to bring her mind to the present.

She blinked hard and stopped, looking around to discover her surroundings.

Lori's ears perked to the ebb of the river and the sounds of the city in the distance. The tall lights of the warehouse lot winked overhead, providing weak illumination in the dark of the night. Ahead of her, a steel door creaked open and two shadowy figures emerged. Their gait was slow and sure and they walked with the easy roll of men who menaced for a living.

Victor's smile came alive under the lamplight and Howard trailed two strides behind him. He stopped about five feet from her and chuckled softly.

"Hello, Lorelei," he drawled in a voice that dripped honey. "I'm so glad you decided to reconsider." His face hardened. "Hand it over."

"You realize you won't get away with this?" she asked, pulling the black pouch from her bag. She dangled the ties from her outstretched hand and began to start feeling for the dark rush of power she knew was coming.

Howard barked out a short laugh.

"How trite," Victor replied. "But it's already over. We both know this is just a formality." He motioned Howard forward to take the pouch with his left hand and pulled the nine from his waistband with his right.

She smiled as Howard moved closer. "You think that's going to scare me?" she laughed. "I don't think so."

Howard reached out to grab the pouch and she drew harder, primed to strike.

Nothing.

Surprise flashed in her body and she reached again. The darkness was there at the edge of her mind, but she couldn't grasp it. She felt it start to slip away as if her fingers were greased and choked back a small cry. Panic set in and she listened for the whispers, craning her ears to hear.

Silence.

She swallowed hard in fear and curled her fingers, refusing to release the pouch.

"Ah, ah, Lorelei," Victor chided as Howard tugged. "We had a deal."

Her eyes widened and she shook her head and whispered a strangled, "No!"

She pulled and pulled and felt nothing. No fire, no darkness, just nothing. And then she heard one whisper, one soft sound that made her blood turn to ice.

You do not control us.

Howard's fingers tugged again and the pouch fell into his grasp. His evil smile filled her vision and his mouth opened in a sinister laugh.

There was no power, no nothing, and as she opened her mouth to scream, she heard Victor's command.

"Do it."

Howard's fist swung up and crashed into the side of her face. Pain jackknifed through her skull and she fell into darkness, hearing nothing but the echo of mocking laughter.

This time the scream managed to burst forth from her lips as she felt the bite of two sets of fangs and the cut of blades on her flesh.

Her mind melted into the anguish and she felt death creeping toward her. She tried to rally against the onslaught, but it was too much and she felt herself sliding down further into the spiral.

"Victor!" She heard a voice bellow in the darkness but she saw nothing.

Suddenly, on the jagged edge of death's precipice, the familiar whispers returned. Louder now, they were angry, snarling and unwilling to die. She felt them claw at her consciousness and take over her body as tendrils of power filled her. In that tiny moment of clarity, she realized they were right. She did not have the control. So she did the only thing she could. She let go and hoped it didn't kill her.

Lori's eyes flew open and Victor and Howard looked up with bloody faces into green eyes awash with fire. She recognized the instant fear in their eyes as the voices within her swelled and erupted in a loud roar.

"You will not defile us! You will burn!"

Fire consumed her and a geyser of flame came pouring out of her eyes and mouth, blasting the vampire and the human toward the front of the warehouse.

She felt her body begin to roll with power again for another strike, but as quick as it came, it was gone with another touch on her bleeding body.

"Victor!" Varian cried again with a harsh yell as his hands beat out the flames on her clothes. He rolled her to her side and she saw Victor and Howard, still alive, struggle to their feet some thirty feet away. *The vial!*

She tried to get to her feet, but agony in the first move of muscle kept her grounded.

Victor stood and kept his eyes on Varian as he lifted the pouch in triumph. Neither brother moved in that frozen moment until Howard shouted.

"Victor, come on!" He turned and grabbed the vampire by the sleeve and they disappeared into the darkness.

Varian dropped to his knees. "Lori? You with me?" His voice cut in over the painful pounding in her brain.

She coughed and wheezed and felt her lungs gurgle and fill with blood as she gasped for air. Haziness set in with each labored breath and in the back of her mind she became scared. They wouldn't make it to help in time.

Varian shoved his hands beneath her body to lift her into his arms, but she grabbed at him as she went limp. She didn't want to die here, in some riverfront lot like a rat. She wanted to die in safety, security. Somewhere warm and comforting where she knew peace. Home. Her fingers clutched Varian tight to anchor herself and she let her mind drift toward somewhere she wanted to be. Every ounce of will and concentration she had left were poured into one single vision. She closed her eyes.

Marcus' face filled her mind and then suddenly, she and Varian were gone.

Varian felt as though time and space were turning him inside out when it all twisted together in one moment and he hit the ground hard. He grunted as the stone steps of Belle Ombre's facade cut painfully into his back under the weight of the fall and of the bleeding woman in his arms. His stomach rolled violently under the dizziness and he set her aside to vomit. He wiped a hand across his mouth and sat up to check on the witch.

Lori's eyes were open and glassy and her breathing was shallow and had an eerie rattle. He waved a hand in front of her eyes. Not a hint of consciousness. Blood was still gushing steadily from points all over her body. She was sliced to shreds and punctures peeked out from her torn clothes. He jerked his head up as he got to his feet and carried her to the front doors. He hefted her over one shoulder and banged a fist on the old oak, beating it until the flesh began to shred and bleed. Varian threw his head back and started screaming.

"Marcus! Cain! Somebody!"

Decker stretched out on Cain's couch and folded his arms behind his head and tried to erase the last couple of days from his memory. A bullet to the brain would have been easier and probably less painful.

I bit her. The thought kept repeating like a bad song. *Even worse, I liked it.* Decker snorted and ran a hand over his face but his focus didn't change. *And now it's over.*

"It's not just about looking good, you know."

He was only half-listening to the young vampire. "It's not?" Decker asked, turning to face the kid. Cain's ego was amusingly massive when it came to the opposite sex, he was discovering, as he prattled on.

"Nah, man, though you need to look good. Chicks like their man-candy."

The urge to laugh was becoming uncomfortably difficult to restrain. He didn't know how much more of this he could take. At least he was distracting. "Who doesn't?" Decker quipped.

"Dude," Cain said soberly, "I'm serious. Like I said, hotness is not everything. You gotta be smooth...sensitive."

This time the barked laugh slipped out. "Right. Let me guess, you read them poetry?"

"Sometimes." Cain smiled wide. "I've been known to quote some B.S. to get a little motion in the ocean."

"B.S.?"

"Bill Shakespeare. Duh," he stressed. "Chicks love it. I think it's the iambic pentameter." Cain sighed. "Yep, anything remotely romantic with a rhythm and the panties come flying off. It's *awesome*. You should try it. I'll bet V's a sucker for The Bard."

"I wouldn't know. Don't think I'm going to find out, either." Shock came over Cain's face as he continued, "It's over between us. I let her know this can't work."

Cain's bling jingled as he shook his head. "Whoa, whoa, whoa," he said, holding up his hands in earnest. "Back. The. Fuck. Up." He narrowed his expression on Decker and arched a disapproving eyebrow. "You're telling me that you just bailed? You're gonna walk away from her? Just like that?"

Exactly like that. The kid couldn't understand. He didn't belong here. He would never belong here. Biting her made that point crystal fucking clear.

Cain let out a loud snort as he came over and clapped Decker hard on the shoulder. "I wouldn't expect this from a guy with a set like yours, but hey, things have been majorly fucking weird ever since you showed up." Cain thrust a hand in his face. "Congrats. You're a douche."

Decker sat up. "You don't get it," he said, waving off Cain's hand. "She needs someone who is a part of her world. I won't ever be that. The longer it goes on, the harder it would be to say goodbye. Early on, I thought it could work, but," he

264

paused and ran a hand through his hair, "now I see I can't deal with it. And there's other things, things neither of us can ignore." Like how he had never felt the urge to bite his wife, to possess her so completely.

Cain shook his head again and plopped down next to him on the couch. "Dude, and I say this with all due respect here, man, but you gotta nut the fuck up. I've seen a couple of dudes come and go after what she went through. Not one of them ever put a sparkle her eyes like you, Deck. Not one. She's yours." He sniffed and looked Decker straight in the eye. "You want to know what I think?"

"I thought that's what you were doing, Dr. Phil. Telling me what you think."

"Maybe, but this is the part I want you to remember. Sister Mary Agnes, she was one of the nuns at St. Max who helped raise me before I came to live here, well, she was a pistol. She always told me the same thing when I would bitch about my situation."

"And what might that be?" The lapsed Catholic in him was rifling though old Bible verses. There was no telling what kernels of wisdom the sweet nun had managed to impart on Cain.

Cain's toothy grin erupted. "When life hands you a lemon, you fucking eat it and be the man."

Decker frowned, "I assume you're paraphrasing again."

"Nope," he chuckled. "I told you she was a pistol. And you're a fucking moron if you think it's just the whole 'she's a vampire and I'm a human' shit. I see you, dude." He pointed to Decker's head. "You got a helluva lot more rolling around in there than you let on. Even I can see that."

Decker returned Cain's smile. "How did you get so wise, Cain?" Cain's face shadowed and looked almost sad. The brightness in his eyes flared down as he shrugged heavy shoulders.

"Dunno. Sometimes I feel really old, like I've lived hundreds of lifetimes. Like I've lived through a lot of shit." The shiny bling jingled as he pounded a fist into his chest with a small thump. "It gets me right here. I just can't remember any of it. I feel out of place on several planes of existence. So, I do have some idea of what you're feeling." Cain's head shook. "I don't think I've ever been in love, though."

Decker put a comforting hand on Cain's shoulder and gave it a quick squeeze. "I'm sorry, man."

"No worries, Deck," he said, standing up. "Like I said, every now and then I get a little down when I get confused about where I fit in." He adjusted his leathers and the goofy grin returned. "Then I get a sack of lemons from the Piggly Wiggly and eat the whole fucking bag. Makes me feel better."

Suddenly the trilling notes of Cain's "SexyBack" ring tone chirped in the air.

"Yeah?" he answered. Decker watched the kid's face go white and his eyes widened in extreme shock. "We'll be right there." He shoved the phone in his pocket and grabbed Decker's arm, pushing him to the door. "That was Marcus. Varian's just brought Lori to the infirmary. Victor's torn her up good." Cain was a flash as he pushed past him down the stairs and hit a dead run.

"Decker!" Vesper's voice made him turn and look. She was in step behind them and her face was just as white as Cain's. Her fingers curled around the cell phone in her hand. She had gotten the same call. Her eyes pleaded, despite the stiffness in her body. He couldn't let that make a difference. Then why did he feel like such an ass?

He turned without a word and headed for Cain.

Vesper hit the door to the infirmary, only to be met by a bloody Varian, who grabbed her shoulders and spun her to the side.

"I couldn't get to her in time. I don't know if she's going to make it. He-" Varian's blue eyes were liquid with tears. She couldn't tell if they were for the witch or for his brother. He swiped a hand across his face. "I-I've got to see Artemis." He pushed past her and was gone.

She entered the room to chaos.

Lori's body was laid out on the exam surface and Gideon moved over her, taking stock of all the damage. Marcus and Cain were across the room, facing off in a tense confrontation.

"This is your fault, you bastard!" Cain screeched, launching himself at Marcus. He was a whirlwind of leather and chains as he yelled, "You were supposed to be watching her back! You knew what would happen if he found her! You hate her! You wanted this, you fuck!"

Marcus caught him in the air and slammed him to the floor with a heavy thud. Cain coughed and sputtered as he turned murderous eyes on the tall vampire.

Marcus stepped back and said, "Pick a fight with me later, kid." He pointed to Lori's body on the table. "She needs you, and if I stomp your punk ass right now, who's gonna do your thing?" He outstretched a hand. "There's no time for this, Cain. Come on."

"You let it happen. You *wanted* it to happen," Cain growled, pushing aside the sides of his jacket and reaching for the Desert Eagles.

"Don't be stupid, Cain!" Marcus shouted.

"Can you two quit dicking around? I need some goddamned help here!" Gideon snarled over his shoulder. He was ripping open sterile gauze and pouring saline flush over the cuts, trying to get every wound to stop bleeding. Gushing blood pumped from several cuts on her leg. Gideon turned to

Decker. "Get me a surgical pack from that cabinet over there," he said, pointing a bloody finger.

Decker snatched it in two seconds and placed it next to Gideon, who swiftly opened it and began pulling out instruments, clamping off the rush of blood.

"Are you a doctor?" Decker asked, peering over his shoulder.

Gideon never looked up. "How are you doing? Are you all healed up?"

"Pretty much," he answered.

"Then yeah, I'm a fucking doctor. Now, do you want to be useful and help me save her or do you want to get the fuck out of my way? Because I don't have time for this shit and if she dies, so do you," Gideon said through tightly gritted teeth.

Decker backed up.

"Wise move." Gideon called back over his shoulder, "Cain? You coming? I need you, kid."

Cain got up and shoved past Decker, having ignored Marcus' proffered hand, to stand next to Lori. He took one of her hands in his and cradled it to his face, hot tears streaming down his face. He swallowed once and then closed his eyes and began to murmur softly.

Marcus stepped forward, but Cain's head whipped up sharply. "Get out. Get the fuck out. Don't come near her," he snarled. Vesper watched as Marcus froze under Cain's hateful glare. The kid meant it.

Gideon was still working on applying bandages and stitches. "Just go, Marcus. Don't piss him off anymore. He needs to focus." This time, the dark-haired Penitent looked up.

Marcus met the look and nodded. "Yeah," he said quietly. "I'll go." He turned and left the room without even looking the witch's way.

Vesper quietly stepped back, removing herself from the commotion surrounding Lori. Cain had the witch bathed in a bright white light, the glow the only thing visible. She'd only gotten a glimpse of her friend, bloody and broken, as Varian rushed her into the infirmary, but as the fight ensued, she was able to see just how bad it was. Lori was covered in blood from head to toe, her clothes nearly hacked off. Bite marks and deep cuts wove a chilling path of depravity across every inch of her exposed flesh. The sheer number of wounds made her stomach turn. Even under the thick coat of blood on her skin, Vesper could see that her friend was deathly pale and barely clinging to life. Decker, Gideon and Cain completed the circle around the table and she couldn't bring herself to get closer.

Her head still ached from whatever spell Lori had used to knock her out, but a steely resolve was slowly overtaking the haze as she watched Gideon, Decker and Cain try to get Lori stable. *He did this to her. Victor. He did this to me.* The knowledge infuriated her. But she would make it right, and no one would stop her. Not Decker, not Lori, not her brother.

She would find him and deliver his death and the cycle of justice and punishment would be complete. Her failure redeemed. She wouldn't have to wait long.

The BlackBerry buzzed as the heel of her boot hit the doorway. She backed out of the room and turned, pressing her back to the wall as she pulled out the phone and checked the screen. *Lori's cell.* The confusion was momentary and then the icy chill hit her.

"Vesper." Her voice was like steel. Victor's soft chuckle moved her lips into a snarl. "Hello, princess," he breathed. "Is she still alive?"

"Barely."

"Ah, well, that's unfortunate. I was hoping to kill her. Maybe she can just chalk this up to one of life's harder lessons." His mocking undertone was sending her anger throttling ever higher. She wanted to shove her hands into the phone and wrap them around his neck and squeeze until something popped.

"Which is?" she ground out.

"Don't fuck with me." He sighed. "I have something you want."

She headed to a back set of stairs and took them two a time to the second floor and went to the door at the end of the long hall. She tilted her head and held the phone to her shoulder.

"What's that?" she asked as she pulled the black zippered pouch clipped to her jeans and withdrew two thin metal tools.

"I think you know," he replied. "If you want it, come and get it."

She dropped to her knees in front of the door. "Where are you?" She inserted the tools into the small keyhole in the doorknob.

"Our little love nest." Grainy flashes of blood, tile, and concrete moved past her eyes as she recalled the place. "We have unfinished business, princess. Don't disappoint me."

Victor hung up.

One soft snick and the lock turned and the door opened. She stood up, pocketed her phone and the tools and stepped inside.

There was no way in hell she could get the Vantage past the front gate without security calling back to the main house, so it was time to improvise. Vesper adjusted her gear and went to the closet. Finding exactly what she needed, she turned back to the open door, retrieving a set of keys from the dresser on her way out, locking the door behind her.

Minutes later, the guard station at the front gate waved out the leather-clad helmeted figure on the bike. The motorcycle's engine throttled noisily as Cain's Harley sped off into the night.

Victor snapped Lori's phone shut and shoved it into the satchel with the rest of his things. *Good. The bitch was coming.*

"What the fuck was that?" Howard snapped. "Why do you want to involve her anymore? It's done, we're free and clear."

Victor rounded on him and dropped his fangs in Howard's face. "Because now it's my turn to have a go at how we do things." He stabbed a finger in Howard's chest, loving the roll of anger he saw flare in his eyes. "And I want her."

Howard stiffened. "You want the Penitent?"

Victor stared at him for a moment then relaxed, the pointed finger becoming a full palm on Howard's chest. "It's not just for me," he whispered, shaking his head.

Howard's face was cold, all his hatred for the Penitent bitch evident in his eyes. He moved in closer, watching the other man's nostrils flare slightly in anticipation. "They're a pair, aren't they? Just like us. Where one goes-"

"The other follows," Howard finished, understanding glittering in his stormy eyes.

Victor smiled wide. "Exactly." He dragged his hand up Howard's chest to cup his cheek. "Give and take." He went over and grabbed their gear and pushed a bag into Howard's hands. "Let's go. I want to make sure everything is perfect for her arrival."

They piled the bags into the back of a late-model dark van and sped off to the west, upriver.

Vesper pulled the Harley off of Jackson Street onto Tchoupitoulas and the waft of the river permeated through the air into the helmet. She was close. Even though she hadn't been down to this little bend in the river in forever, her body was telling her it could have been yesterday. *Just keep it together, Vesper. Use the emotion. Focus. He's just another target.* She rolled the bike to a slow stop in the parking lot of the cluster of buildings and warehouses and got off. A soft breeze from the river blew in and ruffled her hair as she removed Cain's helmet and the slight chill made her skin prickle. She checked her knives and headed toward the building.

The outside of the whitewashed building made her think it was abandoned. It had been the last time she was there. Lots of heavy graffiti was scrawled in bright colors all along one side and rusted washboard sheets of metal and cast aside wooden pallets leaned up against the facade. There were several entry points, three doors spread at least thirty feet apart from one another, all of them with small signage proclaiming this building to be part of a marine repair operation. The couple of overhead lights that winked out from the second floor shot down her theory of abandonment.

One of the doors slowly creaked open. That was her invitation. She looked up over the door frames and noticed the cameras. The red lights blinked, indicating they were on and rolling. *Fuck you, Delacroix. You will not get to enjoy this.* She adjusted her jacket and walked toward the door, giving the camera the bird as she broached the threshold.

Vesper stepped from the shadows and walked across the concrete floor. "Hello, Victor."

The vampire's eyes brightened and a sinister smile broke the line of his face. "Well, well. You're looking as lovely and dangerous as ever." He paused. "Isn't she, Howard?"

Vesper's head whipped to the side and she noticed Grainger hanging back in the open door frame, lounging against it, blocking her path to the outside. He must have doubled back out a side door to come up from behind. Her head turned back to Victor as she slowly reached up underneath the back of her jacket to produce the deadly twin blades. She heard Howard's dry chuckle behind her.

"She is," he said. "And the outfit. She must have remembered how much I liked it. All that leather and sharp steel." He hissed through his teeth. "She's perfect, Victor. Just perfect."

Her eyes never waved from Victor as she turned the blades out in her hands. "If you think I can't take the two of you, you're mistaken."

Victor's eyes darkened in evil appreciation. "I don't think so, love. You see," he rasped, "I'm counting on it."

Her arms came up from her sides to fan out, the blades twinkling in the low fluorescent light. "Don't."

The vampire's mouth was slightly agape as he panted a little. Victor licked his lips and smiled wickedly. "I think you've made an amusing, yet clichéd error in judgment."

"Really, and how's that?" she asked, sliding a foot back for balance.

"Didn't anyone ever tell you not to bring a knife-" The nine appeared out of nowhere in his hand and leveled on her, "to a gunfight?"

The sound of Howard's laughter and the double pop of the gun were the last things she heard as her knees exploded and she crumpled to the concrete.

Decker hefted the duffel higher on his shoulder and rapped twice on the guest house door. Vesper wasn't in the room when he packed his bag and it was just as well; he didn't want to have to face her when he gathered up his shit and left. He heard some shuffling from inside the house and then the door opened onto a bleary-eyed Varian.

The sight of Victor's twin made his breath catch for a minute and his body stiffen in unconscious memory as his mind flashed back to the fight at Absynthe. It was like peeking into death's open door, but he hadn't expected death to look so sad.

"Sent to check up on me?" Varian asked quietly. The vampire's face was drawn tight.

"No. I'm moving in for a while," he replied, stepping forward.

Varian opened his mouth, but caught sight of the duffel and paused.

"Problem?"

Varian shook his head and let it go, moving aside. "Entré."

"Thanks. I don't think I'll be in your hair long. Hopefully, we'll get word soon. I'm anxious to get the hell out of Dodge."

The door shut behind them and Varian followed him into the living room.

"Yeah, Artemis looked pretty grave when I saw him and told him about the witch. I think he's in a tighter spot with the Council than he's let on. How is she, by the way? Lori, I mean."

Decker dropped his bag next to the couch and looked around. "She's going to live. Cain and that Gideon guy patched her up. It was touch and go for a while, but she pulled through. She's a fighter."

"Yeah," Varian let out a long sigh. "That was rough. I knew sooner or later I would be face to face with him, but I didn't...I didn't expect to see what I did."

I hear that. "Your brother not quite what you remember?"

He chilled as Varian's eyes went hard. "He's worse." The vampire sniffed and shook it off. "You can put your stuff

277

upstairs," he said, looking at the stairwell. "Take any room you want, I've settled in down here."

Decker nodded, picked up his bad and headed upstairs. He opened the door of the first room he found, threw his stuff on the bed and sat down on the edge with a slow, heavy sigh.

Relegated to the outside again. Just like before.

Time seemed to ripple out in front of him in black and white waves as voices came floating in to bring him back into years long gone.

The high trill of Howard Grainger's laugh as he was slipped into the back of a cruiser, hands cuffed tightly behind him, rolled over him.

"You're too late, Detective. Much too late."

Then his phone rang and on the other end his world had ended as his captain had sadly confirmed Miranda's death. The damn Crown Vic almost blew a tire as he barreled across the city like a bat out of hell and he'd laid out two uniforms that had tried to keep him from the scene. He only got a three second glimpse of her, shredded, bloody, defiled, before he was tackled and hauled away like a perp.

And Victor had been there. He realized that now. Grainger had sacrificed his freedom to protect Victor from being discovered.

Hot tears sprang forth as he put his head in his hands and wept. Her sweet face smiled back at him as he sobbed. The heartache welled until he thought his chest would burst under the pressure. She wanted to go to Paris for their anniversary, but he couldn't leave the job. She wanted to have a baby, but he couldn't stand the thought of leaving her alone with a child to raise if something happened. And she had put it all aside for him, because she loved him. Because she trusted him. And in the end, he betrayed that trust. He couldn't keep her safe. There would never be Paris, never be a child. There would never be anything.

He ran his hands over his face and wiped away the wetness. Downstairs there was a man with firsthand knowledge of what she had experienced. He was tired of getting jacked around. He flung open the door and headed for Varian.

"What happened between you and your brother?" Decker asked, bounding down the stairs.

"Excuse me?" Varian looked up with an angry glare.

"You heard me," he snapped. "What the fuck happened? Did you know about my wife? Were *you* involved?"

Tension coiled tightly in the vampire's body as he slowly rose from the couch and the two men squared off in the middle of the room.

"I don't think I like what I'm hearing," Varian warned, dropping fangs.

"Fuck what you heard, Varian. Answer the goddamned question."

"You better back up, Decker."

"Make me." The anger was growing, itching under his skin. He knew the line he was walking here, but he didn't care. He just needed to know.

"Whatever you're thinking, I suggest you un-think it. I am *not* my brother."

"Then how is he the killer and not you? How do you explain-"

"I can't!" Varian exploded. "I can't! How can I even try to explain what happened when I have no fucking clue!" He backed up from Decker and turned around, throwing frustrated hands into the air. "I thought I could find answers if I left, but there are none. Fuck!" he bellowed. "No one gets it! No one understands! We were alike for so long and then...then he was someone else. He wasn't part of me anymore. He was something dark. Something dangerous." He turned back to look at Decker. The vampire's eyes were filled with pain. "People...people were hurt."

"Like my wife?" he snarled.

"I'm not certain," Varian said quietly. "From what I understand, that happened after our break. After I left for Prague. After he hurt Vesper. After he found-"

"Grainger," he finished.

"Yes." Varian sat down hard on the couch. "I don't know how they met. I should have known if someone like that entered his life. I should have, but there was no connection anymore. Even now, there's nothing."

"You're sure?"

Varian nodded. "Yeah." His eyes were dark as he turned them on Decker. "Just remember I lost a brother before you lost a wife." He paused. "And that's all I'm going to discuss with you. If you want to have a go at me," he said, rising from the couch, "then come on. But I don't think beating the shit out of me will make either of us feel any better."

"I'm not so sure. I feel like kicking some ass right now." Understatement of the century.

Varian chuckled. "If you're set on a fight, I could call Cain. That kid would take on a gator with a switch in the swamp at night. I give you two hits before he pops you with those hand cannons."

Decker relaxed and smiled at the thought of shiny, noisy Cain. "They are fucking big guns, aren't they?"

"Goddamned huge."

Her blood rolled across his tongue and he moaned in ecstasy. She tasted hot, sweet, decadent. Nothing would ever taste the same again and he wanted more. More. Forever.

"Mine," he growled against her. She gasped in pleasure and he released her, needing to see the desire in her eyes. She was his. Decker eased back from her and devoured her with his gaze as she lay beneath him. Her skin was slick with sweat and blood and she undulated against him as his fingers stroked the heated satin folds of her sex, extracting low

and hungry moans from her throat. The sound thrilled him and made him hotter.

"Look at me, Vesper," he whispered. He wanted to see the darkness in her violet eyes. The heat. The need. Her eyes fluttered open.

Soft brown eyes stared back. Miranda. Her mouth opened on a sigh. Miranda's voice.

"Decker."

He bolted upright, sweat pouring down his face as he barked out a harsh cry of surprise. Decker untangled himself from the clinging sheet and got out of bed. Shit. Why couldn't he let this go? He pulled the pair of jeans off the floor and tugged them on, not bothering with a shirt, and jerked open the door and bounded down the stairs, determined to find something alcoholic. Preferably very cold and very strong.

The lights were off downstairs, save for the flickering of the television. He saw the top of Varian's blond head over the sofa. Guess he wasn't the only one who couldn't sleep.

"You awake?" the vampire called softly, not turning around.

Decker snorted. "Sort of. You got anything to drink around here?"

"There's a stash in the cabinet next to the fridge. Vodka's almost gone." Varian's arm appeared in the air with a clear glass bottle, very close to empty.

Decker opened the cabinet and pulled out a bottle of his own. "No thanks. I prefer scotch."

"Suit yourself."

Decker sat down at the other end of the sofa and pulled a long swig from the scotch and hissed as the liquor burned its way down. "Yeah." He turned to Varian. "Listen, about earlier-"

Varian held up a hand to cut him off. "Forget it. End of story. Got it?"

He relaxed against the cushions and nodded, taking another swig of the scotch. "Yeah."

"You should know Vesper and I were together once." Varian's voice was calm.

"Really?"

"Yeah. It was very brief."

"How brief?" Decker turned to look at him.

"Couple of months. It was," Varian paused, "a mistake."

"I can't imagine why," Decker said dryly.

Varian tipped the vodka bottle at him in agreement. "On the nose, my friend. We were both struggling after everything that happened. Just trying to make sense of it all, you know. It was the innocent mistake of two very damaged people. I think we thought we could fix each other. Work out each other's demons. You know, shared pain, and all that."

"Didn't help then?" Decker swallowed hard, finding it difficult to think of Vesper and Varian clinging to one another for comfort.

"Hell, no." Varian chuckled. "The bastard knew what he was doing. We were too broken to be any good for each other. Or anybody else." He cast a glance a Decker. "Sorry. At least for me anyway. So, I went to Prague and she stayed here."

"Find anything there?" Decker asked.

"More emptiness. More pain."

They sat there for a few minutes, watching the antics of a late night sitcom, when Varian let out a loud sigh, closed his eyes, and threw his head back. "I still love my brother."

The confession hung in the air. Decker kept his eyes on the television and took a long swig from the bottle of scotch. "If I have the chance, you know I'm going to kill him, right?"

"Not if I do it first."

"Fair enough."

A soft buzz rumbled in his back pocket. He'd forgotten to take his phone out of his jeans earlier. Decker reached back and pulled it out, checking the screen. Vesper.

He pressed the button and the photo loaded. As more and more of the picture filled the screen, the bottle of scotch slipped to the floor and the amber liquid began saturating the rug. Varian sat up with a start.

"What is it?"

His voice was frozen in his throat and all he could do was turn the screen to Varian, who went white as he processed the image. Even though Victor was nowhere in the frame, he was all over the screenshot. Howard Grainger held Vesper's hair back, exposing her throat. One of her large knives was in his hand with the tip just digging into her neck. Her shirt was gone, but her black bra remained and the expanse of white flesh was marred with blood. And just above the swell of her left breast, a shallow jagged heart was carved into the skin. Vesper's eyes were glazed with pain and Howard's dark smile stared directly at them.

The phone buzzed again and Decker turned it around to view the incoming text message.

There's still time.

CHAPTER TWELVE

As he swung the Aston-Martin out through the front gates, Varian said, "You didn't call Cain or Marcus."

"Nope. You're the one I need. Your brother's a bit high-strung and I have a feeling that if he sees me with anyone else, he'll just kill her, because where's the fun in that? Being confronted by a couple of pissed-off Penitents with guns kind of puts a kink in his fantasy, you know? And you, he's not expecting you. I think that might just throw him off enough to give us the upper hand," Decker explained. "So, be useful and program the GPS so I know where the hell I'm going." *Hold on, Vesper. I'm coming. I'll make it this time.*

"Done." Varian sat back. "You're headed riverside to Tchoupitoulas. The signal came from a business complex near the water."

Decker said nothing and stepped on the accelerator. The Vantage shot forward into the night.

The trip to the city was made in record time and cruising down Tchoupitoulas had all of Decker's senses on alert when he spotted Cain's Harley in one of the lots. He pulled the Vantage alongside it and he and Varian got out and made their way to the open door of the building.

"Here, take this," Decker said to Varian as he handed him a Glock nine. "Be careful, okay."

Varian nodded and followed behind.

The light was on inside the building, and they stepped into the open room. Two doors branched off of either side of the room leading down long corridors and Decker could see a stairwell at the end of the right hall. Decker motioned for Varian to move to the left and take the far hallway. As Varian moved alongside him, Victor appeared in the far doorway, a nine raised and level.

"Welcome to Hell, Detective. We've been expecting you." The vampire's eyes widened at the sight of his brother and he sucked in a harsh breath. "Varian," he hissed, as his twin raised his own weapon. "Well, this does make things more interesting."

Decker started to come forward, the SIG dead on Victor's chest. "Where is she, Victor?"

Victor raised his gun to Varian. "In due time. I think my fraternal obligations come first."

"Whatever. I'll just shoot you now, then." The safety clicked off.

"And take your chances that you find her before she dies?" Howard's voice came in mockingly from behind him. He stood in the doorway, a large metal pipe in his hands. "That didn't go so well last time. That's right," he laughed, "she was already dead."

Decker snarled and swung the SIG around to Howard, preparing to put a bullet in his brain.

Howard lifted the pipe and swung it hard to knock the SIG from Decker's hand with a loud crack. Decker cried out and lunged for him, but Howard gave the pipe one more swing, baseball style, and it crashed into Decker's left knee, bringing the detective down hard on his right. Howard dropped the pipe and grabbed a fistful of Decker's shirt and slammed his fist into the cop's jaw twice before he could react. Decker lolled back, unconscious.

Howard sniffed and took a deep breath. "Where do you want him?"

"Take him upstairs," Victor said as he turned back to Varian. "I'll be up shortly."

Howard grunted as he began dragging Decker from the room. "Don't make me wait too long," he huffed. "Or I might have to start without you."

Varian watched the human exit with Decker and he lifted the gun higher onto his brother. His voice wavered slightly. "Then, *I* will shoot you, Victor."

"Put the gun down before you shoot yourself in the foot, brother." Victor shook his head. "Using one is much different than reading a manual. Don't be stupid."

"I will, Victor."

Victor laughed. "I really believe you want to." He let the nine dangle from a finger as he spread his hands in open invitation. "Go ahead, Varian. Shoot me."

The gun shook in Varian's hand and his finger curled around the trigger, and then froze. A thousand reasons why he should squeeze flooded him but he couldn't move. He couldn't do it.

"Give me that," Victor snapped, wrenching the gun from his brother's grasp. "Christ, you were always so predictable." He grabbed Varian's shoulder and spun him around and shoved the muzzle of the nine in Varian's back. "Now move."

Victor walked him out the door and down the corridor off into a small work area with a wooden table, a couple of chairs and a giant tool chest in one corner. Engine parts were scattered around the rest of the room. Victor muscled him down into one of the chairs and went around the other side of the table to face him.

"Sit. Put your hands on the table."

290

Varian did as he was told as Victor tucked the guns away in his jeans and produced two small black-handled blades. He held them up for Varian in the light.

"You recognize these?"

They were Vesper's. He nodded.

"She knows her stuff, our girl."

Our girl? Varian's mouth opened in surprise and Victor smiled at him.

"Oh, yes, I've kept track of you, brother. I know where you've been and what you've been doing. It's a shame you couldn't make it work with the Penitent bitch, but I guess one brother is a poor substitute for the other." He inspected the knives closely. "These are superbly crafted." He nicked his finger on the tip and drew a bead of blood. "Razor sharp, too." He lifted a dagger in each hand and tossed them end over end in the air with a flourish.

Varian's eyes followed the glint of steel as Victor caught them easily and slammed the blades down into the backs of his hands, pinning him to the table. He threw his head back and howled in pain as his brother leaned across the table to snarl in his face, "You should have stayed in Prague."

Varian whimpered in pain and looked into the face of his twin and saw nothing but calm resolve. He could see that the bond that was once so strong between them was now severed beyond repair. He did not want to let his brother go. He couldn't die without trying.

"You knew I would come for you eventually. We are two halves of the same whole, Victor. It has always been that way," he managed. He watched as his brother's eyes narrowed. "Why did you forsake us? I would have helped you. I would have done anything for you, bro-"

"No," Victor sneered, pulling back. "He is the half you never could have been. It should have been you, Varian, but you betrayed us to your saintly Artemis and his precious Council. And they tried to destroy me. We were part of each other. We should have been together. You are just like me, Varian."

"No!" Varian cried. "I could never do the things you've done. I am nothing like you!"

"But you should be!" Victor screamed. His brother's eyes bore coldly into his. "And maybe you are a tiny bit. Deep down in the darkest part of your soul, you crave the ugly little things. You want them. The pain, the blood, the sex. You need it, just like me. We could have had the world on its knees, but you were too weak to reach out and take it. I have found what is mine and I will not be denied. Do you know what I see when I look at Howard?" Victor lowered his face to Varian's until they were a breath apart, not waiting for an answer. "I see me." He smiled wickedly. "How sad that I couldn't find that in you, brother, with a face the mirror image of mine." He sniffed and backed up a step, and pulled one of the daggers from Varian's hands. "This is your fault, Varian. All of it." Victor wiped his hand over his face and looked skyward. "And as much as I love him, it kills me that I still love you more. You should have loved me, Varian." Victor's voice choked on a sob. "If you had just *loved* me." He stiffened and looked back to Varian. "Now you will pay for your betrayal," he said, nodding. "Yes, you will pay."

Victor came around behind Varian and fisted a hand in his brother's hair, pulling his head back and bringing the blade to his throat. Varian swallowed hard under the flat of the steel and closed his eyes. *His brother was gone.* The emptiness consumed him and he let out a small breath and prepared for the pain, a single tear escaping from the corner of his eye.

He felt Victor's lips at his ear. "No tears, brother. I will weep for you."

Decker shook his head to focus as he came around. His jaw ached and his knee was killing him. The twinge of pain got to him as he remembered Howard and the metal pipe.

"Glad to see you're finally awake. Thought I was going to have find a more interesting way to get your attention," Victor said.

From somewhere behind the vampire, he heard Vesper cry out.

"Shut it!" Howard yelled from the dark of a corner. There was the wet sound of a quick slice and Vesper screamed again.

Decker grunted loudly as his injured knee protested and he fought to stay on his feet as he moved forward to find her.

"Not so fast, Detective." Victor lifted the gun. *His SIG.* "You're fine right where you are." He turned his head slightly and called back over a shoulder. "And put a muzzle on the bitch. She can scream when I'm ready for it."

His vision was clearer now and he was able to get a good look at their surroundings. The room was a large open space, almost like a loft. Several doors banked the walls and a set of elevator doors were off to his right about thirty feet away. Fluorescent tube lights winked overhead and the line of stars out the high windows suggested they were upstairs. The rest of the room was fairly clear, and there were several dark stains on the floor. Blood and drag marks. A wide metal table was pushed up against one far wall and he could see lengths of thick chain and various other metal components piled at one end and an open leather satchel at the other. Several bladed instruments were scattered next to it. They were all bloody. His stomach clenched. Vesper's jacket and knife holster lay next to them along with her phone.

"Show me Vesper," he ground out.

"Are you sure about that?" Victor sneered. "She's looking a little rough."

His voice cracked. "Bring her out."

Victor snapped his fingers and Howard dragged the metal frame into the light and Vesper groaned.

The sight of her almost dropped him to his knees. Hair that once rippled around her head in a tide of silk was stringy and matted with blood. Alabaster skin streaked with rivers of dark crimson. He growled. They had stripped her of her shirt and her feet and ankles were bare and bloody, shackled to the bottom of the frame. Her hands were cuffed to each side of the frame, and heavy cuts were sliced into her flesh. Tight leather pants that had accentuated curves were shredded in places, the ripped fabric allowing for the deep slices to her legs and thighs to show through. Two rags, red with blood, were tied around her knees and her weight hung limply as she tried to support herself as best she could on damaged joints and muscles.

And there, above her left breast, the jagged heart stared back at him. His lips curled back into a feral snarl. All sense of justice and loyalty to the law vaporized. Whatever the outcome, the vampire and his lover were going to die.

She lifted her head to meet his gaze and he saw the same resolve mirrored in her eyes. She was weak, but she was still alive. And he intended to keep it that way.

"I really don't know what you thought to accomplish other than getting yourself killed. But I think that it's great that you tried. It restores my faith in the simplicity of the human race." Victor smiled coldly.

"And what about him?" Decker jerked his head in Howard's direction. "Is he aware you think less of him because he's human? How far do you think his loyalty goes knowing you hate him for what he is?"

Howard's fists clenched and he headed for Decker. Victor's arm snaked out and caught him by the elbow. He shook his head at Decker. "In body only. In spirit, we are the same. But, there are ways we can be together forever. We plan to explore those." Victor stroked Howard's cheek and the other man closed his eyes, leaning in to the vampire's palm.

"Death is a good start," Decker snarled.

"And as for his loyalty-" Victor sniffed hard, "you're about to find out how deep that well goes."

"Why couldn't you just be a normal couple? Get a couple of cats, an apartment in Marigny, hit the bars in the Quarter at night. You know, get your rocks off without killing people?" Decker chided.

Howard lashes lifted on stormy gray eyes as he smiled over Victor's hand and rumbled softly, "We're experiencing an *alternative* alternative lifestyle."

Victor looked at his lover and chuckled. "Yes, I suppose that's what you could call it. Has a decidedly progressive ring to it, doesn't it?"

"It's sick and twisted. Just like the two of you." Decker replied.

"All good things must come to end," Victor grabbed Howard's face and pulled him into a deep kiss then turned back to Vesper and Decker. He cocked his head to one side with a rueful smile. "Sadly, Detective, ours is now." He handed Howard the gun and stepped away from to haul the rack where Vesper hung closer to the wall, an eternity away from him.

She grunted in pain behind the gag as she was jostled bodily, still trying to keep herself upright. Her wrists bled from the where the cuffs dug tightly into her skin and her heels and ankles were torn and bloody from the drag of the concrete.

"Leave her alone," he growled.

Victor ignored him as he went to the table and plucked one of her large, nasty knives from the holster and placed it in Howard's waiting hand, taking the SIG for himself. The two men shared another long look and then kissed again. Howard went to Vesper and fisted a hand in her hair, pulling her head back roughly, the big knife hanging still in his left hand. She let out a muffled gasp and Decker's eyes narrowed and his hands became boulders.

"Let's do this like gentlemen, shall we?" Victor sniffed. "You've got the right idea, then," he said, nodding to Decker's tight fists. Victor dropped the gun on the floor and kicked it to Howard. "You ready, Detective?"

"And waiting, you fanged fuck. Bring. It."

Victor glared at Decker. "This is not your ordinary I hit you, you hit me. No, no, no, no. This is I hit you, I hit you, I fucking hit you." He turned to Howard. "Every time he touches me, cut her."

Victor turned back and then both men launched themselves at each other. They grappled for a moment, testing the waters and then Victor's hard fist swung out and caught Decker's jaw.

He felt his teeth tear into the side of his cheek and his lip split. Blood streamed from his mouth.

"Well, well," Victor chuckled. "Look my dear, he wants to bleed for you. How chivalrous." He inclined his head at the detective and chided, "But don't you think that's a little dangerous considering your present company?"

Decker put a hand over his mouth, holding the flesh together and snorted, "What, because blood turns you on? You gonna eat me then fuck me?"

Victor's smile was dark as he jerked his head at Howard and laughed again, "No, Detective. He'll fuck you. Then I'll eat you."

Vesper watched as Decker threw himself full-force at Victor and began slamming fists into the vampire. The second he connected with Victor, a stinging burn pierced her as Howard sliced into her.

"I'm going to enjoy bleeding you. I want him to watch. I missed that with the last one," Howard rasped in her ear. "She wasn't nearly as exciting as you are." Decker landed another punch and she felt another slice and cried out behind the gag.

Victor held up an arm and blocked another punch, lifting his leg and kicking Decker back against the wall. He landed with a hard thud but sprang right back to his feet and dove for Victor. The vampire caught him in the air and slammed him down hard into the floor and Vesper could hear the crack across the room. Decker howled and rolled to the side as Victor backed away.

"Come on, Detective," he snarled, spitting blood onto the floor. He hissed as he dropped fangs. "You have to give this a fighting chance if it's going to be any good for either of us."

"It's gonna be good alright, motherfucker," Decker wheezed, rising slowly to his feet. "It's gonna be so good to watch you die. Because when I get my hands on you again, I am going to choke the fuck out of you."

Victor's voice was loud and commanding. "Make it real for the detective, please."

Vesper screamed as the blade stabbed deep into her flesh over and over and white hot pain exploded in her body under the relentless kiss of the blade.

"Vesper!" Decker bellowed.

"Let's finish this. Once and for all." Victor turned back to Vesper as Howard nodded and raised the blade to her throat.

Miranda's voice cut in through the fog. *Always the hero, Decker. Now. Save her.*

With a guttural cry, Decker focused everything he had left and launched himself across the room, ready to go out swinging. He had only seconds to register the wide-eyed disbelief that crossed Howard's face and the high, hysterical wail of Victor's "No!" before his eyes found the discarded SIG on the floor and dove for it. His hand closed around the grip and he lifted it into the air and began pulling the trigger. As he emptied the gun into Howard's chest, everything went red.

The gunfire was fireworks in her ears and Vesper's head whipped up to focus on Decker as Victor tackled him and slammed him to the concrete. Howard lay on the floor, dead eyes staring into nothing as blood pooled in rivers around him. The electric surge of adrenaline pumped life into her limbs as she thrashed against the metal prison.

She had to get free.

Decker and Victor rolled on the concrete, grunting and trading crunching blows as blood from mouths and noses flew everywhere. Victor grabbed Decker and pushed him down hard as he hissed and bared fangs.

"You're still too late, Detective. You won't get out of here alive. Neither will she," the vampire growled as he reared back to strike.

Something silver glinted from beneath Howard's body and she lurched for it with one giant heave. The metal frame creaked as it toppled and Vesper came crashing to the ground with a painful cry as woman and steel landed on the dead man.

I am the Penitent. I am the Penitent.

Vesper held her breath and pulled against the cuffs. Her scream bounced off metal and concrete and she felt the bones in her hands and ankles snap and crush while the flesh ripped and tore as she forced them through the handcuffs.

She pushed hair matted with blood out of her eyes and fumbled with a bloody hand to grope for her blade.

"Vesper!" Decker's voice shot her head up and she watched as he kicked Victor off and the vampire flew back and slid across the floor, coming her way.

I am the Penitent. I am the Penitent.

Decker watched as Victor reached out to try to grab Vesper and the blade and he leaped forward to pull him away. Blood trailed from several cuts over his eyes and obscured his vision, but he was able to see enough to keep Victor down and pound several more good hits into the vampire. Suddenly, he heard Vesper's voice chanting loudly and the room began to glow in a soft blue light.

Victor's eyes were wide with horror and he screamed as he flailed underneath Decker.

"No! This cannot happen! Howard! *No!*"

Decker held him down hard against the floor as the blue light came closer. He made out Vesper's silhouette and backed off as she neared the end of the execution litany.

Vesper's chanting grew louder, coming to an ominous crescendo as she raised the blade high above Victor.

"I AM THE PENITENT!"

Decker rolled to the side and her blade hit home, sliding into Victor's chest with a wet hiss as it penetrated his heart. As she twisted the hilt, the blade flashed in a blinding burst of blue and then went out.

Vesper let go of the blade and turned to him. She was ghastly pale and streaked almost black with blood.

"Decker," she whispered.

Her eyes rolled back with a horrible flutter and she collapsed to the ground. Next to him, Victor's body stiffened and rendered to ash and he crawled to her and gathered her in his arms and buried his face in her neck. She was still.

You're too late, Detective.

Decker crushed her tighter to his chest and threw his head back and roared.

"Vesper!"

He laid her down gently and put his ear to her chest. She was still alive, but she was fading fast. Her breath was coming in such shallow gasps that there was no visible rise and fall to her chest. Blood covered her everywhere and she was still slick in places. He paled. He was going to lose her. Like hell.

Wiping blood from his face and sniffing back tears, he struggled to his feet and half-crawled over to the pile of stuff in the corner and snatched the BlackBerry off the table. He needed help or she was going to die. He scrolled through her call log. Marcus. He dialed.

"Vesper, where the hell are you?" Her brother's voice was beyond angry. "Cain and I are tearing this city up looking for you. Artemis-"

"Marcus, it's Decker. She's...Victor....oh God, she's-"

"Slow down! What? Where are you?"

"A building complex off Tchoupitoulas. Marine repair. Tell me what to do, because I'm gonna lose her. She's barely alive, man! Come on!" Decker shouted.

"Okay," he breathed. "You got to calm down, cop. Is she breathing?"

Decker scrambled back over to her and put his face to her nose. "No! Fuck, Marcus!"

"Okay, check her for a pulse. Her heart might still be beating. If it is, then you have to get blood into her. You hear me? You have to get her to drink." The phone went silent for a second and then he heard, "Cain! Come on, kid! Decker, you with me?"

He slid his hand up her neck and felt at her jugular. It was faint and soft, but it was there. He bit his lip to keep from screaming. "Yeah, I'm here. She's...oh thank God, she's-"

303

"Alive. So, let's keep her that way. Leave the phone on and we'll track the signal. We'll find you. Just keep her drinking, got it? If you don't, then she dies, understand? We're coming, so just hold tight until I get Cain there. It won't be long."

"Yeah, just fucking get here," he rasped.

Decker tossed the phone aside and sat up, pulling her into his lap with a grunt.

"Come on, baby, we got to do this. You have to drink for me. Come on, Vesper. Do it for me." He shoved his wrist past her lips, feeling for the points of her fangs. They lightly scraped his flesh and he held it there and wrapped his other hand tight in her hair for support. He brought his arms together and cried out as he forced his wrist into her teeth.

Blood dribbled from the side of her mouth as it pooled out. She wasn't drinking.

"No! Come on, Vesper! Drink! You have to drink!" He pushed harder and tilted her head back, allowing the liquid to slide down her throat. She had to drink. She had to live. The icy hand of fear was creeping up his spine and hot tears spilled onto his cheeks. "Please," he whispered. "Please, Vesper. I-I can't lose you." He leaned down and buried his face in her hair letting the muffled sobs wrack his body. "I love you."

He felt her stiffen and cough. Decker eased back and looked down.

Her eyes were open. They were glassy, unfocused. But they were open. Suddenly, the violet rings narrowed and darkened and her lips pulled back over his wrist and she clamped down hard. He yelped in shock, but held her still as she drank.

Pain splintered in his arm and began traveling through his body at light speed. This was nothing like before. Instinct had him pulling away, but her hand shot out like lightning and kept him to her. She groaned in a low, deep voice and her eyes fluttered shut. She sucked harder and harder and he began to feel dizzy.

"Vesper, please-"

Her eyes snapped open and she pushed him over onto his back and straddled him. He had little time to react and she released his wrist and dove straight into neck, sinking her teeth in with a hungry hiss.

His vision blurred and the pain spread like fire through his veins. He pushed at her with futile hands, but in this moment she was stronger and she kept him pinned down as she drank greedily.

The fire began to ebb and a hazy, dreamlike fog whispered over him and felt his body begin to detach from his mind. As he felt his strength drain, he could feel the power in her body, feel the life. *She was alive.*

He wanted to cry out and rejoice. Finally, he understood. All of his doubts and fears melted away and a sense of completion washed over him.

Miranda.

Vesper.

He relaxed and let go.

Her body burned with need, with hunger. Her teeth sank deeper into flesh and her mouth sealed around it as the precious liquid filled her mouth and ran down her throat. It was so good she wanted to choke on it, have it fill her into infinity. Strength pulsed in her veins and she felt her body grab hold of the feeling and run wild. She would drink it dry.

"Vesper!"

The voice was a distant buzz in her ear. She ignored it and sucked harder.

"Christ, Vesper! Cain! Help me!"

Rough hands tugged at her and she lashed out with her arms and her feet, hitting solid muscle. She kept her mouth on her prey and snarled through her lips. She needed this feed.

"She's killing him, Cain! Come on!" Marcus cried out as he managed to grab hold of both of her arms and wrench them behind her back. She let go of Decker and screamed as Marcus twisted up at the same time Cain hit the door with a limp and bloody Varian hanging on to him.

"Yeah, we're here. Where is-oh, holy fuck!" The young vampire eased Varian to the floor and ran over to help Marcus.

"I've got her, you fix the cop," he said, hauling Vesper to the corner.

She kicked and railed against her attacker. "No!" she screamed. "It's mine! Mine!"

"Vesper!" The slap to the face knocked her head back and jarred her into the present. She blinked and focused. Marcus' lean face was a breath away from hers and she gasped.

"Marcus! What-what happened?" She looked over his shoulder. "Oh, no, Decker!" She pushed against Marcus and scrambled to get past him. Marcus grabbed her.

"No, no. Sit down. Cain's got him. Just sit. I'm going to take a look." He stood up and she shot past him straight to Decker.

He was pale and breathing in hollow gurgles, despite the bright light Cain had over him. Two massive punctures bled at his neck and wrist. The sight of the wounds made her stomach roll. She did this.

"Cain?" Her voice was broken.

He looked past her over his shoulder to Marcus with grim eyes. "I don't think I can heal this. He's taking everything I got and then some. He's fading faster than his body will heal. What do you want me to do?"

"Save him!" she screeched, grabbing handfuls of Cain. "You've got to save him!"

Marcus came over and looked down at Decker with sad resignation. "He won't make it back?"

Cain shook his head. "Nah, man. He'll be lucky if he makes it to the freeway."

"What about what Lori did with me and her? When she brought us back to Belle Ombre? Artemis said you've been working with her. Can you do that?" Varian's voice was weak as he sat in the open doorway, his eyes focused on the pile of ash. He swallowed hard and forced his eyes to Cain.

"I've never done it before. I don't know. I mean, Lori's only told me how it's supposed to work. I'm not supposed to try it on my own."

"Since when do you listen?" Marcus asked.

Cain looked at him. "You sure you trust me? I could kill us all. Or worse."

Vesper flung herself at Cain. "Do it. Just do it. He won't make it any other way."

Cain blew out a long breath and held out his hands. "Alright, everybody hold hands or something. We have to all be connected."

Marcus went to the door and brought Varian over. "Okay, kid. Strut your stuff."

Cain closed his eyes. "Good. Now, everybody just relax."

Vesper watched his face draw tight in concentration and beads of sweat popped out onto his furrowed brow. *Faster, Cain, come on. Please.*

Cain's features suddenly slid into a slow smile. He breathed out with a sigh, "Oh yeah, I got this shit."

Vesper felt her body tingle with electricity and then time warped itself into strange spirals and she lost herself to the sensation. *Please let us make it in time.*

They reappeared in the open expanse of the mansion's foyer and Marcus grabbed Decker and heaved him over his shoulder and began running, bellowing for Artemis. She took Cain's hand, ignoring the stab of nausea, and they both helped Varian to his feet.

"Come on, V. Let's go." Cain said softly. "It's not over yet."

When they reached the infirmary, Marcus had already laid Decker out and he and Artemis were sharing a long, heavy look.

Vesper's voice was frantic as she rushed forward to the Elder. "You've got to do something. He's *dying*!" She broke into hoarse sobs. "Victor-"

"Is dead," Artemis finished. "Price is no longer your concern."

"No!" she shouted, tears streaming down her pale face. "It can't end like this. Please," she pleaded. "I love him! You can save him. If you turn him, you will save him."

Artemis' face broke into anger as he set her back from him. "You want me to do this? Go against the Council? Turn someone without their knowledge? They will have my head."

He shook his head. "And Price? What does he want? Did you think of that?"

"I don't think he would want to die like this."

"And that's your decision to make now, is it?"

Artemis looked at Decker, lying pale and cold on the metal exam table, and then back at Vesper.

"Please," she cried, "I am begging you."

Artemis stood firm and held up a hand. "Enough!" He looked to Marcus. "I want you and Cain. Get everybody else out."

Vesper lunged forward. "I'm staying."

Artemis ignored her and pushed her toward her brother. "Put her outside."

"No!" she barked. "I'm not going anywhere! I won't leave him!"

"Then you stay quiet and out of the way. If I hear you, you're out." He turned around and she backed up against the wall. Time was precious. *Stay strong, Decker. Stay with me.*

Artemis looked at Cain. "Is he stable enough for this?"

"He's still alive, but barely. You might end up killing him. But I will do as you command, Excellency." Cain bowed his head.

"Fine," Artemis sniffed. "Grab his arms and his legs. Marcus, you get the other side. He's going to protest. Strongly. You might break something, but keep him still."

Cain and Marcus moved to opposite sides of the table and laid hands on him.

"I mean it. Hold him tight. Understand?"

The two nodded.

Artemis came to stand at the end of the table, at Decker's head and he placed a hand on either side of it, murmuring in the Old Tongue. A bright orange light flared out and over Decker as the Elder spoke, causing Cain and Marcus to turn their heads and Vesper to shield her eyes.

Decker's eyes flew open and he screamed in agony while his limbs began to twitch and jerk.

"Hold him!" Artemis shouted. The Elder continued his litany and the orange light grew brighter and brighter and the air in the room became dry and hot. Decker's cries echoed louder and he threw his head back as he shouted. Cain and Marcus were hanging onto him for dear life as Decker thrashed and writhed on the table.

A gasp from the doorway make Vesper turn and Lori stood there, open mouthed, as they watched the spectacle underway.

Artemis' voice became louder as his hands curled into the side of Decker's head in an effort to keep the man still. With one final shout, the High Elder released Decker and the orange light was snuffed out and Decker stilled.

His eyes fluttered closed and a deep breath escaped him as his limbs went still. As Decker slipped into unconsciousness,

Artemis' gaze swept the room. "I trust the lot of you will walk him through this?"

Vesper's eyes couldn't break from Decker's still form. She merely nodded as she walked over to the table and took his hand in hers.

"Yeah," Cain added softly. "We got his back."

"Good. I'd like to know that I haven't risked my standing and all of yours for nothing. Now," he finished, "the Council must be notified." He turned to Lori in the doorway. "Ms. Masters, if you're up to it, the pleasure of your company is required," he intoned, offering her his arm.

Warily, the witch took hold of him.

"Don't look so worried, Ms. Masters," he said, folding his hand over hers. "The Council is going to hear all about how valuable you were on an...advisory basis. We couldn't have done it without you, my dear." Artemis patted her hand as her shoulders relaxed. "Your uncle, I'm afraid, is a matter in which I cannot interfere. I will say, however, should you require it, sanctuary is within these grounds. Your debt to us is paid. We will expect you to deal with the vials in due course."

Vesper turned her head at the surprising note of sincerity in her Elder's voice as Lori responded, "Thank you, Artemis. I don't know how things are going to go for me, but I thank you."

"You two," Artemis snapped at a confounded Marcus and Cain, "quit gawking and find Varian. Get Gideon to look him over and let me know how he's holding up."

With that, he and Lori took their leave. Cain and Marcus both gave her one last look and then they were gone.

Vesper leaned across Decker and brushed her hand across his forehead, caressing his brow. Probably for the last time. Maybe he could find some happiness now, some peace. He had a very long time ahead of him to look for it. At least she had given him that.

"Vesper-" Decker's eyelids fluttered open, the blue depths slightly glazed and usually bright.

"Shhh," she said, putting a finger over his lips. "Just rest. You'll need your strength. The next few hours will be difficult."

"No," he sniffed, trying to rise from the table. "I feel good. I mean, I feel....*really* good." Her hands pushed his shoulders back until he was resting on his elbows. "It's strange. I feel like I should be in pain, but I'm not. I feel like I could do rope drills all day long. And I haven't played football in years." He wiped a hand across his brow. "Christ, it's hot in here. Are you hot?"

She shook her head. "It was part of your change. When Artemis-"

"My change?" he frowned. "What-?" he paused for a long moment then worked his jaw from side to side. His tongue

313

darted out and ran across the edges of his top teeth. His eyes met hers as he found the sharp points of brand new, perfectly pointed fangs. He swallowed nervously. "Vesper? What's going on?"

The disturbing look his in eyes shattered her heart. All she could do was apologize.

"I'm sorry, Decker. It was the only way to save you," she managed. Tears filled her eyes as she looked at the floor, unable to bear the burden of his gaze any longer.

"Save me?"

She nodded, sniffing, eyes still plastered on the tile floor. "When you gave me your vein, I was disoriented...confused...I didn't realize it was-" She shook her head. "I lost control and nearly killed you." The weight of the admission buried her and her head shot up, wanting him to see the anguish of her decision in her eyes. "You lost too...I took too much blood. And the only way to save you was to get Artemis to turn you."

"Turn me? You mean?" his voice trailed.

"You're one of us," she said with heartbreaking finality. "One of the powers of the High Elder, I'm afraid. But, he's not allowed to turn a human without Council approval. He did it for me." She smoothed her hand over his forehead again. "I couldn't let you die," she whispered. She moved closer to him and curled her fingers on the edge of the table and steeled her resolve. The storm of emotions across his face seemed to ease as if a breeze had suddenly blown in. Hope flared in her heart.

She continued gingerly, "Decker, I'm sorry. I'm sorry for everything I said. I know you still love Miranda and that's okay. I know that I didn't give you a choice, but I couldn't let you die. I wanted you to live. Even if it was without me. It was selfish, I know, but...but I love you. And now you're alive," she smiled. "That's all that matters. I hope you can be happy." She paused, but he said nothing. Her stomach turned. "I know that this isn't a life you wanted, but-"

"You," he stopped her. "I want a life with you. However I can get it, Vesper. I was holding on to a memory of something beautiful with Miranda. And you were right." He took in a deep breath. "Nothing will ever be same as it was with her."

Her eyes misted over and she felt her lips beginning to tremble. "I know. I'm sorry."

His eyes gleamed like sapphire jewels as his hands came up to cup her face. "Just because it's not the same doesn't mean it doesn't exist. I can let her go. I let her go. Because she would have wanted me to find more beauty however I could find it." He smiled. "And even though what's between us is raw and dark and passionate, it's still beautiful. I want to keep that beauty between us forever. I told you, remember?" he breathed, filling her senses with his dark, spicy scent as he pulled her lips down for the kiss. "Whatever it takes."

About the Author

Tara Wood divides her time between creating domestic bliss and creating hot paranormal romance with the occasional side of kink. When not playing June Cleaver for her hubby and daughter, she can be found at the local Starbucks slamming back Frappuccinos and plotting out her next idea. Or she's watching the BBC. Tara resides with her wonderful and tolerant family in the suburbs of Houston, Texas. She is currently at work on several projects, one of them being the next book in her In Blood series. Redemption in Blood is her first novel.

Connect with Tara Online:

Facebook: http://facebook.com/twoodwriter

Blog: http://tarasphere.wordpress.com

Twitter: @twoodwriter